# The P

# &

# The PureLight Order

A NOVEL

by

Brandon Ellis

First Edition, July 2013

*Copyright © 2013 All Rights Reserved*

ISBN: 978-1492103271

Editor: DB Gregg
Proof Editor: Chris Bailey

www.brandon-ellis.com

Dedication:

To Hunter, Jenna, and Lilyana. May your path in life always lead you to joy, truth, and love.

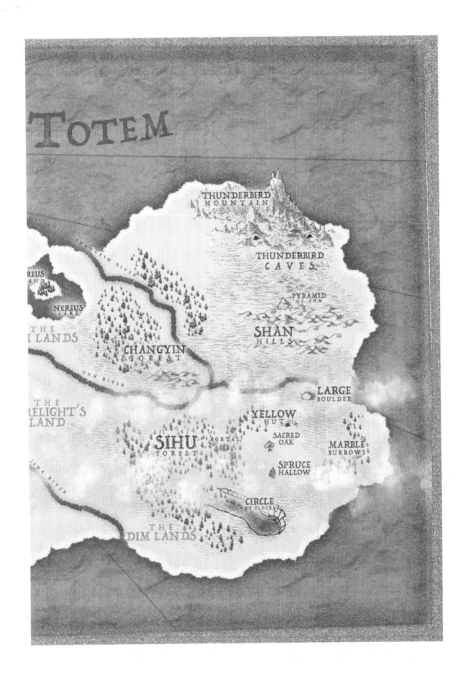

# Chapter 1

Zoey lay face up on a wooden raft, strapped down by an invisible force that grew tighter and tighter each time she tried to move. A soft breeze blew against her, as the raft bobbed up and down. All was quiet and she hadn't any idea where she was, or where she was going.

As if in answer to her thoughts, she heard a voice. "You're on my river, the Miyajima. You're heading to my home and you aren't going to like it there."

Zoey moved her eyes, glimpsing the black silhouette of Crepus Dim against a waning moon. He moved directly over her, so she could see him more clearly. "How do you like being a prisoner?"

Zoey shook her head. *How long have I been on this raft?* She winced in pain as something poked at her side.

"You're so easy to control, Zoey." Skint came into view. He looked very pleased, standing on his hind legs like a human and holding a sharp, pointed stick between his paws. "I thought you should know that I have a new best friend."

Zoey tried to get up, but the invisible force holding her down gripped even harder, slamming her head against the raft. Anxiety coursed through her as reality set in. She *was* a prisoner.

"Do you want to know who my best friend is?" asked Skint. "She was the reason we captured you so easily."

She didn't know what Skint was talking about.

He continued, "She made you so, so sad. She made you miss her. She made you cry. It drained your energy to be so gloomy. After all, you thought she was killed." He laughed as though he had just let her in on a big joke. "Because your energy was so low, you didn't use your petty little powers to stop us from snatching you, and—"

Crepus smacked the back of Skint's head with his tail. "You babbling brook! Just get on with it."

Zoey heard a young voice crying, and then it suddenly screamed, "No, no. Please don't!"

Skint pulled on someone struggling against his strength. Zoey saw a wing and instantly knew who it was, although she didn't want it to be true.

San squirmed in Skint's grip and her eyes were full of tears. "Zoey, they made me do it! They made me bring you to them! They made me take you on a ride in the Zolts—they made me do it all!"

*It can't be*, thought Zoey. *San's alive?*

She didn't want it to be real. San wouldn't betray her, would she? From the sound of her voice, let alone San's recognizable silhouette, she knew it was her. Is this a hallucination forced by Crepus?

Zoey wanted to look away, but couldn't. Then the invisible force made Zoey lock eyes with San. *How could she be alive? I saw her die.*

Sadness overwhelmed Zoey. She wanted to cry, but the energy lock wouldn't allow it. She tried to speak, but her mouth was held shut. Then she saw Crepus' eyes. He leaned over Zoey, searching her soul, his black crystal pulsating over and over again, turning from gray to black.

Her mind started to spin and her eyelids became weak, closing against her will. Abruptly, a scene appeared in her mind. She saw herself hovering over Coda at the Circle of Elders, right before the fight began. Her stomach was in knots, full of nervous energy. As she hovered over Coda, she was snatched out of the air by a large eagle. It swooped in with incredible speed, grabbing her with its sharp talons. She saw herself struggling against its strong grip, but to no avail.

Suddenly, a wild screech filled the air, disrupting Crepus' mind control over Zoey and her eyelids opened with a start. A sudden commotion erupted.

8

"The Ghost Shadow," whispered Skint.

The shadow of a large bird drifted over Zoey, and a moment later she could see an owl coming into view, high above them.

"Aderyn," stated Crepus. "Get ready."

The owl swooped down, making a close pass on the raft. With all of the resulting chaos on the raft, Zoey could tell there were a lot of Dims on board.

She heard a scream, and then a splash. A Dim either fell overboard, or was thrown. Then another splash and Crepus ran out of view, yelling for everyone to get a grip on themselves. Zoey heard several voices scream in terror, accompanied by more splashes. All Zoey could do was listen and stare blankly at the sky.

Then she felt the swoosh of the owl as its shadow cast over her. Then the owl climbed high, arched in the air and dove straight at the raft. More pandemonium, then another splash and then another. Out of the corner of her eye, she could see several Dims swimming toward the shore.

"You can't have her, Aderyn!" shouted Crepus.

The owl came into view again, and then spiraled straight into the river, disappearing from sight.

"Did you get her in an energy clasp?" asked Skint.

"Yes," replied Crepus. "I'm going to drown her."

The remaining Dims on the raft were silent, waiting in anticipation for whatever was going to happen next. The waves gently rocked the raft, making a sloshing sound. Zoey desperately wanted to move, and to escape the lock that Crepus had on her. She'd done it before when Skint had tried it with her, so she knew she could do it again.

Abruptly, like a missile, the owl erupted out of the water, soaring into the sky until it came to a peak, and then dove straight down. Zoey gasped in shock–the owl was heading right at her!

The owl extended its talons and grabbed her. Zoey rose into the sky, dangling while being carried off in a westerly direction. Zoey wanted to look around, but still couldn't move and her energy was draining.

"Crepus is sucking your energy. I'm getting you to safety."

*Who's carrying me?*

By her voice, Zoey could tell that the owl was a female, but Zoey's thoughts were cut short as her body weakened and her eyes got heavier. The owl screeched loudly, saying, "You, who walk the path of the Sacred Heart, must stand alone in the eyes of the Shaded Crystal, and wait for the protection of the Ghost Shadow. Fear not, for she will be there."

Those were the same words Zoey had read on the scroll that Taregan found in the Spruce Hollow. *How does she know what the scroll said?*

"I was the author of the scroll," said the owl. "I was also its messenger."

Zoey's body became limper; her energy was quickly dwindling away. She couldn't keep her eyes open much longer, and just before she lost consciousness she heard the owl speak again, "Fear not, child. I'm taking you to the PureLight Order, where you'll train under my tutelage until you can spread the PureLight Order throughout Ohm Totem. Thus, your destiny awaits!"

# Chapter 2

Lying on the soft earth, Coda looked gratefully into Nova's tranquil eyes. She had just complimented him on how brave he was for walking through the northern Fog. He disagreed, keeping his lips tight. It was difficult enough to face the Fog, let alone walk through it. His sister, taken by the Dims, had been the main force driving him forward, and causing him to brush aside the Fog's attempts to turn him back by pumping him full of fear.

Coda was overwhelmed with sadness. He had to get his sister back. What would he do without her? He'd found out how much he loved her while being in Ohm Totem. In fact, he respected her, and was inspired by her newly awakened talents while on this strange and incredible island. He knew beyond any doubt that he truly was her protector. He sighed. *This isn't going to be easy,* he thought. He was now in the Dim Lands, and even though he'd never been here before he was sure that things were going to be more difficult from this point forward.

He looked around. *Where's that hawk with the indigo crystals? I think her name is Shikoba?* Coda gazed around some more. "Did Shikoba make it?"

"Not yet," said Chev, who was lying on his back, slowly rolling back and forth. Coda wondered if it had been as hard for Chev to get through the fog as it had been for him.

"Any moment," said Nova. "Watch the Fog."

Coda turned, eyeing the Fog once more. It fluctuated, ebbing in and out like an ocean wave trying to suck what it could while withdrawing from a shoreline. Then the Fog started to shake, as if something was forcing its way through it at an alarming rate of speed. It was the hawk. Coda was sure of it.

*Shikoba!*

Like a jet fighter, Shikoba rumbled through the Fog, wings spread wide and spinning as she exited, and then flying high into the air and dropping like a dive-bomber. Then she turned a flip, diving toward them while spreading her feet as she swept in for a landing. She touched down softly on the ground beside Nova.

Mission accomplished and completed, and without any expression on her face.

"You know," teased Chev, "You could've just flown over the Fog, instead of through it."

Shikoba grinned. "There's no challenge in that."

"Let's go." Not wanting to waste another moment, Nova dashed ahead. Talking over her shoulder, she advised, "We mustn't be seen. We can rest in the Changyin Forest, on the other side of the hills."

Coda ran after her. "Where's Crepus?" he asked worriedly as he came alongside of her.

Nova picked up her pace. "Due west."

Confused, Coda did his best to keep pace. "Then, why are we going north?"

"We're going to rescue Zoey from the north. Crepus won't be expecting that."

∞

Because of their size, the hills ahead were daunting. And they were dotted with thin patches of grass and small, spindly trees. The sky above was an unhappy gray and Coda wondered if all of the Dim Lands were like this. The weather was so different here. In fact, it seemed chilly on this side of the Fog.

Shikoba glided over Coda's shoulder, landing on Nova's back. The snow leopard didn't break her stride, as if she'd been expecting Shikoba's arrival.

"Shikoba," said Nova. "Be my eyes."

12

Shikoba spread her wings, darting forward, and flew between the hills, vanishing from sight.

Nova veered to follow Shikoba's direction. When they reached the base of the two converging hills, they slowed down and Coda exhaled in relief. He was glad the path between the hills was flat. He didn't want to have any part of having to climb over them.

Chev sluggishly plodded past Coda, looking exhausted, his big feet dragging with each step.

Numee caught up with Coda. "Zoey's fine," she assured him. "I have a feeling."

Coda wished he felt the same. Over the past day, he'd been antsy, and if he could have it his way he'd go directly to Crepus and get Zoey back, instead of going this roundabout way. He'd face that awful Dim leader and fight him. He didn't care how clawed up he'd get in the process, just as long as he got his sister back in one piece, safe and happy.

"Nova thinks she's safe, too." Chev said, hopefully.

"Keep your head high, Coda," counseled Numee. "Here in the Dim Lands, you never know when something is going to snatch you." She prodded his shoulder to make sure that he was paying attention. "Understand?"

Coda nervously eyed his surroundings, expecting someone, or something, to come out from behind a rock or a bush to snag or bite him at any moment. But Numee's advice was simply common sense. From now on, he'd be ready at all times.

Nova's tail pointed ahead. "Forward."

∞

The sun was beginning to hide behind a hill, shading the path Coda and the group was traveling. Coda had been in Dim country for hours, following Nova and the rest of the small group consisting of Chev, Shikoba, and Numee. Coda shook his weary head, finding it hard to accept this path to the north. He'd rather travel west, straight to Crepus.

He blew out a deep breath. *How long have we been walking? Where's Shikoba?* As if in answer, Shikoba swooped low, landing in front of Nova. Nova raised her tail for everyone to stop and huddle around her.

"What have you found?" asked Nova.

Shikoba looked around the huddling group. "It's gloomy," said Shikoba. "Everything has changed since the Shan Tribe was wiped out of this area. I came upon spirit animals, deep in the Changyin Forest. They looked aggressive and had gray crystals. They also looked like they were under a lot of stress, but I got the feeling that they weren't on Crepus' side." Her voice carried very little sadness with it. She was a matter-of-fact, to-the-point kind of hawk. Turning her head, she pointed with her wing. "We should camp just around the other side of this hill. There's plenty of shelter there."

Nova nodded. "Thank you, Shikoba. Rest on my back as we walk."

Shikoba dipped her head. "Thank you, Nova." She hopped onto Nova's back as Nova twitched her tail, signaling the rest of the group to follow her.

*Doesn't she ever rest?*

Coda, feeling like he was in military school and not liking it, kept going. Chev walked next to him. "Do you need a lift?"

"I'm okay," replied Coda. It was a strange question, because out of all of them Chev looked the most fatigued. His large feet were dragging along on the ground and Coda noticed that his legs were trembling from fatigue. Chev was growing weaker and weaker with every step, giving it his all to keep up, and paying dearly for it. He held his mouth open with his tongue hanging out, trying to get enough air to supply his big elephant body. Numee walked over to him and tapped him on a hind leg. Chev stopped and looked down at her, only all too happy to stop for a moment. The others continued as Numee placed her raccoon paws on Chev's hind leg, infusing him with life sustaining Prana.

14

A rock suddenly clanged down from a hill on Coda's left, rolling to a stop in front of the group, prompting an abrupt halt by everyone. They all looked at the top of the hill and saw a thick tail wag from the edge, then move out of view.

Numee padded up to Nova. "Shall we make ourselves scarce?"

Nova nodded, and then looked at the hill on their right. It was lined with brush, large boulders and sporadic patches of tall grass.

*That'll take all day to climb,* thought Coda.

Thinking twice about it, Nova nodded as if in agreement to Coda's thoughts.

"Do you want me to take a look to see who was watching?" asked Shikoba.

Nova shook her head. "Whoever that was may not be of any threat to us. If, by slim chance, it didn't see us down here, then I don't want to reveal our position. If it did see us, then so be it—let it attack if it so wishes, and suffer the consequences. Let's keep going and find our camp for the night."

As they rounded the base of the hill, Coda's mouth formed a shocked 'O'. There, before him, stood the biggest forest he'd ever seen. The trees were massive, all the size of the Spruce Hollow. The ferns were twice as big as the ferns in the land of the Sihu Tribe and the moss covering the ground was glowing a strange green color. *What is this place?*

Numee whispered in his ear. "This is the Changyin Forest, the largest forest in all of Ohm Totem. It glows at night, and has the oldest trees."

"Wow," replied Coda.

Chev, reinvigorated from the prana, softly cuffed Coda's ear with his trunk and smiled. "Shhh." He pointed to Nova.

Nova's back was to them, with her head pointing forward, surveying the forest. Then she crouched low, placed her ear to the ground for a lingering moment, and then walked over to a gigantic tree that stood at the entrance of the forest. She sniffed at it, gave it a respectful nod of her head and moving forward like a curious cat, she padded into the forest.

∞

It was cold in the shade of the Changyin Forest, and Coda's hind legs were dragging. *We've been walking through the forest for hours*, thought Coda. *I'm tired and this is boring.*

The sun had set and the wind was ricocheting from tree to tree, seemingly to consume him, and only him. Why wasn't the rest of the group as cold as he? In fact, it felt like it could snow at any moment.

Nova stopped. They were in a small, circular clearing surrounded by trees with very little brush. The ground was covered with the glowing moss he had seen upon first entering the forest.

Nova eyed them all. "We'll stop here for the night."
*Good!*

Coda and his group had been walking the entire day, and he wondered how his pads remained on the bottom of his feet. He took a deep breath, enjoying the comforts of the thick air, and then sat on his haunches. His tongue hung out as saliva involuntarily dripped from his mouth.

Nova padded over. "You look tired."

Coda fought to keep his eyes open. "I am."

Nova placed her paws on his, instantly sending him energy. He sat up straighter, feeling his body become more alive and healing all of the aches and pains he had felt only moments ago. He blinked a couple of times, and then took a deep inhale. "Thank you."

"I wanted to speak with you earlier about your breathing technique, but we needed to find a place to camp."

Coda gave a puzzled look, thinking, *What technique. I don't have a breathing technique.*

"As I watched you breathe, I saw that you took shallow

16

breaths through your mouth, and exhaled it out your mouth. This activates the 'fight or flight' mechanism in your brain and takes your *own* energy away, blocking vital Prana from entering your body."

Nova continued, "Walking or running isn't designed to sap your strength. It's designed to enhance it. There's a trick to it, though." She wrapped her tail around his shoulders. "When you spend all day walking, it's best to take long, deep breaths through your nose, using your solar plexus like a billow, drawing your breath deeply, filling your lungs, and then exhaling through your mouth or nose. Never inhale through your mouth, like you were doing. While breathing correctly, you also want to concentrate on taking longer breaths. This allows more Prana to enter your body, thus rejuvenating you. It would be a good idea to imagine a line of white energy coming from The Great Spirit above, down into your body from ear to tail tip during each inhale. Make it a habit. That's why the rest of us don't look tired or feel the frost in the wind." She leaned in with a sly smile and winked. "With the exception of Chev, of course."

Coda glanced over at Chev. He was laid out, fast asleep.

Nova licked Coda's shoulder. "The longer the breath—the longer the life. It would be wise to sit in one place and practice. Breathe slowly and deeply. As you do, tap your foot. Count the number of taps while inhaling, and then exhale with the same number of taps. Do your best to increase your inhale and exhale as you go along. The more you practice, the more natural it will feel and the breaths will become longer. Does that make sense?"

Coda nodded. Sometimes the new information Nova gave him was a little out there, and even though he'd been in Ohm Totem six days, he still wasn't used to such talk. He remembered, however, that if he didn't understand exactly what Nova was talking about, he'd somehow remember and understand it later on.

"Wonderful," exclaimed Nova. "Now, we're going to have five observing shifts tonight to watch for any signs of danger. Each of us in the group will take one shift. I'll take the first, Shikoba will have the second, Chev the third, you the fourth, and Numee the fifth. You have the fourth because it's the darkest time of night and you have the best night vision among us. Does that sound suitable to you?"

Coda shrugged his shoulders. "Sure. But, what do we do in the meantime?"

"We sleep," replied Nova.

Coda followed Nova to the center of the circle of trees. She woke Chev and sat down. Then, curling her tail around her forepaws, she addressed everyone, explaining their shifts.

"When you feel you should wake up the next spirit animal for their shift, then do so. It will be their turn to watch and your turn to rest. Is that clear?"

Everyone nodded their head except Coda. He stepped forward. "How do I know exactly when to wake up Numee?"

Nova looked at the canopy of branches and needles above. She was assessing the best way to answer his question. Her answer was short and simple. "When you feel you must, then you wake her. Nothing more, nothing less. The feeling will prick at you until you wake her."

*That's it?* He knew there had to be a little more to it than that. Regardless, he nodded his head.

"You ready, buddy?" asked Chev.

"Ready for what?" replied Coda.

Chev wiggled his butt. "Ready for the best part of the long day? What you've been longing for since the sun was high in the sky?"

Coda cocked his head in confusion and looked around, wondering if anybody else was listening. Numee was conversing with Nova, while Shikoba sat on a large branch in the middle of the clearing with her eyes closed. Twitching his whiskers, he looked back at Chev. "What I've been longing for?"

Chev nodded his head up and down. "Yep. Watch this." He walked in a circle three times, then bent down on his

18

front knees, shook his toosh, and lay down on the soft moss. He closed his eyes and fell fast asleep.

*Sleep?* Coda glanced up at Nova. She was wearing a slight smile, bowed her head, and for a second, he thought he heard her voice whispering in his ear. *Go to sleep. Rejuvenate your soul.*

Coda decided to mimic Chev. He circled three times and laid down, placing his chin on his front paws and closing his eyes.

∞

Coda felt his body jerk and heard a whisper. "Coda?"

Coda pushed whoever it was away, mumbling, "I'm sleeping."

"Coda!" shouted a loud whisper.

Coda thought, *Crepus Dim!* Jumping up and going into a protective crouch, he was ready to dend his friends! As his vision cleared, he could see Chev's big face and eyes staring at him. Startled, Coda leaped to the side, and hurriedly backed away.

Chev jokingly rolled his eyes, feigning annoyance. He grinned. "You about done protecting us?"

"Protecting us?" Coda looked around to see everyone peacefully asleep. "Protecting us from what?"

"Well, you woke up like I was going to clobber you or something."

Coda waived his tail in the air, his brow crinkled by irritation. "You could have woken me a little more gently, you know."

"Oh," replied Chev. His trunk came up and curled above his head as he yawned widely and spoke. "I guess I could have. Good point, my friend."

Chev walked over to his spot to sleep, yawning again. "I'm going to shut my eyes now. You do what you do best."

"What I do best?" asked Coda.

Chev opened his eyes and winked. "Protect us." He

19

started to lay his head on the ground, but then lifted it. "Oh, if you see anything, or hear anything, let Nova know."

*That's easy*, shrugged Coda. He watched Chev quickly doze off into a deep slumber.

Coda looked up. The canopy of branches and needles hid most of the stars from view and the moon was covered by a dense cloud, dulling its shine. The green glow from the moss allowed him to see his breath flow like a small fog in front of him, dissipating seconds later.

*My breath.* He remembered Nova's words about breathing. *I should practice.*

He took a breath and started tapping his foot as he inhaled, counting. When he reached nine taps, he exhaled. He did this over and over, doing his best to make his breaths longer and longer. When he reached eighteen taps, he realized that Nova was right. He did feel more awake, and more energized.

A sound stopped his tapping. Someone, or something, had just stepped on a branch. Was it someone in his group?

He eyed everyone and they were all sleeping cozily in their make-shift beds.

He looked around, and then peered deep into the forest. His panther vision allowed him to see extremely well in the dark. In fact, it was easier for him to see in the dark than it was while the sun was up.

But, seeing nothing, he exhaled and thought he was just hearing things. He walked to the edge of the group, practicing his breathing exercises again, allowing the rich air to enter his lungs which pulsed energy through his veins, waking him up even more.

Another sound, but this time it was dull. It reminded him of the sounds of his own footsteps in soft dirt, but he wasn't walking right now, and this was farther away than the first sound he'd heard. And whoever it was didn't seem too worried about being detected. Then he looked around again, and thought it was probably nothing more than an insect. *Wait! I never see insects in Ohm Totem.* He wondered why there weren't any ants or beetles scurrying up the trees, or crickets chirping up a storm. *Why aren't they here? Maybe because all of the animals are spirit animals? What about the insects? Are there spirit insects?*

He shook away his thoughts, continuing to survey the area and hoping to find the intruder. *When am I supposed to wake up Numee?* He nodded his head, remembering to wake her when he felt the urge, which wasn't the case at the moment.

He sighed, glancing around, his ears perking up in concentration. It was eerily silent and he was a little cold and frightened. He felt vulnerable, as if at any second a creature might jump out from a tree, land on him, and claw him to pieces. *Mom would probably tell me to stop watching late night horror movies.*

A movement out of the corner of his eye brought him back to his senses. He lifted his head and looked to the left. *What's that?*

Something was hiding behind a tree about twenty panther lengths away. Coda remained still, not wanting the creature to know that it had been seen. After a couple of minutes, Coda took a step toward the tree, making sure to move at a snail's pace so the creature wouldn't notice what he was doing. As Coda took another step, something poked its head out. Coda froze and the creature moved back into its hiding spot behind the tree.

*Should I get Nova?* Then he saw it move again, but this time he got a clearer look. It was an animal with white and yellow fur, with black spots.

It quickly moved from behind one tree to another and, whatever it was, it was fast. It didn't seem to know, or care, that Coda had seen it. *What's it doing?*

The creature's head poked out again. Coda could see that it was a large cat, about the size of Nova. *Does it know that I'm staring at it?*

Again, the creature moved to another tree. It was skillful with its moves and approaching Coda quickly.

21

Coda was about to turn to wake Nova, but stopped as the strange, invading cat gestured with its front paw for Coda to come closer. Coda didn't respond and remained still, acting as if he didn't see it.

The cat gestured again, in addition to its mouth moving to form the whisper of two words. "Come here."

Coda's eyes widened. *Why does it want me to come closer?* Coda slowly shook his head no.

The large cat looked up at the sky with an exasperated face, and then gave a rather large sigh. It looked at Coda again, gesturing with larger movements for Coda to come closer.

Coda looked left and right, considering his options. If he walked over there, would he be walking into a trap? He looked over his shoulder at Nova peacefully sleeping. He didn't want to wake her if this large cat wasn't a threat.

He looked back, but the creature was gone. Coda walked to his left to get a better view, but saw nothing. He walked to the right, but again, didn't see anything.

*Did it just disappear into thin air?*

Coda padded back to his position. He lay on his stomach, placing his chin on his forepaws, watching for the creature and wondering if it would show its face again. After several minutes, Coda became more uncomfortable witht the situation. *What do I do now? Should I go look for it? No, that would be stupid. Should I wake up Nova and tell her what I saw?* Nodding to himself, he stood up, stretched his legs, and padded toward Nova.

He nudged her shoulder. Nova stirred, and then opened her eyes. "Yes, Coda?"

Coda frowned. "I saw a large white and yellow cat, with weird black spots on its fur." He pointed at a tree. "It was hiding over there."

Nova tilted her head. "Interesting. Did it seem hostile?"

Coda shook his head no.

Nova looked down in thought. "Okay. Thank you, Coda. Now, it'd be best if you got some rest. I'll stay up and keep

22

an eye out."

"But you didn't get much sleep. It's Numee's turn next. Do you want me to just wake her?"

"Not tonight."

Something cracked in the distance, echoing loudly through the forest. Coda froze. Nova bent low, her eyes searching for the culprit. Another crack sounded, but this time, even louder. Coda crouched defensively.

Nova sniffed the air. "It's coming closer."

Another loud crack filled the forest, waking the rest of the group from their sleep. Coda was amazed at how quickly they went into a defensive stance, ready to protect each other.

"Get ready!" shouted Nova. "Something's coming." She shook her head, squeezing her eyes shut as pain shrieked through her skull. She opened her eyes. She had sensed something. "It's not a spirit animal."

"It's not a Dim?" asked Coda.

Nova shook her head. "I've never sensed a creature like this. It's not anything I've ever encountered."

# Chapter 3

A warm light flickered next to Zoey, casting orange and red beams across the ground where she lay. Blinking her eyes a couple of times, she wondered if it was a figment of her imagination, or if the colored lights were really there. Groggily, she looked around and knew they were real, and then confusion set in as she noticed that the night was still upon her.

*How long have I been asleep?*

Her back and head ached. She didn't know if it was caused by the stone-like earth she was lying on, or if it was because of Crepus' energy lock.

*Crepus!*

Frantically, she remembered how she had been taken by the Dims, strapped down on Crepus's raft by some unknown force, and then plucked into the air by a big, mysterious, bird.

*Wait! Where am I?*

She went to get up, but fatigue prevented her from doing so. It felt like she had a concussion, although she had never had one before, so she didn't know for sure. A streak of pain shot through her body, making her wince, but it disappeared after a moment.

She took a deep breath.

"Keep your eyes shut," said a female voice. "You're safe now. The warmth and energy of the fire will bring back your life force."

"Where...?" The words came out of Zoey's mouth as a breathy whisper. Zoey cringed, squeezing her eyes as she struggled to lift her head. But her head dropped back to the ground as the weakness in her muscles took over.

"You're in the old country of Gwenfree, at the base of my

home. My name is Aderyn."

Aderyn's voice soothed Zoey. It reminded her of her mother, which conjured up a gigantic pain in Zoey's heart. She missed her mom and wanted to be in her arms at home again, where life was normal and familiar. She felt a knot in her throat as tears began to fall from Zoey's eyes, then her cheek feathers, and then to the ground.

"Good," said Aderyn. "Tears are an exit for impurities and cleanse the soul. You'll feel better soon."

Zoey's eyes welled up with tears so she closed them, but she kept her ears focused on the movements of Aderyn and the sounds around her. She could hear a river close by, rushing loudly. She didn't feel or hear anyone else around Aderyn, and was pretty confident that they were the only ones present. Everything else was quiet.

Zoey sniffled. "I...my..." She took a deep breath, and another tear fell. "...brother...Coda." Zoey let out a bigger cry, which she didn't expect. She wanted to get to her brother. She wanted to help the Sihu tribe from the attack. They were outmatched.

*Did they survive?* thought Zoey.

Zoey heard Aderyn shift with a slight uneasiness. "I don't know the location of your brother and I don't know where your home is, young one." She set something down, next to Zoey's beak. It sounded like a rock. "Water is in the bowl I've set beside you. Drink and it will heal you more quickly than I can right now. Crepus zapped my energy while I was rescuing you."

*Crepus? Is he here? Am I still a prisoner?*

Zoey opened her eyes as she rocked to the left, trying to get up to fly away as fast as she could, but weakness wouldn't allow it. She attempted to roll to her right, trying to get up with all of her strength, but again, couldn't manage it. She felt hopeless.

"Drink the water," said Aderyn.

Zoey, taking everything she could muster, inched her beak over to the edge of the rock bowl. The first sip seemed to fill her body with cool energy that traveled from her head to her wings and down to her toes, instantly returning life to her. She took another drink and her muscles pumped with much needed strength.

Taking a deep breath, she lifted her head, seeing firelight flickering across Aderyn's body silhouetted directly in front of a tree. Aderyn's wings were much larger than Zoey's.

"What..." Zoey's voice was hoarse, and slow in catching up with her thoughts, "...are you?"

"I'm a snow owl," replied Aderyn.

"A snow owl?" Zoey tried to get up again to examine her new friend more closely, but dropped to the ground.

"Stay put." Aderyn walked out of view and Zoey heard Aderyn's footsteps shuffling around on the dirt behind her. "My strength is improving, somewhat, and my energy is slowly returning. Do I have your permission to place my wings upon you?"

Zoey screwed up her brow in confusion. "Sure," she said, not knowing why Aderyn would want to do that.

Zoey felt the warm, subtle tips of Aderyn's wings touch her head, reminding Zoey of the time when Numee had done that to her, so she understood, and melted into a state of relaxation as warm heat filled her body, energizing her.

"You were energetically attacked by Crepus, who drained your energy. If I hadn't come, you would be a Dim and your crystals would be gray."

Within minutes, Zoey felt her body twitch with electric energy as her body began to recover. Soon, she felt new again and took a deep breath, allowing air to fully expand her lungs. She stood up slowly. Her legs were a bit shaky as she took her first few steps, but steadied as she walked around.

She looked up at the moon to see clouds slowly passing by, obscuring its light. Then she looked around at her surroundings as she stepped closer to the campfire. She observed the firelight dancing across a large, red rock wall slightly to Zoey's left, illuminating it. She peered up,

26

scanning the wall's height, and gasped out loud because of the sheer immensity of it. It seemed to extend into the air for miles, and was like the Circle of Elders' canyon but ten times larger.

Once again, she was aware of the sound of rushing water, but couldn't determine the source of it. She kept looking, peering past a large gap in the rock wall to see a waterfall crashing into a pool of water near them. The pool eventually emptied into a river just behind her.

"That's Hafron Falls, or what I like to call Mirror Falls," spoke Aderyn.

Zoey nodded and her eyes moved past the waterfall, along the lines of the red wall in the other direction. She noticed two large passage ways, one leading to the east somewhere, and one to the west. She spread her wings, stretching them long and wide, and glanced at Aderyn as she did so.

Aderyn smiled. "You're in Carwyn Canyon. Welcome to my home."

"How do I get back to the Sihu Tribe?"

Aderyn lifted her wing, as if gesturing at many things. "The Sango River flows through the canyon passage, here. It brings me news of the Dims and their whereabouts. Right now, it's not safe for you to travel and you'll need to remain here, in hiding, for several moons."

Aderyn sat as she looked into Zoey's eyes. "What's your name, child?"

"Zoey."

Aderyn's eyes grew wide for an instant, but then normalized. "Ah," said Aderyn.

Zoey tilted her head, a little baffled. *Why was she shocked when I said my name?*

"It's been ages since you and I have seen each other," said Aderyn. "You had a different name then."

*Another name?* Zoey shrugged and looked around. Nothing seemed familiar, here in Carwyn Canyon, so how could they have met before? She frowned. "We've met?"

27

Aderyn stood and walked toward Zoey, gesturing with her wing for her to come closer. "Come with me. The sun is soon to rise. You need your rest."

Zoey didn't move. "Where are we going?"

"We're going to The Redwood." She pointed at a large red tree behind them. "Do you think you can fly right now?"

"I don't know," said Zoey as she spread her wings, ruffling them up and down. They felt strong and able, so she nodded. Then she flapped, lifting herself a few inches off the ground, and then landed gracefully back on the hard dirt. "Yes, I can."

"Excellent. Follow me!" Aderyn pushed off with her strong legs, flapping her wings in the process, and flew in a diagonal line toward the gigantic red tree. Once she was about an inch or two from the tree's bark, she zoomed straight up.

Zoey was impressed, and then sighed. *I can't do that!* Nonetheless, she opened her wings and jumped high, flapping her wings hard and fast.

They flew swiftly, with Aderyn in the lead, climbing higher and higher. The wind blew against Zoey's feathers as she struggled to keep pace with the snow owl.

The higher they went, the more Zoey tired. *Does this ever stop?* Just as Zoey was about to slow down through necessity, Aderyn landed on a large branch. Relieved, Zoey gave a couple of hard flaps, pushing with all of her might to reach the top side of the branch Aderyn had chosen.

Then Aderyn walked along the thick branch, toward the tree, and knocked on the trunk exactly how you would knock on the door of Spruce Hollow. Three knocks, then two, and then one.

A door slid open.

Aderyn nodded her head to the right, indicating for Zoey to follow her. "Welcome to my home." Aderyn jumped through the entrance, vanishing from view.

Zoey inched her way toward the entrance, and then looked down at the ground. It was dark, but the small fire on the ground below still blazed brightly, showing her how far up she really was. *Wow!* thought Zoey. *The fire looks almost as small as a sesame seed.* She'd never been up so high—at least, not in a tree. If she wasn't a bird, she'd be terrified.

Aderyn poked her head out of the entrance. "Please join me."

"The fire is still lit. Won't the Dims see it if we don't put it out?"

Aderyn closed her eyes, and then opened them a moment later. "Do you feel better?"

Zoey cocked her head to the side. "No, why?"

"Look down."

Zoey peered over the edge of the limb, seeing only blackness below. The fire was out. *Is she a VioletLight?*

"Please come in, Zoey." Aderyn's head disappeared into the hole. Zoey took several steps toward the entrance, hopped through, and was instantly enveloped by darkness. Then then the door shut, making it blackness.

"Aderyn?" echoed Zoey's voice.

"Over here."

Zoey could hear Aderyn's movements, but couldn't see her. Zoey walked slowly toward the snow owl's voice, and stopped when the ceiling above her slid open horizontally, introducing light. Zoey stumbled backwards in surprise.

"Relax," hooted Aderyn. "You're safe."

Zoey eyed the lit area where they both stood and it looked like it had been gouged out of the tree by a drunken beaver. Everything was cut this way and that, and the floor was jagged with large gashes in it. But, as she looked above, she saw something quite different. Just above where the ceiling used to be and well beyond, Zoey saw a perfect, circular space, like a wide, hollow tube, extending up as far as she could see. Up there, the walls seemed to be as finely polished as the walls of Spruce Hollow. Zyte lighting lined the gigantic hollow just above the open ceiling, spiraling along the walls all the way up, until she couldn't see them anymore. There seemed to be several perches, or landings, positioned up and down the walls, as well.

"Wow," Zoey said in awe.

"And that's my home," said Aderyn, as she spread her wings and flew up in the hollow to sit on the first landing.

Aderyn pointed at the landing where she was perched. "Come."

"Okay." Zoey opened her wings and flew toward Aderyn. Just then, Aderyn closed her eyes and took a deep breath. A floor magically slid shut underneath them, about five feet above the jagged floor below. Aderyn hopped off her perch to land on a nice, polished floor. Zoey hovered in mid-air for a second before she felt safe enough to land. "How did you do that? You know, make a floor?"

"It's nothing special. What you didn't see was that this floor opens and closes with my command. It doesn't just manifest out of thin air. It retracts into the wall to open the upper section of the tree. Once I fly above the opened ceiling, I ask it to close and it retracts out of the wall to make a floor. I simply ask with my heart."

Zoey saw violet colored crystals on Aderyn that had glowed brightly when she said 'heart'. For the first time, Zoey could see that the snow owl was, indeed, a VioletLight.

"Remember this. To open the floor, drop the image of it into your heart and surround it with bright light. Imagine it opening and it will respond accordingly."

*That sounds easy*, thought Zoey.

Aderyn flew up to the first landing again, gesturing for Zoey to sit next to her.

Zoey flapped her wings, landing beside her. She looked around and saw an elegant nest tucked away on a ledge just a couple of stories above them. *That must be Aderyn's bed.*

Aderyn shook her head. "That's *your* bed. I'm content to nap on the perch, here. You need to get your beauty sleep. We'll converse in the morning."

At first, Zoey was surprised that Aderyn had read her mind, but remembered that Aderyn was a VioletLight.

30

Aderyn yawned. "Do you know how to open a window?"

Zoey shook her head. "I've seen it done, but I've never tried it myself."

"Well," replied Aderyn. "I'll teach you tomorrow. You have to promise me to keep the windows closed at night, though. This tree is very large, and can be seen above the vast forests in the Dim Lands. At night, the Dims may be able to see the light coming from the zytes if the windows are open. Do you understand?"

Zoey nodded.

"Any suspicious Dim who sees any light peering out windows will come crawling over here." She sighed. "They do that enough, already."

A little dismayed, Zoey frowned. "The Dims come here often?"

Aderyn nodded. "They send search parties for me. They like to keep me on my feet. They know I'm in the area, but they don't know exactly where."

*If they come here a lot, then why don't they just chop down the tree?* Zoey pondered for a moment on that thought. These are spirit animals and probably don't have axes or chainsaws.

Aderyn nodded at Zoey, as if reading her mind again, and then gestured for Zoey to fly to the nest above. Zoey did so, and as she settled into the nest she noticed that it was soft, pliable, but very large. It was fit for a large owl, not a small skylark like herself, but she liked the room it gave her, anyway. Plus, the zyte above her gave off soft, comforting warmth that she very much needed. She was in a different place now and apparently under the protection of a VioletLight.

31

# Chapter 4

Coda could see his breath against the green glow of the moss he stood upon. It was getting even colder, and not just in temperature. Something felt wrong—very wrong. The others quietly waited in a defensive position, listening to the approaching sound.

Another crack filled the air. To Coda, it sounded like thunder, and there was a different tone to it that Coda couldn't quite place. The sound fizzed out at the end, almost as if it was malfunctioning or something. He shook his head. He didn't know what it was.

"What could it be?" asked Numee, eyeing the forest around her and looking as if she were expecting the cracking 'whatever-it-was' to land on her at any moment. Shikoba sat perched on a branch just above Nova, looking as calm as could be. Chev, on the other hand, looked everywhere, twitching nervously. His open mouth was gaping and he kept backing up a few steps, then he would patter a few steps forward. It was an odd display that Coda had never seen him do before.

"I don't know what it is," said Nova, shaking her head. "It's not one of us."

Coda didn't understand that comment. *It's not one of us?*

Nova looked blankly past Coda as if she was in thought. He'd never seen Nova with a blank expression before. Her eyes usually revealed something, but this time they didn't. She moved her eyes to meet Coda's. "I'm certain it's not a spirit animal."

Chev walked over to one of the large trees and rubbed his back up and down against it, flinging small slivers of bark to the ground. "Then what is it?" He crinkled his eyes in delight as if he had just gotten an itch that had bothered him for eons.

"I'll fly ahead and take a glimpse," volunteered Shikoba.

Nova's eyes grew wild, another sight Coda had never seen on Nova before. "You'll do no such thing!" She eyed Shikoba as if she'd just said the worst thing in the world. "I'll move ahead, but no one follow. Do you understand?" She looked away, not waiting for a response from the group. "Never before in my life have I felt such a creature." She crouched low. "Stay here!"

With that, she was off faster than Coda had ever seen her travel. The sparse, small brush flicked back and forth as she zoomed through it. In an instant, she was gone, disappearing into the night.

Numee padded up to Coda. "I've never seen her like that." She looked worried, turning to Shikoba. "What do we do?"

Shikoba blinked, yet remained still. She was true to form, never showing a lick of expression. "We stay."

"I don't know about you," replied Chev, clumsily hopping over a large branch in the middle of a small clearing. "But by the way Nova looked at us before, and ran off makes me want to leave here this instant."

"You have free will," stoutly nodded Shikoba. "Do as you please." She stared into the direction Nova had gone.

Numee sat on her haunches. "I'm doing as Nova said. I'm staying."

Chev shrugged his shoulders. "Yeah, positive things usually occur when listening to a VioletLight."

A large crack whipped through the air. Then the ground shuddered beneath their feet and Coda instinctively ducked. The crack had sounded far away, but the ground shook right where they stood. This was baffling.

*Did the entire forest just shake?*

Shikoba jumped and flapped her wings, hovering about fifteen feet above the ground, doing her best to get a clear view of this racket. The expressionless hawk then made an

33

expression. Her mouth widened and her eyes about bulged out of her head as she flew forward, yelling: "Follow me! Follow me!"

Coda ran after Shikoba, jumping over fallen branches that were as wide as a regular sized fir tree. The ground shook again and Coda fell on his side, slamming against the base of a gigantic redwood. He laid there dazed with the wind knocked out of him. Before he could get up, Chev's soft trunk grabbed and lifted him to his feet, then dusted the dirt off his fur.

"Come on, good buddy." Chev gave a weak smile, hiding the layers of fear that penetrated him through and through.

Numee ran by. "Come on!"

Coda shook off the rest of the dirt and dashed forward, easily passing Numee. Looking behind, he saw Chev in full stride, picking up Numee and putting her on his back. At that moment, Coda realized that Chev's long, thick legs may have made him look slow, but in reality, he was fast.

As Coda followed the zigzagging hawk, he could hear a commotion up ahead. It sounded like Nova, but he couldn't quite make out the words and she sounded close by.

Rounding a tree, Coda came to a screeching halt. There before him, Nova stood face to face with something Coda had never seen before. And by the look of Shikoba, she had never seen this either. Hovering just above Coda, she moved her head from Nova to the thing, and back to Nova again, as if waiting for an order from the snow leopard.

*What is that?!* thought Coda.

A towering black shadow with ghost like features hovered back and forth in front of Nova. Even though the lighting was dark, Coda could see it well. The glowing green moss highlighted the creature's base where a robe-like silhouette hid any sort of legs—if it had legs at all. The creature was fluctuating in and out—transparent, then solid black, then transparent, and then solid black. Its face looked ghastly and dead and its eyes formed wide slits that created a piercing black stare. And inside of its form, every so often

34

a dark blue electric charge would vibrate through it. It would crackle like lightening, only to fizzle out a second later as it made the same sound they had heard back at their camp.

"Do not come any closer, Shikoba! Make sure they all stay back!" shouted Nova. She stood motionless in front of the creature. Coda could tell that she was assessing it, searching for its strengths and weaknesses. What she'd do after she found them, Coda hadn't the slightest idea.

The creature lurched upward, growing taller than it already was, and spreading what looked to be huge, black wings, that it slammed down on the earth, shaking the ground.

A second later, Coda heard a couple of gasps behind him. Turning his head, he saw Numee and Chev just arriving.

Nova stood still. "I know you fear for my life, my friends," said Nova. "But please listen to me when I say don't come closer! I've not gathered what this might be yet."

Quickly, Shikoba dipped her head. "We apologize, Nova. We disobeyed a direct order." The shadowed figure moved back and forth as all eyes followed it. Nova stared at it, as if she was peering into its soul. Then she whipped her head around, suddenly understanding. "It's a dis-incarnate!"

"What?" asked Coda.

"A shadowed spirit. A soul without a body," replied Nova. "This one preys on fear and in so doing, creates fear everywhere it goes. If a spirit animal takes in that fear, it creates even more negativity. This dis-incarnate then feeds on the fear, sucking all of the negative energy it can. It's their food. This dis-incarnate is very powerful. I've never seen one like it."

Then Shikoba screeched, "Let us at it, Nova!"

Nova stepped back from the creature and took a deep breath as she scuffed the earth and slowly shook her head 'no'. She looked at Coda. "Orion was a wise counselor and the most impressive of tacticians. He was quick and precise with his decisions. Remember that, because that's who you

35

are, deep down inside." She looked worried, as if something was about to happen.

The dis-incarnate then lashed and lunged at Nova, smashing her body with his, covering Nova in blackness and swallowing her from view. An electric charge pulsed through the creature, and then blasted outward. The sudden blast singed Coda's fur and he dropped to the earth, stunned by the sudden jolt. Chev ran toward Coda, jumped over him, and positioned himself in front of his friend, hoping to block a second attack.

Shikoba flew at the shadowed figure as Numee ran toward it as well. Another blast of electricity filled the air and Coda saw Numee tumble past him, slamming against a large bush.

Coda jumped up, side-stepped Chev's body and ran forward, stopping in mid-run. But where was the dis-incarnate? Where was Nova? Coda looked around, running left and right, searching for the strange black shadow. He found Shikoba behind a bush, lying motionless on the ground and slightly breathing.

Coda scanned the area, but again, couldn't find Nova anywhere. *Where is she?* he thought, pleading more to the forest than to anyone else. "Nova!"

"Over here," said Chev. He was standing over a burnt hole in the ground, surrounded by broken rock and charred soil.

As Coda peered at it, he saw that it was maybe five feet deep, and what was inside of it saddened him and grieved his heart. At the bottom of the crater was a tuft of white fur with black spots dotted with dried blood. It was Nova's. "Where is she?" whispered Coda, not wanting to even speak.

Chev shook his head. Nova wasn't there. Was she alive? Did the dis-incarnate kill her, or simply kidnap her? The dis-incarnate had disappeared in a matter of moments, and because of that there was no way to follow it and no way to tell where it went.

*This can't be!* Frantically looking around, Coda was

36

speechless. Then he gazed into Chev's eyes, trying to find an answer that Chev didn't have. He padded around, peering inside bushes, looking behind trees, and searching the area in a calculated circle. Again, Nova was gone. *How can this be? It's Nova! She's a VioletLight!*

Numee nudged her body against Coda's. "She's gone. Vanished." She shook her head, "Where? How?"

Chev patted the top of her head. There was melancholy in his voice when he spoke. "Right now we have to take care of Shikoba. We'll find Nova and Zoey soon."

Numee looked down as a tear fell from her eye. She walked over to an unconscious hawk whose feathers smoked from the electric charge it had received moments ago. Chev picked her up, holding her gently in his trunk. Coda padded over to the smoky indentation in the ground and stared at the bloody fur. "We need to keep moving north," he said.

∞

A sliver of light rose from the forest's horizon as Coda's group traveled, gifting them with the first rays of light since yesterday. They'd been walking for hours since the shadow creature had attacked and taken, or maybe even killed, their cherished VioletLight.

They had started out walking in the darkness of early morning when it was easiest for Coda to see, but slightly difficult for the others. The first signs of the rising sun was a welcome to the group, even though not much would lift their spirits right now, unless Nova or Zoey somehow walked up to them.

Chev carried Shikoba with his trunk and Coda walked in the lead with his head low, not knowing where he was going. Numee closely followed. They were all numb in mind and spirit.

Coda stopped next to a huge tree with red covered bark. He sat down, eyeing the ground and noticing that the day was starting to shed more light, passing through the holes in the forest's canopy above, sprinkling yellowish rays upon the ground before him. The moss was losing its glow, but that was fine since the sun far out shined the moss. Plus, moss didn't give warmth like the sun. He took in a deep breath. The day was starting to display itself as being a hot one, which was much better than yesterday's chill.

"You won't be alive in this forest for too long if you think you can take on those crackling shadow creatures," said a female voice behind them.

They all turned to see a white, yellowish jaguar with black markings. It looked familiar to the large cat Coda had glimpsed last night. In fact, it was the same spirit animal.

She sat calmly, grooming herself as if she had seen this type of event take place before—a shadow creature taking or killing a spirit animal and disappearing moments later. Coda remembered that Nova had called the beast a "dis-incarnate."

Coda sighed, and then examined the jaguar. She had gray crystals, but didn't seem to be dangerous at all. She had a cut across her left ear, as if she had been in a fight not too long ago. Other than that, she looked rather healthy, fit, and very determined.

"Who are you?" asked Numee.

The jaguar shook her head. "I'm nobody you need to learn the name of. But, if you want to survive, then come with me."

# Chapter 5

*You betray her. Your thoughts, your feelings, your actions—all betray her.*

Maldwyn sat chained against a cold, gray wall. The stones he sat upon were flat and hard, creating an ache in his back that wouldn't leave. He'd been there for days. *Its morning*, he thought, welcoming the slit of light making its way through a barred window.

The ape pulled on his chains, doing his best to break free from their hold. It was useless, he was too weak. He had been thrown down here in Crepus's dungeon and held against his will because he assisted Zoey in the tunnels a couple nights ago. He didn't help her physically. He helped her with a whisper. He mouthed the words, *procede from the heart* and Zoey saw it. She performed brilliantly after that, just like he knew she would. She listened to her heart and shot a powerful energy at the Dims, making them tumble backwards. Except for Crepus, of course, who stood like an impenetrable rock against Zoey's rushing energy.

*You betray Aderyn. Your thoughts, your feelings, your actions—all betray her.*

The thoughts again crept in, taking Maldwyn away from his memory of the tunnels, back to the cold dungeon floor. The more Maldwyn tried to get Crepus's thoughts out of his mind, the lower his head drooped. It wasn't easy; especially since Crepus did everything he could to push negative thoughts deeper into Maldwyn's own thoughts. It was getting to the point that Maldwyn was agreeing with them. He was being brainwashed and Crepus was doing it slowly and methodically.

A drift of snow blew through the barred window,

fluttering against his leg and distracting him. He stared at the white flakes, knowing what they were, but not truly understanding why such a wet, cold substance would serve any purpose in life. It was beautiful, yes. And maybe, just maybe, he thought, beauty held the secret of its own purpose.

Maldwyn shook his head, *No. Snow is death.*

"You continue to impress me, Maldwyn. You're getting closer and closer to the truth. But one thing is eluding you. Do you understand why you betray Aderyn?"

Maldwyn looked at Crepus standing in the shadows at the top of the stairs. "How long have you been watching me?"

Maldwyn continued to stare at the shadows, waiting for Crepus to come into view.

"Not long." Crepus walked slowly down the stairs, purposely tapping each claw against each stone with every step.

Maldwyn looked down, hiding his eyes from Crepus's crystals. "Leave me alone, Crepus, and stop feeding me these thoughts and lies. They aren't mine, you wretched soul! What can I do to harm you?"

"A lot," replied Crepus. "Regardless, I need you. I need your mind. You're going to lead me to Aderyn. We can't find her, but you know her best. You know where she hides, and *what* she hides."

Maldwyn closed his eyes. It was not by his choice, though. Crepus had a way of forcing another's will to follow his own.

With eyes closed, Maldwyn's mind opened up. He watched as his mind floated through Crepus's castle, out the large wooden doors and into a dense forest. His mind moved through the paths of the forest and into an open field where long yellow grasses went on for miles, stopping at the base of a large canyon. *Carwyn Canyon,* thought Maldwyn. He forced his eyes open, breathing heavily. Crepus had his mind again, and was trying to force Maldwyn to reveal

40

where Aderyn was hiding.

"You can't control me, Crepus."

Crepus grunted. He was almost there, almost to Aderyn. He gazed into Maldwyn's brown eyes. "I will." His black crystals pulsed again. "Look at me."

Maldwyn shook his head. "No."

"Look at me."

Again, Maldwyn refused, but something invisible pulled at his head. Maldwyn did his best to hold back, but the force was too strong. His head came up slowly and Maldwyn was staring at the pulsing crystal embedded in Crepus's forehead.

*You betray her. Your thoughts, your feelings, your actions—all betray her.*

Maldwyn's eyes closed. His mind was at the base of the cliff, gazing up at the miles of red and yellow stone of the canyon wall. He drifted upward, moving at a quick pace, and flew over the lip of the canyon, heading toward a large redwood tree—the only redwood in sight.

He forced his eyes open again.

"Impressive. You have a strong will and you aren't easily manipulated." Crepus nodded and walked toward Maldwyn. "Trust me, though, I'll soon break you and you'll show me everything." He sniffed at the flakes of snow that lay against Maldwyn. "I see you don't pay too much attention to the cold."

It was true, no matter how cold it was Maldwyn had control over his body temperature, but he wondered why he couldn't control his mind when Crepus crept into it. He jerked on the chains. "Let me go!"

Crepus tilted his head. "I fear I can't do that. You've betrayed the ones you've loved. That alone should be punished, don't you think?"

Maldwyn dropped his head and hung it low. He looked exhausted, which pleased Crepus. Maldwyn sighed heavily. "I beg you. Please let me go."

Crepus's crystals pulsed again and Maldwyn's eyes

41

closed for a third time.

Maldwyn's mind gazed at the redwood tree, and peered up its entire height. His mind started to travel up the tree, but halted and turned around, glimpsing the base of the eastern canyon wall, and then dragging his vision to the Sango River. Maldwyn was now in control. His mind flew forward, following the river toward the Zola Tribe and stopping at the foot of the Northern Fog—the boundary between the Dim Lands and the PureLight Lands. He suddenly halted. The spirit animals of the Zola tribe were Maldwyn's friends. Even though Crepus knew the location of the Zola tribe, Maldwyn wasn't going to give him the pleasure of spying on them.

Maldwyn opened his eyes yet again. They showed betrayal and sadness. Crepus flew into an angry fit. He growled and scratched the stone floor several times with his claws.

"She's with the Zola Tribe?" He slammed his tail against the ground and turned on his heels, heading toward the staircase. The light streaming in through the window streaked across his body. "You lie!" Glancing up the stairs, he yelled, "Guards!"

Two large apes, built much like Maldwyn, came racing down the stairs. They must have been somewhere on the platform at the top of the staircase the entire time, because Maldwyn didn't hear a door open. They huddled next to Crepus with their backs turned to Maldwyn, waiting for orders.

"You can do what you want with him, but don't kill him." Crepus placed one foot on the first step, and then froze. He sensed something—something coming from Maldwyn. *Is he putting together an escape plan?* He was about to turn toward Maldwyn, but was interrupted by a creak of the door just beyond the top of the staircase. "Who is it!"

"Fric," said a low male voice. The door creaked as it opened wider.

"Come," replied Crepus, who took his claws off the step

and backed up a few paces.

With one giant leap, a large white, shaggy wolf landed next to Crepus and the apes. It had an old scar on his left cheek and was breathing at a fast pace, his tongue hanging out slightly. He was doing his best to control his breath after being on a long run.

Fric jerked his head back when he saw Maldwyn, then growled. Fric and Maldwyn weren't the best of friends. The scar was one of the reasons why. "Do you insist on keeping this ghastly ape around?"

Crepus ignored the question. "Why are you here, Fric?"

Fric stood tall. "I spotted PureLights in the Dim Lands. I watched them enter through the Fog, and then walk on the paths between the hills. They were heading toward Changyin Forest."

Crepus frowned. "How many?"

"I saw five, but there could be more ahead of them."

Crepus tapped a claw against his chin. "I doubt that." He paused as if in deep thought, and then sighed. "Was the Snow Leopard there?"

"Yes," replied Fric. "She was in the lead."

"When did you see them?"

"Yesterday morning, my lord." He paused, as if he'd done something wrong. "I ran as fast as I could to relay the message to you."

Crepus spat on the ground in front of Fric, not pleased that he took so long to travel to the castle. Shaking his head, Crepus glared at the two large apes and pointed his tail at Maldwyn. "Do your best to abuse him."

The apes nodded as Crepus followed Fric up the stairs, leaving the room and closing the door behind them. Maldwyn sat motionless. His head hung low, hiding his face as he waited for the brutal attack about to come. His mouth moved—not to form words, but to form a smile. He'd been ready for this moment.

The two apes snickered as they looked at each other, silently asking each other who wanted to take the first shot.

One of the apes shrugged his shoulders, stuck out his lower lip, and gestured to his friend. "You first."

As the other ape reared back to deliver a massive punch, Maldwyn swiped its legs out from under him, flipping him backwards. The ape landed hard on his head, knocking him unconscious. The apes hadn't seen that only Madwyn's hands were in chains. His legs were free, allowing him to use them, and use them well.

*That was easy.* Maldwyn turned his focus on the other guard.

*Uh oh!*

The other guard was quick and landed a heavy knee against Madwyn's chin, causing him to bite his lower lip. Blood filled his mouth, making Maldwyn spit on the floor. As Maldwyn turned his eyes back toward the guard, he saw the guard's fist coming at him, punching his cheek. Pain coursed through his face and neck as Maldwyn's vision became blurry, but came back into focus an instant later.

Grasping the chains that held his arms tight to the wall, he pulled with all his might, then let go once another volley of punches landed on his face.

He shook it off and pulled the chains again, this time with success. He felt the wall give a little, but had to tighten his body when the guard smashed his fists against Maldwyn's torso and stomach, knocking the wind out of him.

The guard laughed. "You had enough yet?"

Maldwyn nodded a yes, hoping for a little reprieve from the onslaught this ape was handing him.

"I don't think you have!" The ape kneed him under the chin again and more blood filled Maldwyn's mouth. Instead of weakening Maldwyn, it angered him, giving him an adrenalin rush that coursed new energy through his veins.

The next volley of punches came and landed, but Maldwyn was already in the process of pulling on the chains with all of his might. The guard's eyes widened when he saw what was happening, but reacted too late. Maldwyn pulled so hard that the chains broke from the wall, slamming onto the ground in front of them. The guard hesitated, not something you want to do around Malwyn. With the chains still fastened to his wrists and now attached to nothing else but the air, Maldwyn swung the chains, wrapping them around the guard's neck.

The guard, now being strangled, put his hands against the chains, gasping for much needed oxygen. Maldwyn pulled the guard in close, eye to eye and nose to nose. "I think I've had enough of this negative attitude of yours." Maldwyn gave a quick tap and a twist on the guard's gray forehead crystal, dropping the guard instantly to the floor, stunned and knocked out.

*I've got to get to Aderyn.*

Maldwyn glanced around the small room, searching for anyone else hiding in the shadows and ready to attack. When he saw no one, he unwrapped the chain from around the guard's neck, and then wrapped them around his own forearms, making sure they wouldn't make any noise by dragging against the heavy stone. He then quietly tip toed up the stairs to the landing platform, and toward the large wooden door. It was closed, and perhaps locked. Plus, the door always creaked, which may turn some heads if anyone was in the castle hallway. This wasn't good. His sudden freedom might be short lived.

He stood in thought for a moment, eyeing the two unconscious guards below. There they lay with small flakes of snow settling on them. Then it came to him.

*The guards! I look like them. Anyone who sees me will mistake me as one of them.*

Thinking this was the only plan he could muster, he pushed the door open. Just as expected, it creaked loudly, echoing down the hallway. He walked out into the hallway, closing the door behind him. He turned, seeing the lock on the door which was nothing more than a heavy latch, and flicked it shut, locking it. This may buy him some extra moments in case the guards wake up soon. He turned and walked down the hallway. He felt lucky that the area wasn't well lit, though it didn't matter much since the hallway was empty.

"Guard! Stop!"

*I was wrong, there's always someone watching in this castle.*

Maldwyn halted and narrowed his eyes. He didn't recognize the voice. He went to turn, but realized that would give him away. He forgot he still had the chains around his arms. He had to hide them.

Carefully turning, he slowly slid his arms behind his back, making sure it looked natural. He stood straight, arms behind his back, and then nodded to a white wolf strutting toward him. For a second he thought it was Fric, but saw no scar.

The wolf eyed Maldwyn, then sniffed him up and down. "What are you doing?"

"Going to find Crepus," lied Maldwyn. "The prisoner is causing a nuisance."

"Don't bother the dragon. He has important business to attend." The wolf's mouth turned into an evil grin. "Why don't we show this prisoner a thing or two? I'm in the mood for fun."

Maldwyn hesitated, and then spoke. "I must get to Crepus." He furrowed his brows. "Now leave me be!"

"Then I'll report you for disobeying me."

"Who would I be disobeying?" replied Maldwyn.

"I'm second in command of the White Wolves." He said that as if he was the most important wolf in the world. He stood proudly. "We're Crepus's deadliest assassins."

Maldwyn wanted to roll his eyes. He gestured with a nod of his head for the wolf to proceed back to the door.

"That's a good boy," said the wolf. They approached the door, staring at it. It was locked, so the wolf stood on his hind legs, unlatching the lock with his mouth. He took his first step down the stairs, halting the moment he saw a guard lying motionless on the ground. He peered over his shoulder to see a wide smile on Maldwyn's face. Maldwyn kicked the wolf's backside, causing the second in command of the White Wolves to yelp in surprise. The wolf toppled down the stairs, crashing against the cold dungeon floor. He shook his head and looked up to see the huge ape jumping down the entire flight of stairs, baring his teeth, hands above his head in a fist, chains flinging in the air. Maldwyn landed in front of the wolf and snatched him in his arms. The wolves eyes were full of fear, wide and confused.

"Good night assassin," growled Maldwin, and before the wolf could reply, Maldwyn twisted his crystal, stunning him to sleep.

Maldwyn slapped his hands together, jingling the chains as he did so. His next stop—Aderyn.

# Chapter 6

The sound of muffled voices woke Zoey. She yawned and stood up in her nest, doing her best to get the voices out of her head. *Why are the trees waking me up?* Then an erratic knocking of some type echoed through the tree. She shook her feathers and stretched them high, getting the sleep out of her body. Then she peered over the edge of the nest.

She was expecting to see Aderyn somewhere on the floor moving things around, or something. Perhaps smashing rocks against the floor because that's exactly what it sounded like, but Zoey saw nothing like that going on. Aderyn was gone and she saw a perfect, shiny redwood floor.

A loud voice caused Zoey to quickly duck back into the nest. She realized that the trees didn't wake her up at all. There were spirit animals somewhere, perhaps the Dims, but she didn't know where. She closed her eyes to listen more intently, and when the voices grew louder she knew that spirit animals of some type had to be inside the tree.

*Who's here?*

"Be still and quiet, little one," came a whisper from above. Looking up, she saw Aderyn putting one wing feather up to her beak. "Shh."

Zoey mouthed the words. "Who is it?"

Aderyn mouthed back. "The Dims."

Zoey was at a loss. No matter where she went, the Dims seemed to follow and worse yet, they always seemed to find her. *Can't I have a day of peace?* Zoey's stomach flipped in circles as fear of the worst entered her mind. *What if they capture me again? What then? Will they kill me?*

Zoey looked around only to see zytes glowing throughout

their area of the tree. She was glad the nice and shiny floor below hid them from where the voices were coming.

*Is it morning?* Zoey wondered, though she didn't know since the windows were closed, but she figured it probably was. She felt rested. *And these Dims in the tree—who are they?* wondered Zoey. *Maybe they were just flying along and found the entrance to the tree? Wait! They would need to know the special knock to even open the entrance! How would they know that?*

Zoey quickly understood that whoever was down there knew the knock. She glanced at Aderyn, who shook her head. "We're fine and safe," Aderyn whispered.

Zoey wasn't so sure. She thought she was fine and safe with the Sihu Tribe. Experience told her otherwise. If she could only get back to the Cornell Forest and be home again, then all of this drama and chaos would be over. She remembered her old forest, and even though it had only been a week since she'd been away, she missed it terribly. She felt alone, even though Aderyn was here. She wanted her parents, even Coda, sitting next to her, telling her everything was going to be fine and that this was just a dream. She sighed as the thoughts rang around in her mind.

A pound, much louder than the previous sounds, took Zoey out of her daze. *Do they know we're definitely up here? They have to!*

Then a loud crack startled Zoey, causing her to fall in the nest and on her rump. It sounded as if the floor had just split in half. She peeked over the lip of the nest, but saw nothing disheartening. Off in one of the corners, however, proved differently.

*What is that?*

It was orange. The longer she stared at it, the more perplexed she became. She frowned slightly. Then she craned her neck to look at Aderyn, who was also looking at the orange object, as well, and she seemed very impressed. Then Aderyn whispered something similar to what Taregan had told her once before. "You have quite the imagination."

49

Zoey looked back at the object, and in an instant knew exactly what it was. The orange object was that same suitcase she saw when she had first walked into the Spruce Hallow. She apparently had imagined it then, but completely forgot about it until now.

*Why is it so significant, anyway? It's a stupid little suitcase. And, why do they keep saying that I have quite the imagination whenever that suitcase appears? This place is baffling sometimes. What does this have to do with my imagination?*

She crouched when another loud bang echoed across the giant, circular room. She ducked again, hiding in her thick nest. She stayed there for a few moments, until she looked over the twigs and feathers that formed the edge of the nest.

*Yes, still safe!*

But, glimpsing around the floor, she saw that the suitcase was gone.

"Well done," whispered Aderyn.

*What's so well done with an appearing and disappearing suitcase?*

"I know you're here, Aderyn!" came a voice from under the floor.

That didn't sound like Crepus. It didn't sound like anyone she'd ever heard before. Zoey looked up at Aderyn, who rolled her eyes, shook her head and smiled. Whoever it was didn't put one drop of fear into the snow owl's heart. In fact, it looked as if Aderyn was holding in a big laugh.

This went on for what seemed to be hours. Aderyn simply closed her eyes and fell asleep. Zoey, on the other hand, couldn't shake the fear that whoever it was down there was going to break through the floor at any second.

A loud crash dulled her hearing for a moment. She squinted and shook her head, trying to get her hearing back. She peered over the nest's edge again, seeing nothing to worry about. Everything was still the same. The walls themselves were glowing like usual, and looking up, she saw nothing to make her think danger would be tumbling down upon them anytime soon.

"Let's go!" came a voice from below. Zoey heard talons clacking against the wood in the entryway, then one by one, the dull sounds of wings flapping in the wind echoed around her, then slowly faded the farther away they went.

She glanced up at Aderyn. "Are they gone?"

Aderyn frowned. "Three flew from the redwood, leaving one to spy."

Zoey tilted her head. *How did she know there were four?*

The fourth stayed for a short stint and Zoey heard it leave several minutes after the other three.

Aderyn spoke, "Open."

Just as the order left her mouth, a small crack opened up, across the hollow of the tree and just above a small landing, allowing the morning light to peer in through a window that had formed.

"Zoey," said Aderyn.

Zoey looked up and saw the snow owl pointing her wing in an open gesture for her to fly over to the window's landing.

Zoey opened her wings, jumped high, and glided to the perch. She landed softly on the wooden plank and peered out of the window.

"Wow!" involuntarily came out of her mouth. She couldn't help it. She was higher than the rest of Ohm Totem. She felt like a giant. She could see a sliver of Mirror Falls smashing against the Mosazi River, creating a mist as it did so. The canyon looked small, as well. It had red and yellow walls that stood like guardians over the river. Beautiful green trees that spread into a vast forest stood off in the distance. She could see a large lake to her left, and as Aderyn landed next to her, the snow owl commented, "You're looking at Nereus Lake. There's a sacred island in that lake that no Dim or PureLight can set paw, talon, or hoof on. It should be avoided in all cases."

Zoey scrunched her brow. "Really? Why?"

51

Aderyn groomed her wing by flinging it over her head, then poking her beak into it over and over again. She stopped and peered out of the window. "We don't know."

Before Zoey could reply, Aderyn gasped and stepped back. She lost her balance for a moment, but kept herself under control. "I wasn't expecting this so soon." Her voice was serious.

Zoey followed Aderyn's gaze. To Zoey, nothing looked different. "What's the matter?" she asked.

Aderyn looked down and shook her head. "The Shiver is upon us." She pointed to a large structure, gray in color, off to the east. It was huge and topped with snow. And the tips of the trees that stood around it bore snow on them as well. Zoey could see that the snow stopped there, but small patches of it were sprinkled across the forest near them. Other than the mountains to her right, the rest of Ohm Totem looked warm and alive with color.

"What's the Shiver and why is it so scary?" asked Zoey.

"It's snow. That's why it's called The Shiver. Snow is something that hasn't been seen in this part of the world in...well...I don't know how long. The Shiver represents death. Crepus has reached the tipping point. What that means is that he has been able to successfully manipulate the majority of the population's thoughts in the Dim Lands. When this occurs, the weather patterns follow the thought patterns, mimicking them. In this case, the negative thought patterns of the Dims have created cold instead of warmth. If this isn't stopped soon, it will rapidly spread and change the island. Trees, foliage, and spirit animals will die because of it. This is a way for Crepus to control others with a heavier claw. He knows that it's easier to control a small population, rather than a large one."

Zoey's eyes widened. "He's meaning to kill most of us?"

"He is. And he wants you to be by his side. Do you understand why, Zoey?"

Zoey stepped back, nearly falling over the edge. She was shocked that Crepus wanted her. *Why can't he just get somebody else?* Gathering herself, she asked, "Why me—I don't understand."

"You will. We're protecting you until you do."

Zoey's shoulders drooped and rolled her eyes, mumbling something under her breath.

"Look up, child."

Zoey raised her head, but her eyes burned of fury. She was tired of everyone dangling a carrot in front of her, and then taking it away the moment she wanted to take a bite. *Why won't Aderyn just tell me why Crepus wants me by his side?*

"Patience, young one." Aderyn took a deep breath, lifting her wings as she did so. Then she dropped her wings to her sides while she exhaled. She did this a couple of more times, nodding to Zoey to imitate her. Zoey obeyed, and in a few moments she was calm again.

Zoey walked over to the window and looked out over the land. It quickly changed her mood for the better. "It's so beautiful here in Ohm Totem. It kind of tricks you, though, because everywhere I go someone wants to hurt me."

Zoey felt a wing fall across her back. "Not everyone."

"Can I just go home?"

"You can, but I don't think you will," responded Aderyn.

Zoey nodded. She knew she wouldn't be able to leave, at least not yet. Her heart had a string attached to this place, but why that string was there she did not know. She had the choice of leaving just after she first arrived in Ohm Totem, but had decided against it, even refusing to leave when Coda wanted to run through the portal.

*Coda!* Her heart about sank. She missed her brother. She missed everything—her home, her room, her toys, her friends, and most of all, her parents.

"Will I ever see my brother again?"

"I don't know." The owl looked out the window.

Zoey followed her gaze. They were again staring at the gray structure with snow on it.

"What *is* that big gray thing anyway?" asked Zoey.

"Oh, yes." Aderyn closed her eyes and the floor below them opened up. Aderyn flew down to the gashed floor in the entryway. She craned her neck. "Come."

Zoey glided down, landing next to the snow owl. The owl put her wing around Zoey. "Are you ready to see what it is?"

"To see what the gray thing is?"

The owl dipped her head. "Yes."

Zoey shrugged her shoulders and looked down. She mumbled. "I guess."

"That's our first training," replied Aderyn. "To fly unannounced and unseen, to the gray *thing* over there."

*Oh no!* thought Zoey. She almost rolled her eyes, but saw the excitement on Aderyn's face and decided not to. The last thing Zoey wanted to do was train. She was able to somehow get out of all of her training in the Sihu Tribe. Aren't they supposed to be hiding from Crepus until she can somehow get back to the Sihu Tribe, and do whatever it was she was supposed to do here? Zoey brought her wing to her beak and bit on the tip. "Training?"

"Yes, training. The Great Spirit led you to me. You are to be trained in the ways of stealth, the Art of Defense, and speed. Your natural talent of a Skylark is song. You will practice that as well." Her face seemed proud, as if she hadn't taught in a long, long time—as if she had been waiting for this moment for ages.

Zoey held her shoulders and face up with great effort, knowing that if she didn't they'd droop and droop until she was laying on the ground, wishing she could be somewhere else. *Ugh! I don't want to train.*

"Also," Aderyn's face became stern. "We are to train you in the thoughts and memory codes of the PureLight Order."

For a second, Zoey felt a large weight lift from her shoulders. The PureLight Order was something the Sihu Tribe had spoken about alot and she really wanted to know what it was and why it was so important. She didn't know what memory codes were, but nevertheless, she was excited. The moment, however, disappeared as quickly as it came.

54

Down below and hundreds of yards away appeared thousands of Dims. They were in a march, coming out from the Gwenfree Forest. They were heading toward the redwood tree and right for Aderyn and Zoey.

"What do we do?" asked Zoey, pointing to the Dims.

"We don't panic," replied Aderyn. She squinted her eyes, observing the area below. "Stay here. If you move, make only slow movements. The Dim's have eyes just as good as ours and I don't want them to see you." She hopped onto the ledge of the entrance opening, and then dropped like a lead weight out of the tree. Zoey gasped as she looked over the ledge, scanning the width of the tree, expecting to see Aderyn flying. She saw something quite the opposite.

Aderyn didn't fly. Instead, she dove straight down like a missile. Her feathers nearly matched that of the redwood tree, camouflaging her. *How did she change the color of her feathers?* Aderyn was a white snow owl moments ago, and now a redish-brown snow owl?

She continued to watch as Aderyn flew only millimeters from the bark of the tree. The skill that Aderyn had was astonishing. Just as Aderyn was about to fall lower than the edge of the cliff that stood next to the redwood, she shot to the left, over the edge of the steep cliff and around to the back of the redwood, disappearing from Zoey's sight.

Realizing that she was holding her breath as she watched, Zoey exhaled. She was amazed, but the amazement vanished the instant she looked past the canyon walls to the oncoming field of Dims. There were more and more of them coming out of the forest, trampling and flattening the long yellow grasses in front of them.

*Are they coming for me? What should I do?*

# Chapter 7

Tiny flakes of snow started to fall against Coda's fur. The sun created a pale glow against the eastern gray sky, giving little brightness to the cover of trees around them.

Coda and the group, minus Nova, had been following this jaguar for many miles. The change in temperature and the overcast sky came too quickly, something they'd never experienced before in Ohm Totem.

They walked in silence, and all but the jaguar were thinking about Nova, wondering about what happened and why.

Coda's head sank lower to the ground as he remembered Nova being swallowed up and vanishing with that shadow thing. He wished he could have seen where they went, but Chev was in the way when Nova went missing. *Did they just disappear? Is she dead? She can't be—she's Nova!* Coda shook his head. *Stop thinking that she's dead!*

His eyes were sullen and he wondered if the rest of the group's eyes mimicked his. Perhaps they knew something that he didn't? Did they suspect that she was alive? Did they feel her? He didn't want to ask, just in case the answer would devastate him. His heart ached and his mind filled with fear. *If she's not with us, how are we going to save Zoey? How are we going to save ourselves?*

The forest was cold under his paws and the snow started to increase, sticking on the land all around them. A gentle breeze buffeted his fur, but did little to comfort him. It only made him colder. The trees creating shadows on the ground were goliath—like all of the trees here in the Changyin Forest.

Numee walked by his side. "What do you think, Coda?"

she asked, affectionately brushing her nose against his cheek.

Coda barely lifted his head. "Think of what?"

"Where this jaguar is taking us? You know, this cat that won't tell us her name."

Coda stopped, prompting Numee to do the same. He stared into her green crystal, then into her eyes. He shrugged. "I don't know, but wherever it is I feel that it'll be safe."

Chev, who carried an unconscious Shikoba, walked on by. "I think we should continue to follow the jaguar, don't you?" His voice was distraught, like a child that had lost his mother, taking away his familiar happiness.

"There's not much else to do but follow her," said Numee.

The jaguar peered over her shoulder. "Come on! Hurry yourselves!" She prodded along, knowing her words wouldn't be ignored.

She was getting on Coda's nerves, though, and even though he felt safe around her, she was arrogant and bossy. But, perhaps she was protecting them and needed to be this way? Or, worse yet, perhaps she was leading them into a trap? He didn't really care, a feeling he'd never felt before. It was a feeling that happens when you lose something important to you, making you feel numb to the world. It was a feeling that was now doubled with Zoey gone, and now Nova.

Up ahead, Coda heard the sound of a waterfall, one that seemed very near, perhaps on the other side of the small hill they were coming upon. As the ground gradually rose into an incline, Coda noticed that the trees on the hill grew in strange ways. Many had their bark twirled in a spiral much like the Snow Tree's. He walked up to one of them and sniffed, then peered up its mammoth trunk. It went on for what seemed to be hundreds of feet. The lowest branch was much too high for him to jump and touch. Shaking his head, he remembered the time he thought Nova was hurt—when

57

he almost drowned in The River Ohm. When he went in search of her, he found that he had the ability to jump at a rate much further than anyone he'd ever known. It was a jump that could easily leap over a house.

"Let's go!"

Startled, Coda somberly looked to where the jaguar stood a little off in the distance. Her face was stern. If she were a human, he imagined her tapping her foot with her hands against her hips, slowly shaking her head the way a teacher does when catching a student doing something wrong. He stopped his tree inspection and crept forward, matching his posture with his melancholy state.

The long walk continued, bringing them closer to the waterfall. Its rushing sound echoed through his ears louder and louder. As the incline peaked, they stopped and stood at the top of the hill. Just to the north they saw a small waterfall cascading down thick rock and heavy moss. Ferns grew between and along the edges of the rock, bathing in the water's thick mist.

Chev was the first to speak: "Why are we here? It's beautiful and all, but..." he paused. "...why?" He shrugged his shoulders in a defeated manner. He wasn't taking Nova's disappearance too well, thought Coda. None of them were.

"It's for the panther," said the jaguar.

Coda looked left and right, trying to find what was *for* him. *The waterfall?* He frowned. "What's for me?"

The jaguar lifted her tail, pointing at a spot where the waterfall cascaded into a pool of water. "Behind the waterfall is an opening for you to enter. There, it holds something that you seek. The rest of us stay here."

Coda's eyes widened in delight. "Is it Zoey?"

The jaguar pursed her lips as if in deep in thought. "Zoey?" She looked slightly amused. "I don't know any Zoeys. But, go and find out. If it's her, then it's her. If not, then it won't matter. You'll find what you were seeking all along."

Coda shrugged, and then turned to Chev and Numee.

58

*Maybe they can tell me what to do?* Chev merely shrugged. He took his eyes from Coda, and then eyed the cold ground, the snow thickening more and more.

"What does your heart say, Coda?" asked Numee as she walked slowly toward him.

Coda closed his eyes and dropped to his heart. For many moments he stood in pause, waiting for an image or a feeling. But nothing arrived. He felt like an empty bucket. He sighed and shook his head. "I don't get anything. All I can feel is the snow hitting my back."

The jaguar walked over to him, whispering. "The daylight is running out and you don't want to be here when night comes." Her lips were now mere centimeters from his ear. She whispered. "Trust me."

Coda felt a tingling sensation engulf his body with her last words. He then felt at ease and his pelt warmed, bringing him a vast amount of energy. He took a deep breath, inhaling the rich and thick air, noticing that it's still very healthy to breathe here in the Dim Lands.

Coda brushed his fur against Numee and smiled. "I'll be fine."

Numee smiled back, and then nodded, but her eyes seemed to be filled with anxiety.

Chev butted the end of his trunk against Coda, accidentally hitting Shikoba into Coda. Chev jumped back. "Oh! Sorry Shikoba." He scrunched up his face in embarrassment, knowing she was unconscious and wouldn't be able to hear him anyway.

"She'll forgive you, Chev. I promise," replied Coda.

"Be careful, Coda." Numee sat on her hind legs, watching Coda as he started his descent down the hill.

Coda peered over his shoulder as he padded down the hill toward the waterfall. His friends looked sad, but the jaguar was quite different. Rather than focusing on Coda, she was watching everything around him, almost as if she was on guard, cautious of an attack or an ambush. This made Coda feel a little better. She wasn't out to get him after all—at least it looked that way.

The more the hill declined the faster Coda walked, bringing him closer and closer to the base of the waterfall. Finally, the ground leveled and he padded up to the water, and then sat beside it, overlooking a large bluish, green shallow pool with the waterfall pounding into it. Water splashed wildly about, sending water and mist through the air. He'd never been this close to a waterfall before and now he knew why. The sound of the waterfall was almost deafening to the ears and the gushes of wind it sent outward blew hard against his fur.

He turned his thoughts on the opening behind the waterfall and looked for the best route to get there. Taking a deep breath, he padded around the pool, getting even closer to the waterfall. And, just as he hoped, there was a very dark opening just beyond the fall.

*How am I going to see in there? It's so dark!*

From the edge of the pool to behind the waterfall was a very narrow land bridge formed by rock. It looked very wet and slippery. He decided that was probably the only route. Taking one step on the bridge, he instantly knew that if he took a wrong step, or had an unfocused thought, then it would land him straight into the cold pool of water next to him.

He placed his next paw just in front of his first paw and hugged the inner most edge of the rock wall, doing his best to avoid the crashing water. He knew, however, that the closer he got to the opening behind the fall, the wetter he'd get. He wasn't looking forward to that.

Taking another step, he slipped slightly, but leaned into the rock wall to steady himself, successfully keeping himself upright. He took another step, and then another, until he saw that he was a quarter of the way there.

*Only ten more steps. I can do it. I can do it.*

Looking at his paws, taking step after step, he continued on.

A moment later he slipped again, but caught himself

60

with his back leg just as he thought for sure he was falling. His heart started to beat faster as he panicked. Doubt crept into his mind. The rock acting as a bridge was getting even more slippery. *There's no way I can get across without falling into the ice cold water!*

With his next step, his body started to shake and his foot slipped out from under him. He twisted and landed hard on his side. His tail slid into the harsh, icy water. He went to take a breath, but couldn't. He'd never had the wind knocked out of him before, but he knew this had to be what was happening. It was as if his lungs stopped working and air was trying to come in at the same time that air was trying to go out. It was painful, but the more he concentrated on calming down his body, the easier it was to eventually breathe. Finally, after what seemed to be a very long minute, Coda felt at ease. Now he needed to figure out how to stand up.

Slowly moving his right front leg and his right back leg out from under him, and placing his right paw on the rock bridge, he slowly and methodically lifted himself up into a standing position. To his surprise, it worked like a charm.

Closing his eyes and remembering that by going into his heart and filling any fear he had full of light, would bring him back to balance and away from fear. The result would calm him down immediately. It would bring an uncanny focus as well.

He imagined himself falling into the water, then placed that image into his heart, embraced the fear, and gave it a pink color. Instantly, the picture faded and he imagined himself walking across the bridge with no further incident. In fact, at that very moment it was rather easy for him to picture success. He *could* do it.

He opened his eyes and felt an easiness flow from him, replaced by a sense of balance and knowing that he would not fall no matter what. Taking one step after the other was less about slipping and more about perfect concentration. Any slip under his paw was immediately felt and stabilized that very instant, keeping him upright. But, the more he inched closer to the end of the bridge, the more he had to squint his eyes, shielding his vision from the spray coming off the waterfall. Finally, he saw that he only had a couple of more feet to go. Instead of taking those last steps, he crouched and leaped, slightly brushing against the falling water, giving him an instant burst of energy.

Standing up tall, he assessed the situation. One thing left—the dark opening, the entrance to something unknown to him.

Coming closer and peering into the opening did him no good. Only darkness, just as he expected. He took one paw step inside and looked around. He saw absolutely nothing but blackness. The inside felt hollow and vast, almost as if he was in a large cave. He crept forward, bringing the rest of his body through the opening. A breeze landed against his fur as it swirled around, no doubt coming from the rushing water behind him.

*Where are zytes when you need them?*

He took another step and then another, walking as blind as a bat. Even though his night vision was superb, in here it wasn't. He couldn't see any shapes whatsoever. That didn't make sense to him, since he should be able to see in any darkness. Shouldn't he?

Another step. "Owe!" He ran into something hard, most likely a rock. He shook his head. *I can't see anything. I wish zytes would just turn on and light everything up.*

A moment later, that's what happened. A zyte to the left of him flickered on. Then another and another, until he could see exactly what was what, and he was glad of it, because a few more steps and he'd have slipped down a smooth, rocky hill that leveled out about fifty feet down. It would have been a fifty foot water slide.

Taking a glimpse at his surroundings, he saw that he was definitely in a massive cave, almost as big as the Marble Burrow, but not as deep because the back of the cave was easily seen. He could also see that there were only two ways to go in the cave—out the entrance or down the slope. *I guess I'm going down the hill.*

Gazing at the bottom of the slide, he saw a small, clear pool. He had a sense that it was waiting for him. He thought for a moment, wondering why he had felt such a thing. *How could a pool of water be waiting for someone, let alone me?* He shrugged off the silly feeling.

Crouching and leaning backwards, placing most of his weight on his hind legs, he started down the slope, then slipped. He grunted, steadied himself, and then let his body slide down the slope, knowing he couldn't stop himself now if he tried. He quickly found out that the rock slide was slathered with slimy algae, making this the fastest water slide he'd ever been on.

In what seemed like slow motion, he was sliding faster and faster down the long decline and it wasn't ending any time soon. He could only hope to land right into that pool of water below, no matter how cold it may be, as it would save him from some serious bruises.

Placing his tail straight back gave him more balance and steering capabilities. He leaned on his right side, heading right where he intended. A moment later his loud splash echoed throughout the cave as Coda's fur soaked full of water, covering him from head to tail tip. The water, however, was delightfully warm. It soothed and gave him another burst of energy.

Fortunately, the water was shallow. Placing his feet on the bottom, he walked out of the pool, shaking himself off. Then he glimpsed something out of the corner of his eye, about ten feet away and butting against the back of the cave. It looked like a rolling pin that was outlined in black and made out of gold. He knew exactly what it was.

Inching closer, he took a sniff. It was a scroll. And, again, he wondered, *why do I keep sniffing things? It must be because I'm a panther.*

The sniff had its place though, and he knew just from smelling it that the scroll wouldn't cause him any harm. It would be safe to open.

He placed one paw on the front edge of the scroll and nudged it open with his nose. It was blank.

*Where are the words? Aren't these things supposed to have something special to say?*

And, as if magic came from his thoughts, the words manifested on the gold scroll laid out before him. Sentence by sentence the letters formed, written with beautiful penmanship. He gazed into the scroll, reading out loud: "Only the one who bears the name Orion can decipher my code. Only Orion is welcomed into this abode. There is a message hidden in the chasms of Orion's memory, away from the unenlightened ones, the negatives, and the fools. From all of those who gaze into the majestic pool, it is only Orion who will find the most sacred of jewels."

The scroll had to be talking about the pool he slammed into on his way down the steep hill. But, there was the reference to Orion again, a name that was confusing Coda more and more. He still wondered how it was possible that he was Orion. He didn't feel it, but when he defended himself and the Sihu Tribe he felt something different, something greater than himself, and he knew he'd practiced the Art of Defense before. But when, and most importantly—where? The scroll said that only Orion can read it, and yet he could read it just fine. *Does that mean I am Orion?* He giggle. *No. That's silly.* He wasn't convinced.

Coda rolled up the scroll and scooped it up with his teeth. He padded over to the edge of the pool, and then dropped the scroll onto the stone ground. Sitting on his hind legs, he wrapped his tail around his forepaws and looked into the water.

The water was completely still, so much so that he could see his reflection. It was almost like a mirror, but not quite. It was shallow, with gray rocks protruding through a thick layer of algae on the bottom, giving a green tint to the water. It was quite beautiful, thought Coda.

He stared into the water for several moments, but

nothing happened. He didn't know what to expect, but *'nothing'* wasn't one of them. He gazed into the water even longer and his eyes searched the rocks at the bottom.

He took his gaze away from the rocks and stared at the reflection of the cave's dome-like ceiling reflected on the surface of the pool. There he saw something. Reflected on the water's surface was a symbol of some sort. It was etched in the ceiling. He looked up, seeing it more clearly.

It was that flower of life symbol that he had seen when he was at the Large Boulder. It was composed of multiple, evenly spaced, overlapping circles that started in the middle and radiated outward. It looked like a flower. The memory of San's words echoed in his mind, *It's considered a pathway to a better life. It holds the instructions on how to become a VioletLight. These symbols used to be everywhere..."*

He sighed. Thinking of San and Crepus brought the thought of his sister to the forefront of his mind. The idea of his sister being held as a prisoner in Crepus's castle didn't sit too well with Coda. His shoulder's drooped and his head hung low, making him stare back into the water. He had an angry look on his face, which revealed his true inner emotions. He wanted to get his sister back from Crepus more than anything in the world. He dug his claws into the stone flooring, dragging his foreclaws across it, making a loud scratching sound. Rage was starting to pour through him. *I'm going to get you, Crepus.*

He then remembered Honani's words about seeing the bigger picture. How could he see the bigger picture with his sister in serious danger? Exhaling deep and hard, he peered deeply into the surface of the water, zeroing in on his own eyes. And, that's when it happened.

The water started to ripple. He tilted his head, wondering why the sudden movement. He glimpsed at the entire cave, even looking behind him, but saw nothing that could have stirred the water. No rocks had fallen into it, no leaf, no nothing.

Glancing back at the water, he noticed that the ripples were completely gone. There, standing in place of his reflection, was a wider, more muscular, older and wiser looking black panther. It wasn't Coda. Or, at least he thought it wasn't him. When he took a gander at the large black panther's crystals, he saw that they were violet. Since Coda's crystals were red, he decided that this was definitely another spirit animal. It was a VioletLight and a very confident one at that, standing tall, with his thick chest pushed out, staring with eyes reflecting meaning, depth and soul. Coda then heard this VioletLight's voice in his head. He didn't quite know how he knew it was this black panther's voice, but he somehow knew. In fact, there was no doubt in Coda's mind that the reflection spoke in his mind.

He said, *I have nothing to hide and nothing to fear. I give and accept love without hesitation, without forethought or afterthought. I am all that I am. Nothing more. Nothing less. Take me as you see me, for I will offer you my soul, knowing that I am safe within The Great Spirit. With this knowledge, nothing can hurt me.*

Coda scrunched up his nose. It felt good to hear these words, but it went over his head. He saw, though, that when he scrunched his nose, the reflection didn't mimic him. So, he nodded his head, but the reflection remained the same, staring back at Coda. He put his paw out over the water, just to make sure he wasn't seeing things incorrectly. The reflection remained still.

The reflection smiled, then spoke, startling Coda.

"You are me and I am you."

The words were simple, but Coda's body found them to be profound. His entire being vibrated, and if he'd had skin rather than fur, he'd have goose bumps.

Coda nodded to the black panther. He stared at the VioletLight squarely in the eyes and said, "Hello?"

The reflection smiled, and nodded. "Hello, my friend. My name is Orion. My guess is that Nova has found you."

This made Coda feel much better. Finally, he had some

66

proof that he wasn't Orion and that this reflection staring at him was this great and famous panther. Coda smiled back. "Hi Orion." He looked around, and then back at Orion. "What do I do here?"

"You have to understand something that is very important. It's something that Nova has most assuredly spoken to you about." Orion paused and blinked. "You are me. You are Orion."

Coda's head jolted back. This was crazy talk. He furrowed his brow. "What? How? I don't understand!"

"What you see in this pool is only a small imprint of my energy that I left behind in this cave, before I entered the Cornell Forest, and into your mother's womb to be born again as you. In essence, I've left a small energetic piece of me—of you—in this pool in order to answer your questions on this very day. When this task is complete, this essence you speak to will merge with you, energetically completing you, for we are one and the same soul."

Coda shook his head furiously. "Huh?" Coda's mind was in a boggle. Again, this place—Ohm Totem—wasn't making sense.

Orion continued, "Your memory will start to return and your confusion will begin to erase when I merge with you. This I know and I'll make sure of it. Though, your innocence will remain, which is important for what you must accomplish during your stay here in Ohm Totem." Orion dipped his head. "But for now, watch and remember."

Orion's body disappeared and Coda sat staring at the pool, see that his reflection was missing, along with the reflection of the stone ceiling. An instant later, the water started to form an image, then a scene. The pool now looked like a full sized movie screen, as if a movie projector was projecting an image onto the surface of the water.

Coda watched as he saw the back of Orion and the back of a large tiger sitting on a hill overlooking a large lake. They were speaking as if they'd been friends for a long time, at least that's what it seemed like. *When was this?* Coda wondered. Shrugging his shoulders and not knowing the place, or how many moons ago this was, he simply watched and listened.

"I'm not convinced that Nova knows the way, Orion." The tiger looked down, as if distraught.

Orion gave a friendly nudge to his tiger friend. "Nova knows more than most. I'm not convinced about your thoughts on Crepus. He's been coming by lately, doing his best to convince me, just as you are trying to do now, but I see the error in his thinking. All of us VioletLights see the error in his thought process. I don't know why he wants to create such things."

The tiger slowly shook his head, not understanding Orion's doubt. "Crepus has ideas like none-other. They're revolutionary. Imagine if we used our magic to make the technology that he speaks of. Imagine flying from Ionna Tribe to Sihu Tribe in a hovering craft. It'd only take us a matter of several moments, rather than half a day by the Zolts." Coda remembered the Zolts, the large boulders in the tunnels that took Zoey, San, and him for a ride—an almost deadly ride.

Orion dipped his head. "What's our hurry? Why do we need to be somewhere in such a rush? These things I don't understand. They make me uneasy. We came here to Ohm Totem to get away from all of that, to leave technology behind in order to gain more wisdom and peace. We left to learn life's lessons and to be more in tune with ourselves, the Earth and The Great Spirit. We used to have such things before we entered into Ohm Totem—flying crafts, laser technology, water crafts, and more. All it did was take us farther away from spirit, and almost to our own destruction."

Exasperated, the tiger took a deep breath and stood up. "I'm going to go to the Zolt now and travel back to Sihu Tribe. Please think on all that I have said, Orion."

Orion gave a nod, staring out across the lake. He was calm and composed, but in deep thought or meditation. The tiger pressed his muzzle against Orion's shoulder, a friendly gesture of goodbye. As Coda watched the scene, he saw the tiger turn around, bringing his face into view. Coda jumped back in fright.

*Sigun! Orion was friends with Sigun? He's a traitor!*

As he looked back into the pool, he saw the image of Orion fade and a new scene appeared. Orion was standing face to face with Crepus. They were on level ground and the sky was a perfect blue with very few clouds. He could tell the day was hot and the sun was probably at its highest point. To Orion's right was the large lake. Then Coda's eyes widened when he saw that Crepus's crystals matched that of Orion's—violet. This must be before Crepus's crystals turned black.

Orion grinned. "Dear Crepus, my friend. I don't know why you continue to speak of these things. I'm not going to change my mind. I cannot, and will not, support you on this."

Crepus bowed his head, but his eyes showed sadness. "Orion, please consider what I have to say. If we band together, we can create the most majestic things that creation has ever seen, let alone touched. I have plans for large palaces where we can have meetings, where we can dictate the PureLight Order to the rest of Ohm Totem. I have ideas of disc shaped crafts that hover through the sky. Together, we VioletLights can learn how to create these things. The entire population of Ohm Totem can have large, individual dwellings again, just like we once had in the place we left, and they can be gorgeous creations unto themselves."

"You're leading us astray, Crepus. Creation is right here, right now. We have everything we need right before us, in the air, in the water, in the trees, in the Earth." Orion grimaced. "Lust and desire, Crepus, seep into you. When there is no lust, all things are calm, in harmony with nature, and at peace. You, of all spirit animals, should know this."

Crepus turned his head for a moment, as if hearing

69

words from another source— listening to an invisible someone, or something, whispering in his ear. That's when Orion saw it and felt it. This wasn't just Crepus that Orion was speaking with. Something had taken a hold of Crepus, and changed his thoughts and heart. Orion was speaking and listening to Crepus's speaker this entire day. How long this speaker had a hold on Crepus, Orion did not know. How this speaker found its way to Ohm Totem, and into a VioletLight, baffled Orion even more. This speaker was not of this Earth and was very powerful. Orion understand at that moment that only devastation would come of this. Crepus's speaker would have it no other way.

Orion spoke: "A VioletLight Master doesn't try to be impressive, thus he truly is impressive. A fearful spirit animal keeps reaching out with its paws, struggling for power and control, desiring power and control with all his might, thus never having enough. The VioletLight sees this and as an example of truth, the VioletLight teaches others by interesting himself with the internal and not the external, with the seed and not the plant. Thus he knows where to focus the water—more on the seed and roots, and less on the plant. For what we have in life is not what's outside of it, but what's inside, where true beauty and health originate." Orion paused until Crepus looked back at him. "Does that make sense, Speaker of Crepus?"

A loud hiss resonated across the land, echoing against the blue sky. The hiss was from the mouth of Crepus, and with it came an invisible force, the first act of the Dark Arts on the Island of Ohm Totem, picking Orion up off his feet and throwing him several yards into the air. With a loud thud, Orion hit hard against the grass, tumbling backwards, until he steadied himself onto his feet. He shook the stars away from his vision and tilted his head. He'd never felt such an icy, negative, confined force touch him. It chilled him to the bones, but with one deep breath, his body became warm and free again.

Orion lifted his eyes to Crepus's. "You will not invade my

70

space again, Speaker! I forbid it. Do not step on Ionna Tribe Lands from this point forward."

Crepus smiled and Coda watched the scene unfold, seeing the Komodo Dragon's crystals fade. Crepus's violet crystals turned to gray, then went solid black.

"We tried to do it the nice way, Orion." Crepus's voice was now different, as if someone else was using his mind, his will, and his body to speak. Orion knew this was the case, but remained calm and listened as Crepus's Speaker carried on. "We tried to talk with you VioletLights, but you're all as dumb as you look. You all refuse our genius and turn away from our brilliance. We only want to make this land a more workable place, a more livable, functioning society. We will now take it by force. Your lands will soon be ours."

With that, Crepus turned and ran, hastily heading south toward his tribal lands—where Crepus Castle stood. His speed, like most VioletLights, mirrored that of the fastest animals, but with the stamina to outlast them all. He quickly disappeared into Gwenfree Forest.

Then Coda, still peering into the beautiful water, forgot who he was, or better yet, which one he was. Is he Orion, or is he Coda? For a second, he thought he was Orion, feeling everything that Orion felt on that day.

*Who am I?*

His thoughts brought him back to himself. He was still sitting at the edge of the pool and gazing into the scenes of Orion's life—his old life, the life he had before becoming Coda.

The next scene erupted like no other, and even the water bubbled. It started with Orion sitting comfortably on a hill. It was another gorgeous sunny day and he was in deep concentration, searching for a resolution to the Crepus dilemma. Orion was overlooking Nereus Lake when he found it—the Art of Defense. It came to him from The Great Spirit, like a gift to a child on his first birthday. It wasn't something Orion expected, or something he was particularly looking for, but it came and changed his entire world. He had to teach all nine tribes, even Crepus's tribe— if their crystals hadn't changed yet like their once wise counselor, Crepus.

Orion discerned that this art had never been shared or used in this world and it would be difficult to teach every spirit animal in such a short span. He felt that everything was about to change for the worse. Orion sighed, understanding that if all of the inhabitants of Ohm Totem were VioletLights, then the Art of Defense wouldn't be needed. But, in truth, very few were VioletLights, so he had to teach this new art, and quickly.

An instant later, his heart sank. It was too late, at least for his tribe. Coming near to Lake Nereus, marching in perfect unison out of Gwenfree Forest and splashing through The River Ohm, were thousands of PureLights coming by way of Crepus Castle. Crepus was in the lead, and yes, the spirit animals that followed him had crystals that were drained of its color and turned to gray.

With Orion's incredible vision, he could see that they all had menacing eyes. They were eyes that wanted to compete or worse yet, wanted to end the life of their opponents. They marched with purpose, but with very little light in their auras. From that moment on, Orion dubbed them the Dims. Then many moons later, Crepus took it as his own last name, and then gave it to all of his followers who in turn named every land they took as the Dim Lands.

The closer the Dims marched to Orion's Ionna Tribe, the faster Orion's heart beat. He really didn't know what to do. He hadn't trained the Ionna Tribe in the Art of Defense. They didn't have a chance against these blood thirsty spirit animals who probably had been training for many moons in their style of fighting.

Calming himself down and pushing away his doubt and sadness, Orion turned and bolted down the hill to his tribe-mates. They were doing their usual daily routines.

"Everyone, come quick!" cried Orion, as he stood on a

large boulder overlooking the northern edge of Nereus Lake. His voice was full of alarm and the many spirit animals in his tribe who heard it immediately ran to him, listening intently.

"I've done a grave wrong to you all. I have kept a secret that I didn't take as seriously as I should have. Crepus the VioletLight, our friend and PureLight of the Kasimira lineage, is no longer himself. He is half spirit animal, half something else." Orion paused, sensing the confusion coming over the crowd.

A rhinoceros with indigo colored crystals stepped forward, "We don't understand, Orion. Are we in danger? By the sound of your voice, I feel it to be so."

Orion nodded his head yes, and then spoke again. "Yes, Artax, we are in great danger and we must hide, all of us. As you can see..." he pointed to the other end of the lake where the Dims approached in full view, "...we are about to be attacked, something that has never occurred in Ohm Totem. The Great Spirit and All That IS has just gifted me with a special defensive technique that we can use against our new aggressors, but I have not the moments to teach you, so we must leave our land, hide, and practice this new art."

"What?" came a voice from the crowd. "This isn't making any sense, Orion."

"It would take all night to explain, but trust me—we must leave now. We aren't ready for an attack. We must keep our children and ourselves safe. Is that something you understand?"

The sudden commotion amongst his tribe-mates was something unbearable for Orion to see. He didn't deliver the message as calmly as he would have liked, which caused too much of a stir and too much stress amongst his friends and family. This was a mistake. For certain, they'd go this way and that, instead of in an orderly retreat.

Orion leaped from his spot, walking into the crowd and pushing their backsides with his muzzle, urging them to go west into the Seren Forest where the Seren Tribe and Aria the VioletLight lived—home of the shape shifting spirit animals.

"Go to the Seren Forest. We'll learn the Art of Shape Shifting there, allowing us to hide easily until we are ready to learn the Art of Defense," he yelled. And many did go, but others either didn't hear his words, or thought that fighting was their best and only resort.

Artax, the rhinoceros, came to Orion's side, helping him to urge his tribe to retreat. He pushed his fellow tribe-mates toward Seren Forest.

"Please!" called out Orion. "Find Aria—let her keep you hidden and safe."

Orion turned to Artax, who was trying to get some more stubborn tribe-mates to run, but to no avail.

"Leave them here," said Orion.

Peering over his shoulder, Artax's eyes narrowed as he snorted, "No!"

The Dims had arrived and the worst of them rushed at full speed, their ears pulled back, their crystal's dimmed, and their sharp fangs in full display.

"Artax!" cried Orion. "Go!"

Artax ignored him and faced the coming onslaught, placing himself in front of Orion, his best friend and forever ally.

Orion, knowing the Art of Defense full well even without practicing it, because the Great Spirit had gifted it to him in a way that granted him instant mastery, jumped over Artax and stomped his foot on the ground. A blast of pure energy from Orion's stomp intercepted the first wave of oncoming Dims, spinning them wildly into the air and crashing them into each other as they flipped head over heels. Some were stunned instantly, but after a few moments the majority dusted themselves off, still wondering what had just happened. Then they proceeded with their push toward Ionna Tribe.

Artax was speechless. Where did his friend get such a power and when did he learn how to use it? But, walking forward as if no mighty force could touch him, was Crepus. Artax's jaw dropped and the many Ionna tribe-mates who stayed to defend this land gasped out loud. How could Crepus withstand such a force?

"Get ready!" yelled Orion. "And everyone spread out to form a half moon—quickly! They're coming!"

And the Dims, again, were in a full run, ready to pounce on their opponents. As they ran, the Dims formed a wedge, with Crepus at the apex. Orion knew this was the best offense Crepus could use at this very moment. It would allow a big thrust into Orion's defensive position. But, if Orion's tribe-mates were skilled enough in defense, the half-moon would work well, effectively countering on offensive wedge attack. Orion's group could break into two parts precisely when the wedge hit, but there was no training, no chance for him to explain this to his friends. He just had to hope for a miracle.

The Dim's hooves and paws became louder and louder until they hit the Ionna Tribe at full speed. Orion ducked the first attacker, flipping a lion over his shoulder, forcing it on its back. He quickly stunned it and moved on, facing three attackers coming right at him. He jumped, grabbing a bear's front leg and threw it across the field, hitting another Dim just as it attacked Artax, allowing Artax to make short work of him.

Coda knew that once Artax was trained in the Art of Defense, nothing could stop that rhino.

In the next instant, Orion felt a blow to his side, then a swipe to his face. Blood coursed across his cheek, splattering against his eyes and momentarily blinding him, forcing Orion to shut them. Then it happened. The true Art of Defense.

As Orion kept his eyes closed, he was surprised to see the energy of his attackers. First, he noticed that when a Dim thought about striking a certain spot, he'd see a streak of color shoot to the exact area where the strike was going to hit. Secondly, this allowed him to dodge any swipe, duck any bite, and move without much thought put into it. He could see what was going to happen a second before it actually occurred.

Dodging another attack, Orion stopped and took a deep breath, then exhaled a ferocious pulse of energy at two attackers, sending them flying through the air and slamming into several Dims behind them. Another swipe and he ducked, then grabbed the fore-paw of a bobcat, twisting it, thus making the cat land flat on its back. Orion pressed on its gray crystal, stunning it.

"Argh!" came a loud sound behind Orion. He turned to see Artax fall, bloodied from several Dims and being pummeled as he lay on the ground. Artax did his best to get up, swinging his large tusk, hitting a wolverine and sending it across the grass. But there were too many.

Orion, sprinting toward Artax, reached his friend just in time to see Artax's last moments of life. Artax's eyes were filled with sorrow. He had never imagined friends turning against friends, PureLight tribe against PureLight tribe. His eyes had lost all hope.

In a matter of seconds, the light in Artax's crystals glowed less brilliant and his eyes faded to the haze of imminent death. Orion screamed, "No!" His voice echoed throughout the land, shaking the grasses they stood upon and putting a fright into some of the Dims, making them fall back.

Orion looked around. His shoulders drooped. All hope that he held evaporated. His friends, those who stayed and defended these sacred grounds, were dead. Hundreds of his tribe-mates lay motionless on the long green grass next to Nereus Lake. They were surrounded by thousands of Dims breathing heavily, stained with blood and pulsing with adrenaline, ready to kill more.

And there, no more than twenty yards away, stood Crepus. He held a nasty smile and displayed his body for Orion to see. Crepus had no scratch or pain of injury. Before Orion could speak to his old Komodo dragon friend, Crepus gave an order to his Dim warriors. Pointing at Orion with his sharp claws, he yelled, "Kill him!"

Orion crouched, and then sprang at the first wave of attackers, which was no more than a few Dims. With pin point accuracy, he pressed on their crystals, sending them falling straight onto their backs, stunned. He then closed his eyes and took a deep breath. All sound became silent and he became one with his heart, body and mind, merging them together. On his exhale, he leaped forward and high over the Dims, landing far behind them, and headed to the Shan Tribe, where the Rolling Hills of Shan met the Pyramid of Ohm. He ran with the hope that the Dims would follow him, instead of any potential surviving tribes-mates who fled and hid in the Seren Forest.

He looked back. His plan worked. They did follow, though they were far behind and getting even further. No spirit animal in Ohm Totem had the speed of Orion, nor the stamina—except Crepus. Orion could run for moons if he so chose. And he may have to in order to get to Shan Tribe soon enough to teach them the Art of Defense. Though, as he ran, he wept. Not because of the fight, but because of his friends. Many were now gone, floating toward The Great Spirit. They were brave, but didn't listen. They could have survived if they would have fled like he'd asked them to do, but they didn't. A twinge of anger pricked at his soul.

Heading toward the large trees of the Changyin Forest, he realized that his tribe-mates risked their lives to defend their own ground. Judging them for doing so would lead him nowhere. They did what they did because they thought it was right. It was their lesson, not his.

Coda, completely entrenched and enthralled with everything he was watching, leaned a little too far forward, lost his balance, and splashed into the pool. Surprised and twisting his body as he sloshed warm water around, he gathered his feet beneath him and stood. He walked out of the water shaking himself dry, closed his eyes and calmed himself with several deep breaths. *That's better.*

77

He turned, facing the pool showing only his own reflection. Orion was no longer there. So he stood, peering into the water for several more minutes. Even though he stared into his own eyes looking back at him, nothing out of the ordinary occurred. The only difference now was how he felt—stronger, almost as if his muscles had grown in size. He also felt a little more confident about himself. He sensed that perhaps he really was this Orion fellow before he was born as Coda.

Shaking his head back and forth, he suddenly remembered something. That jaguar outside, there was something about her on the tip of his mind but it just wouldn't come forward. Something he knew. But, what was it?

*Her name!*

He knew her name. He remembered her somehow. Yes, from the distant past. She was his first student. She was always eager to learn the Art, to defend herself and her tribe—the Shan Tribe.

He remembered her like it was yesterday. She helped me give the knowledge of the Art of Defense to her tribe, and to their VioletLight, Lao.

He had to get to her now, to free her. Once he spoke her name, she'd be free of the gray crystal penetrating her soul. She knew this, and that's why she didn't give her name to them when she first met Coda's group of travelers. If she had, she couldn't so easily be changed. That's why she seemed like a loner, a wanderer of the Dim Lands, waiting for him to return. Orion had told her that he'd be back for her someday, to help her and to save her by bringing light to her, making her ready to serve the PureLights of Ohm Totem again—defending all against the Speaker of Crepus.

He crouched, and with one hefty jump, Coda leaped to the top of the hill and landed at the entrance of this deep, dark cave. Instantly, the zytes turned off. Now he only had the dim light coming through the opening to guide his way out.

When he emerged from the cave, it was into a loud world of rushing water slamming against bedrock.

The waterfall.

Inching his way over the rocky bridge, he eyed his friends at the top of the hill. The snow on the ground was much thicker now, making him wonder how long he was in there. And the air was much colder, almost making him shiver. He noticed, and to his relief, that the flakes had stopped falling from the sky.

He dipped his head to his friends as he walked up the hill, feeling the cold crunch of snow beneath his paws.

His friends didn't nod back. Instead, they opened their jaws in silent awe. *What's the matter?* thought Coda.

He reached the crest and dipped his head again in greeting while sitting down on his hind legs. He stretched out and yawned as if he had just had a day of hard work. He laid on the ground, peacefully waiting for their questions.

It was Chev who started first. "Umm, so...huh." He coughed and then 'ahem-ed'. "Well, where did you get those new blue crystals on your head and chest?"

Coda jerked his head up, "Huh?"

Numee sat next to him, saying, "Coda? Your crystals are now blue. That's unusual. I've never seen someone go from red to blue so quickly. Usually, you move up a color scale the higher you evolve. Instead, you skipped orange, yellow, and green, landing on blue."

Coda stood up, looking for a mirror, but he wasn't in Gladstone anymore so he couldn't look at himself no matter how hard he tried. He didn't want to go back down into the cave to look in the pool to see what he'd become. He'd just have to accept what they said as truth, which wasn't too hard to do.

"And," replied Chev. "Where'd those muscles come from? I thought I was the muscular stud, but now look at you?"

Coda scrunched his nose. "What do you mean?"

"Uh, you've got rippling muscles, Mister Muscle Cat,"

retorted Chev, still holding a knocked out Shikoba rolled in his trunk.

"I do?"

"Yes, you do." It was the jaguar who spoke. She had a serious face, but a pleasant expression, as if she knew something that perhaps no one else knew...something about Orion. Or, better yet, about Coda, who was once the mighty Orion and hero of Ohm Totem. "You've merged with the piece of you that has been waiting inside the cave for many moons. You're now feeling the energy of Orion's small imprint, creating a different, more whole you. It's grown you up a little. You are stronger, more confident, and in a sense, wiser."

That was funny to hear. Well, everything was funny and strange in Ohm Totem, and sometimes outright confusing. He shrugged, not feeling any the wiser, but she was right about strength and confidence. He felt thick, balanced, and held his chest out like a healthy, more improved Coda.

Coda perked up, remembering something.

*Her name.*

He nodded his head toward her, silently telling her to come closer. She dipped her head in return and slowly approached him.

"I know your name," he said.

The jaguar bowed before him. "Thank you, Orion."

"That's not my name anymore. I go by Coda, and will from this day forward." Surprising himself, he thought, *Wow, I sound older.*

Chev and Numee simply watched, being patient and holding the space for what was unfolding, though they had no idea what was *really* going on. Nor did Coda. However, he felt that nothing terrible was going to come from this, by telling this jaguar her name.

He brushed his cheek against hers and loudly whispered, "Meli."

As if she'd been struck by a spear, Meli fell back against the mossy ground. She writhed left and right, twisting and turning in pain. Coda's eyes instantly showed worry as he leaned over her. "Are you okay?" He looked at Numee, who was already in healer mode as she padded over the snow toward them.

"What's happening?" Coda asked.

"I don't know." Numee placed her paws on the squirming jaguar, doing her best to bring in Prana.

The thud of Chev's big feet against the snow vibrated in Coda's ears as he came closer. "Anything I can do?"

Numee shook her head as she drew more and more Prana through her paws and into Meli's body. Coda could do nothing but watch. Had he hurt her? Was she dying?

Meli suddenly convulsed and her body went into a fetal position. She moaned, then spasmed again. It looked as if she was having a seizure, and a very painful one.

*What have I done?*

# Chapter 8

"You've forgotten. And I'm sorry."

Zoey stared at Aderyn as if she was an alien from a different planet. She didn't know what Aderyn was talking about. "What did I forget?"

"Zoey, there is so much I want to say and so much that I want you to remember, but alas, I must keep my beak shut and allow you your own journey of self-discovery."

They sat on the jagged wood floor, just behind the lip of the small, shadowed entrance of the redwood tree. Right after Aderyn had flown like a bullet down the tree, disappeared, and quickly reappeared moments later she realized that Zoey had forgotten.

Zoey continued to wonder what it was that she had forgotten as she stared into Aderyn's eyes.

"You're going to have to relearn what you once mastered. You've forgotten the Art of Shape-Shifting."

Zoey tilted her head. "Shape-Shifting?"

"Yes. It's the ability to blend into your surroundings by becoming your surroundings, which is what you saw me do when I flew close to the redwood. I was camouflaged." She grinned. "There's more to it than that, such as changing into another spirit animal form, or an owl into a bluebird, for example. But, I'm only going to teach you how to camouflage yourself."

"So, I can become an eagle?"

"If you wish," replied Aderyn. "However, that's something you'll have to learn on your own. It's a skill that's not easily done, nor is it easily undone."

"Have you turned into another animal before?"

Aderyn blinked, looking as if the conversation was

becoming a little too elementary for her. She nodded. "I have."

Zoey opened her wings wide with surprise. "You can do that?" *I wonder if she was the bluebird who we followed into the blackberry tunnel.* "Can you change into something now?"

Aderyn shook her head. "It's not for play or tricks. It's only used when necessary, like all VioletLight magic. To use it, such as you'd like me to right now, would be abusing its power. It would weaken its strength. It should be used without ego and without desire. Thus is the only way that I use it." She patted Zoey's back with her wing. "We'll train tomorrow and you'll learn, or rather, relearn what you once mastered."

"But, you can't teach me to turn into other spirit animals?"

Aderyn shook her head. "I won't. Like I said, I'll teach you camouflage."

Zoey gave a nod, but was a little bummed. She thought it would be amazing to be any spirit animal that she wanted. Perhaps an elephant, like Chev, or a snow leopard like Nova.

*Nova and Chev. I miss them. I hope they're all safe and taking care of my brother.*

With a little sadness, she glanced outside. And there were the Dims, just on the other side of the canyon, practicing their aggressive fighting techniques on each other.

Looking up, Zoey saw the sky forming gray clouds, bringing a dull haze to the day. Then a cold chill blew in, reminding her of the days of falling snow in Gladstone where she would play in the Cornell Forest, creating snow forts and protecting herself from the snow ball fights her brother and friends would start.

Zoey smiled at the memories, and then wondered if the Dims knew they were being watched. She doubted it, since she and Aderyn were well hidden behind the shaded

83

entrance of the redwood tree.

Aderyn looked out at the army of Dims. "They know we're watching. They do this outside the canyon to intimidate me. They've been doing so ever since they defeated our tribe, the Gwenfree." She made a melancholy face and shrugged. "It's so silly."

"How long are they going to be practicing?" asked Zoey.

"Long. It's a workout just to watch them. They last until dusk, when the sun heads to its lowest point in the west. It's the worst type of training, though. They need rest, instead of daily practice. Crepus has no idea what he's doing to them. He trains them in a way that lowers morale and exhausts them." Aderyn sighed. "If I still had any tribe left at all, those Dims right there would be no match for us, especially if all of the PureLight Tribes were intact and unified. But, alas, only two tribes remain—Zola and Sihu— and they're doing their best to survive."

"Why don't they join together, the two tribes?"

"That would spread them too thin. Right now, each tribe needs to be fully intact to defend the land upon which they live. You have to understand that the Dims outnumber us not by the hundreds, but by the thousands upon thousands."

"What?" Zoey suddenly looked exasperated. "Then how can we win?"

"Win? That's such a strange word. Who decides the victor? What is victory, anyway? Is the winner the side that has fewer piled up dead bodies? Some would say that's victory. Others would say that's a tragedy. Until there is no war, ever again, there will be no victory. When two opposing sides can simply talk things out and find a solution, then that's victory. When we understand that killing one another, suppressing a society and distributing hate affects everyone, including ourselves, then, and only then, will we have "won". That's why you're here, Zoey. I have a lot to train you, but when I'm done you'll be the brightest light among us." She lifted her wings in the air like

84

a kid during Christmas time. "And I can hardly wait!"

A loud sound interrupted their conversation and Aderyn peered out of the entrance. Just as she did, a large falcon lunged at her, its sharp talons missing her by a mere centimeter. Zoey jumped back as Aderyn grabbed the falcon's leg with her beak, quickly pulling it through the entrance hole.

A racket of feathers flew everywhere as both owl and falcon tossed and wrestled, each one frantically trying to get the upper wing on the other. Zoey backed up, but then remembered that she had helped in a fight once before, when Coda and Chev were being attacked by the lion and coyotes. She could help out again.

Zoey hovered in the air, nearly hitting her head against the ceiling, and then darted at the falcon that had Aderyn pinned to the jagged wood floor. Zoey smashed her feet against one of the falcon's broad wings, sending it flying toward the opening, almost flinging it through the entrance.

Aderyn spread her wings and flew at the falcon, grasping its tail and then doing the fastest flip Zoey had ever seen, and landed on top of the falcon. The falcon beat its feathers up and down, doing its best to escape, but Aderyn had her pinned.

The falcon frowned. "That's not fair." She was a female with a very sweet voice. "Two against one? I had you, Aderyn!"

Aderyn laughed. "You're getting better. Plus, you're the one who attacked me. You should have been more aware of your surroundings and noticed another spirit animal in here with me. Hasn't Lao taught you anything?"

*Lao?* Confused, Zoey looked left and right, trying to assess the situation, but could only say, "Wait. What?"

Aderyn stepped off the falcon, allowing her to get up and shake herself. They both giggled, leaving Zoey even more perplexed.

Aderyn pointed at the falcon. "Zoey, this is Luli. She's a PureLight from the Shan Tribe of the eastern lands of Ohm

Totem."

Luli used her wings to continue to brush herself off while saying under her breath, "Or what's left of Shan Tribe."

Luli looked up at Zoey, extending her wing for a wing shake, which Zoey gladly gave her. Luli half smiled. "Hi, I'm one of only a dozen PureLights left in Shan Tribe. Nice to meet you."

Zoey, seeing that the falcon had indigo crystals, relaxed a bit.

"What's your name?" asked Luli.

"I'm Zoey."

"What?" Luli's smile changed into an astonished look. She turned to Aderyn. "How long has she been here?"

"She arrived in Ohm Totem several moons ago. She was kidnapped by Crepus, so I grabbed her and brought her here."

Luli bowed to Zoey. "I'm honored."

*Why is everyone honored when they meet me?*

"Have you anything to report, Luli?" asked Aderyn.

Having regained her composure, Luli stiffened and said, "I do." She turned around and gazed out of the entrance opening, staring at the mass of Dims training below. "They grow stronger. All that's left of us PureLights in Shan Tribe are now holed up in The Pyramid Ohm. It's our last safe haven. I fear a large force could easily overtake us, so just in case that happens I brought you this."

Luli turned and held out her wing to Aderyn, but Zoey saw nothing. Luli whispered something that Zoey couldn't quite hear, and then a moment later something formed as if it had just popped out of nothingness and into physicality. It was a key, sitting nicely on Luli's outstretched wing.

Aderyn gasped, and then took it. Her yellow owl eyes grew wide with shock and she forcefully shook her head. "It was a huge risk bringing this to me. Why would you do that? You don't think its safe anymore with Lao, the VioletLight?" She said VioletLight as if inferring that a VioletLight would be all the protection the key would need.

86

The falcon shook her head. "As the holder of the key, I'm responsible for its safe keeping. However, it's not safe with me or my tribe, anymore. Lao agreed that it should be someplace far away from the pyramid. We thought of you, Aderyn, here in the west—in the redwood."

Aderyn nodded. "I see."

"When the moment arrives, you'll know when to bring it back and use it," added Luli. "I know I can trust you with this. You have a way of keeping things hidden, including yourself and the PureLight Order." She pointed to the long line of Dim soldiers practicing. "And hidden from the Dims."

*The PureLight Order. There's that word again*, thought Zoey. She looked down, mumbling, "What's the PureLight Order?"

Aderyn and Luli leaned in, doing their best to hear her. "What was that, dear?" asked Aderyn. "We didn't hear you."

Remembering Nova and Numee's teachings, she lifted her head and puffed out her chest feathers. She was tired of mumbling, and tired of repeating herself over and over again. She now just wanted to be heard. "What's the PureLight Order?"

Aderyn gave a smile, knowing that Zoey had just made an important decision in her life. Not by asking about the PureLight Order, but by asking with focus and confidence. Aderyn cleared her throat. "It's the most important scroll in Ohm Totem, perhaps the most important in the entire world. It contains The Great Spirit's list of suggestions on how to live a well-balanced, healthy life. The PureLight Order has the ability to change a Dim into a PureLight with just one gaze. It's feared by Crepus Dim."

Zoey piped up. "Why don't we use it, then?"

Luli explained. "It will be used, but not until the correct moment."

Zoey pointed to the Dims below. "Let's go and use it on *them*."

"When you rush into things, Zoey, failure usually

follows. Forcing something that's not ready, ruins what almost was." Aderyn's face was stern. "We may lose the scroll if we take it to a large group of Dims like the one out there." Aderyn showed Zoey the key. "That's why we have the key. It's the secret to awakening many Dims all at once, instantaneously changing them back into PureLights. It's what Crepus fears most, seconded only by his fear of the PureLight Order. The lock the key opens is guarded by his most trusted guards."

Zoey tilted her head. "Where's the lock?"

"At Crepus Castle," replied the owl. "It was created long ago, even before Crepus built the castle in the middle of Ohm Totem, making it the prime location for what this key can do when opening that lock."

Luli nudged Aderyn. "I'm going to take a look across the way. I want to see if there is a clear path homeward."

"I'll point you in the right direction. I know the best ways around this neck of Ohm Totem," said Aderyn. "And Zoey, I'm granting you the privilege of being the key's newest caretaker." She dipped her head in respect to Zoey. "Keep it safe, always, and in all ways." Her beak formed a gentle smile. "Will you accept this most important task?"

Zoey frowned. She didn't want to be the new caretaker of anything, let alone a key. How was she going to carry that around, anyway? Regardless, Zoey nodded, just because she didn't know what else to say or do.

Aderyn, responding to Zoey's thoughts, whispered two words, "Lemla Surita." The key vanished. And with that, Aderyn shrugged her shoulders. "It's done. Thank you, Zoey. I know it will be safe with you."

"Where did it go?" asked Zoey.

"It's in your heart. When you say the words, 'Lemla Surita', the key will reappear." And, as if on cue, the key reappeared, but it was nicely tied with a thin, golden rope around Zoey's left foot.

Zoey lifted her foot to take a look. It shined brilliantly, but felt like it weighed a pound, which was a lot for a small bird. "Is it going to be tied around me at all times?" *I hope not.*

"Yes, but it will not interrupt walking or flying," explained Luli. "You'll go along in life as if it isn't there. You won't feel it until you speak the words that will bring it to the surface of physicality, Lemla Surita."

Again, the key disappeared, and the weight of it on Zoey's leg instantly vanished. It was as if it wasn't there at all, just like Luli had said. *Wow,* thought Zoey. *That's awesome!* She then wondered why do they have to say words at all? VioletLights and IndigoLights don't seem to have to do that with anything else magical.

Aderyn understood Zoey's thoughts. "These words were created by the VioletLights after Crepus stole much of the land in Ohm Totem. We wove magic around certain abilities and items, giving them each words, and then willed the magical words into being," explained Aderyn. "The reason we created magic with words was to keep the abilities and items secret from Crepus and his minions. They know nothing of these sacred words, so it's wise never to speak of these things around anyone else, unless you are absolutely sure that it's safe."

"How will I know when it's safe?"

The falcon put a wing around Zoey. "You're Zoey. You'll know. Your heart will tell you."

Before Zoey could continue questioning, Luli bowed to Zoey, spun around and hopped toward the opening, saying, "Shall we be off?"

Aderyn nodded and Luli flew out of the entrance and straight down, disappearing from view.

"Stay here, Zoey. I'll find Luli a safe route home. I'll be back as soon as I can." Aderyn walked over to the edge, spread her wings, and flew out of the tree as well.

Zoey sighed. *What do I do now?*

"Lemla Surita," she said, and just like that the key appeared at her left foot. "Lemla Surita," she said again, making the key invisible.

*This is amazing!*

She hopped up and down with excitement, like a young child with a new toy whispering, "Lemla Surita," over and over again, making the key appear and disappear.

Though, after a while, she got bored. Glancing out of the opening, she saw that the sun, paled behind the gray clouds, had slowly moved west. And yes, Aderyn was right. The Dims had continued their strenuous workout, looking more and more fatigued the longer they practiced. She watched for what seemed like an hour, and then her shoulders drooped. *What's there to do now? I'm bored.*

Suddenly, a twinge of light came from below the jagged floor, piercing through some small holes and dotting the ceiling with bluish, white light.

*What's that?*

Zoey bent down to examine by closing one eye and looking through one of the small holes with her other eye. All she could see was the calm light coming from zytes lining walls underneath the floor that she stood upon. Zoey, surprised, had no idea that the tree was hollow beneath her. Aderyn had never mentioned it, but why? Was it another one of those secrets that the PureLights withheld from Crepus? Zoey thought that was silly and rolled her eyes. *It's probably just a hollowed out part of the tree, just like the Spruce Hallow.*

Thinking even more, she concluded that it was probably something important, because if it wasn't—then why would there by zytes down there?

Every part of her being wanted to open the floor to take a look. Searching the floor and walking in what seemed to be circles as she did her detective work, she discovered something that seemed a little out of place—a mismatched piece of wood. The flooring was dark brown, but this piece of wood was the size and shape of a nickel and it was in the darkest corner of the entrance and it was a golden color. Why hadn't she seen this before?

She pushed on it with her beak, but nothing happened.

90

She pressed on it with her foot, which had more strength and force than her previous attempt, but again, nothing happened.

Plopping down on her rump, she thought for a moment. *Here we go again.* She was tired of having to figure everything out. *Why can't there just be a button to press on to open things around here?* Sitting there and getting bored, she started to hum a beautiful tune. Then she got so wrapped up in her humming that she forgot about her thinking, and just like that, the floor started to shake. One side of it dipped, while the other side rose. Then the entire floor did a slow spin, opening up enough for her to see zytes lining the walls below. Once the floor spun to a point where the lowest side showed a large opening, she inched her way through the opening and dropped while flapping her wings, making herself hover beneath the floor she had just been standing on.

A loud clunk and Zoey dropped a couple of feet in flight. Looking up, she saw that the floor had stopped it's spin and was level again. *Uh oh! How am I going to get back up there?* Realizing that all she probably had to do was sing, she started humming and humming.

The floor remained shut.

*Oh no! How do I get out of here?* Glancing around as she kept herself hovering, she didn't see any perches to land on. Dropping about ten more feet, she still couldn't see any perches, and all she wanted to do was sit and think her way back through the ceiling.

The lower and lower she hovered, the more and more she saw how tall this tree really was, and there seemed to be no end to it. Down, down she went, thinking to herself that she'd never been inside a building this tall before. But, finally, she detected the zytes' hazy glow bouncing off a light brown area of dirt below. It looked bare, as if nothing had grown there for years. *What kind of a tree is this?* She knew it was a redwood, but how could a redwood grow with no insides to it? It was hollow, just like the Spruce Hallow, and

91

how both trees were alive and vibrant without any insides to them baffled her. *It must be VioletLight magic!*

Landing on the dirt, she found it to be soft and comfortable, as if it had just been tilled—something her father did to their garden each spring. She used to love putting her feet in the soft soil, creating foot prints and hoping they would stay there forever. Her mom and dad, on the other hand, didn't like her doing that. She might accidentally step on the seeds planted in the soil, preventing them from growing.

Zoey grumbled in dismay. She still had that connection with her parents, something she was very glad about, and missing them was still very hard. Like usual, she just wanted to get home. Taking a deep breath, she placed her sadness in her heart and practiced the Snow Tree's technique of love by spreading pink light throughout her heart.

It worked like a charm.

Then she looked up, seeing myriads of zytes glowing up the inner wall of the redwood tree. *Wow*, she thought. *I've traveled far!* She jumped into the air and hovered. Joy filled her eyes. She so loved the feeling of weightlessness and the rush of air against her face. Never in her life did she ever dream of being able to fly, and now that she was actually doing it she loved the freedom.

Taking her eyes off the long journey back up the tree, she landed back down on the ground to look at the surroundings directly in front of her. The lowest zytes were slightly higher than eye level as she stood there, allowing her to see a dark, wooden door near her feet. She walked over to it, bending at her hips to take a closer inspection. It was definitely a door. *A trap door?* If she opened it, would it reveal a deep hole in the Earth? Perhaps leading to that place they call the heart of Ohm Totem? She'd been there in her dreams before, she wouldn't be surprised if she were going to go back again.

On top of the door was a handle, gold in color. She lifted

the handle with her beak, and walked backwards. The door creaked as it opened, bringing in a cool rush of air. She let go of the handle, letting the door drop to the dirt, creating a cloud of dust next to her, slightly hovering above her view of the opening.

Waving her wing in front of the dust, spreading it apart, giving her a better look down the opening, Zoey discovered a pale light coming through. As she continued to stare, she noticed a stairwell leading down, lined by zytes.

Zoey stood in thought for a moment, wondering if it would be okay to see where this led. She shrugged her shoulders and took her first step down the stairway, feeling a chill from cool air coming up the stairs. She shivered. *It's cold down there.*

Taking only ten more steps, she found herself meeting a level, dirt floor. Looking around, she observed that she was in a hallway with stone, rock walls and zytes lighting up the area much more so than the zytes in the stairwell she just came down.

There was a reason for this. As Zoey walked down the long hallway, she saw that the walls had intricate and beautiful etchings of animals, all lit up by individual zytes. In addition, there were two large and powerful zytes beaming toward Flower of Life symbols that were drawn just above each animal figure. As she continued to walk, she could see figures creating a story of some sort. There were spirit animals walking through a sun-like thing, which didn't make any sense to her. She stopped and studied it, trying to discover the meaning of it. *Did they come through a portal like Coda and I did? Is that what the sun represents?* She figured it did and stared at the etching for a little longer, enjoying its beauty.

Then she took a deep breath and continued, seeing a spirit animal that looked just like Crepus surrounded by other spirit animals off in the distance. She could see that Crepus was looking up at a moon with its light shining down on a large scroll next to him. Peering deeper into the drawing, she knew some of the spirit animals surrounding Crepus—Lao the wolf, Nova the snow leopard and Aderyn the snow owl. There was a bear she didn't know, a panther that looked somewhat like Coda, a bird similar to herself—a skylark, and a horse and a large eagle. Again, she didn't know what the scene meant so she walked onward while eyeing the wall.

Next, a large pyramid stood with a bright halo drawn around the apex of it. She saw a large eagle flying toward the pyramid with a scroll in its beak. The eagle was heading toward an entrance in the middle of the pyramid that had a long staircase going to the ground. Then Zoey stopped. A memory started to surface, showing her that pyramid and that entrance and even those stairs.

*My dream. I remember it from my dream.*

Before she entered Ohm Totem, she had had a strange dream about Coda and a snow leopard standing at the entrance of that pyramid. She had watched as a horde of spirit animals came out of the neighboring forest and up those stairs.

Shaking the memory away, continuing to stare at the picture etched in the wall in front of her, she saw that behind the eagle flying toward the pyramid flew the skylark, the snow owl, and dozens of other birds. Further down, on the ground, she noticed that a bear and a horse were either chasing or following them. She didn't know which.

Stepping further down the hallway, the next picture was a round symbol. It showed nine spirit animals within it, all of whom were probably the VioletLight Masters because Zoey saw Lao, Nova, Aderyn, the panther, the horse, the eagle, and the skylark. They were all inside of the circle, although Crepus was at the very top of it.

*Why is he the main one in all of this?*

A little frustrated, she took her eyes off the symbols, knowing she wasn't going to be able to figure them out right away.

A sound from something further down the hallway

94

startled her. She stared in the direction of the sound and shook her head. *I must be hearing things.* Just then, a bright, golden glow lit up the hallway. Gazing into it made her eyes squint. She saw that the light curved around a slight bend up ahead.

Surprisingly, the light didn't scare her. It did the opposite. It made her feel invigorated and happy and it had a magnetic affect that pulled her onward. She wanted to find the source of the light and peer into it, and then sleep in its everlasting glow. She gave an audible "ahhh".

Then, it disappeared, bringing Zoey back to her senses. She took a big breath and moved her little legs in a fast walk down the hallway. She wanted to get to the source of the golden light.

Up ahead, the hallway turned and broke into three more hallways—one that went straight, one that went right, and one that went left. She went into the hallway on the left, the one she was sure would take her to the source of the light.

The hallway took a turn, taking Zoey to a steep stairway that went down. *More stairs?* Zoey frowned, not because she had to traverse down more steps, but because the more she peered down the stairway, the more she realized how far down it went. She sighed, thinking that the stairs went on forever, seeing no end to them, but at least glad it was lined by zytes.

She took step after step down the staircase, but after a couple of minutes passed by, an ahah! thought crept into her mind. *I could fly down to the bottom.* Nodding gratefully to her new found idea, she spread her wings, pushed off, gliding a very long distance to the bottom of the stairs. When she finally landed at the base of it, she looked forward, seeing a branch of hallways.

*Where am I supposed to go now?*

Her first thought was to go to the right, so she did. It turned into a dirt tunnel full of roots coming out of the walls on both sides of her. Some roots even dangled from the dirt ceiling, and some came up through the ground. The roots

95

were thick, twisty, and made some areas of walking difficult to get through. She wondered how far underground she'd gone and thanked the zytes for still giving off light.

A movement out of the corner of her eye made her freeze. She backed up and hid behind a large root jutting out of the wall. She sat for a moment, until she gathered enough courage to peer over the root to see what had caused the movement. Being as quiet and still as possible, she surveyed the area, then ducked back down when she heard a dirt clod fall to the ground ten feet or so in front of her.

Her mind raced. *Who's here? Is it a Dim?*

Peeking out of her hiding place, she saw the back of a furry creature. It looked busy. In fact, it looked like it was reading.

"Oh my, my..." said the furry creature.

*What kind of spirit animal is he?*

It flicked its head and a scroll laid out in front of it jumped into the air, hovered, and rolled itself up, and then flew to a shelf in the tunnel wall. Then another scroll slowly hovered from the shelf, unrolled itself, and floated to the ground in front of the creature.

Zoey was perplexed. *Is this a VioletLight?* She looked up the wall she was hiding next to and just above her was a shelf lined with thousands upon thousands of scrolls. *What is this place?*

"It's Gwenfree's Nueadd Sgrolio, or what some of us like to call, 'Gwenfree's Hall of Scrolls'," said the furry creature.

Zoey hid lower, closing her eyes, hoping that if she was quiet enough she could somehow disappear. Perhaps the creature was just talking to itself?

"I'm of no harm to you, child. I'm just looking for something. Please come out of hiding."

Zoey slowly rose and walked around a root. Sitting in front of her, and profusely sniffing with its twitching nose, was what looked like a very big, fat chipmunk with no stripes down its back. It had reddish brown fur, with about a four inch long black tipped tail. Its eyes were black and beady, but looked gentle. It wasn't going to harm a feather on Zoey. She could easily sense this.

"Hi, I'm Zoey."

"Yes, Aderyn told me about you. But, from my guess, she didn't tell you about me?"

Zoey shook her head 'no' and noticed that he had indigo crystals. During the time she'd already spent in Ohm Totem, she'd noticed that spirit animals with indigo crystals could do some of the things that VioletLights could do. This one could obviously make things hover. He had a bit of magic in him.

The creature walked forward, dipping its head to her. "I'm a prairie dog. I come in and out of this hallway through a secret passageway that only Aderyn and I know about." He shook his head. "There's no way I could climb all the way up the outside of this over grown enormous tree, and then climb down the insides of it to get here." The prairie dog laughed as if Zoey should think that was funny. She faked a laugh in return and he instantly paused and looked down, making a "hmmph" sound. He had obviously noticed that she wasn't being real.

"Well, I'm Gart." He bowed. "Pleased to meet you...again."

*Again?*

He gestured with his head toward the scrolls. "Aderyn has me on assignment. I'm trying to find an explanation for exactly what these shadow beings are that Aderyn and I have witnessed in the forests. We're the only ones left of the Gwenfree Tribe, so we have no one else to talk to about this. We think that perhaps some other VioletLights in the past might have seen the shadows before, so here I am...hoping that I can find any explanations from other VioletLights." He rolled his eyes with a grin, as if knowing that he was searching in vain.

Zoey gazed around. "Why don't you have any tablets?"

He looked at her as if she had just spoken in a foreign language. "What do you mean, child?"

97

"Umm...in the Sihu Tribe they have things that pop up out of the ground. They always have a green emerald-looking thing on them."

He nodded his head up and down. "Yes, yes, yes. I know of what you speak—the sacred tablets." He frowned. "Not every tribe has those, only a few. We have a Nueadd Sgrolio." He shook his head, knowing she wouldn't know that word, and corrected himself. "We have a Hall of Scrolls. When a scroll is granted to a VioletLight, or when a VioletLight creates a scroll, an exact duplicate manifests itself here in this very Hall. It's quite unique. So, if a VioletLight created a scroll that described the shadow beings, then I could read it here."

He scratched his head. "Would you like to help me?"

Zoey was delighted. She wanted something to do, and this would be just fine. "What would you like me to do?"

"I'm searching each scroll, one by one, for any semblance of the shadow creatures, or whatever they are." He looked her over, up and down, with his brows raised. "You can read, can't you?"

Zoey nodded a yes, and then followed him to a scroll laid out on the ground. "You read this one, and I'll read—"

A flash of golden light filled the room and then quickly faded, making Gart pause and Zoey flinch.

"What was that?" asked Zoey.

"Why don't you walk past me and knock three times on the wall at the end of this hall, then pause, knock twice, stop, then knock once. Something wants you more than anything I've ever known." Gart pointed to the end of the hallway, but there was no door. It was just a dirt wall with thin, straggling roots coming out of it.

She did what he asked and took several steps toward the wall. She looked over her shoulder, seeing Gart nod his head. "Go ahead. Do it." It was almost as if he didn't know what was going to happen, but he knew something magical would occur and he was excited for Zoey.

She knocked the way he had said, and then a loud

98

creaking sound followed and dirt fell from a small portion of the wall. Then the wall began to open slowly. A loud click echoed throughout the area when the wall had opened completely, exposing a darkened room. The glow of zytes beyond the wall seemed very faint, creating enough light so she could gaze around the room, noticing that it was a cavern that only had a dozen or so zytes randomly placed here and there. Zoey shifted her feet, not wanting to take a step inside.

She glanced behind her to see a smiling Gart, gesturing for her to move forward. Taking a deep breath, she did just that.

Walking through the doorway, she felt the swoosh of the door shutting behind her, accompanied by a loud bang that echoed throughout the large cave.

The cavern was domed and felt wet—wet everywhere. Water dripped from sharp, narrow rocks that hung like icicles from the ceiling. Small puddles had formed beneath them and they were dispersed everywhere on the ground.

She scanned the cavernous room. There were rock outcroppings high up in the walls and with no vegetation of any sort. Suddenly, Zoey ducked as the golden light beamed again, as if beckoning for her and it was the brightest golden color she had ever seen. It then blinked off a second later. She frowned and opened her wings, flying straight across the cavern, in the same direction she'd seen the light coming from. In the air, she gazed below, seeing puddles, jutting rocks, and slimey gray stone everywhere. It looked slippery and she was glad she could fly.

Reaching her destination, the golden light blinked on and off once more and she saw that the light was coming from a massive scroll shadowed by large hanging rocks above and beside it. She landed and stood in front of the scroll. It looked like it was pinned against the rock wall somehow, perhaps by VioletLight magic. She leaned closer, trying to read what it had to say, but to no avail. She couldn't see so well in the dark. She could barely see her own feet.

*What next?*

She closed her eyes, then pictured the scroll and brought it down into her heart. She put all the love and pinkish white light around it that she could. *Turn on so I can read you, please.* Zoey opened her eyes, and then squinted them shut because the scroll nearly blinded her with its golden beam of light.

Zoey shook her head, whispering more to herself, "No, not that bright. I want to be able to read it—not go blind."

As if Zoey had just turned down a dimmer switch, the light gently faded to a calm glow. She opened her eyes, and saw for the first time the full beauty of the scroll. It was like the others she'd seen, thickly outlined in black and gold in the middle, but the words were intricate and sparkled brightly. She smiled, taking in the wonderful sight of the scroll before her. She could easily read it. It said:

## The Code of The PureLight Order

1. The Great Spirit is Bountiful in Love, Truth, and Patience, and Always Sharing Itself With Every Being. In Me, all Exist and in all Existence, I Am. I Am That I Am.

2. You Shall not Steal or Gather More than You Need or Use.

3. You Shall Inhale the Breath of The Great Spirit, so Health, Wisdom, and Vitality are Maintained.

4. You Shall Use Breath as Your Food, For Dead Flesh Holds the Energy of Fear, Thus Bringing Impurities to Your Body that Lower You and Your Crystal's Vibrational Levels, Creating a Fog Between You and The Great Spirit.

5. You Shall Know and Understand Your Body as an Antenna to The Great Spirit, Giving You All the Wisdom, Imagination, Insights, Inspiration, Truth and Health that The Great Spirit Provides.

6. You Shall Treat Others as You Would Like Others to Treat You.

7. You Shall Listen and Follow Your Heart.

8. You Shall Always Be Honest with Yourself and Others.

9. You Shall do no Harm to any Being, Except in Defense of Your Life and Others.

10. You Shall Be Aware of Your Focus, Positive or Negative, as What You Focus on Grows and Becomes a Reality.

11. You Shall Take Care of the Land, Your Loved Ones, and Those Who Have or Have Not Taken Care of You. No Being, Positive or Negative, is Ever Lost in The Great Spirit's Care.

12. You Shall Cherish and Protect the Weak, and Those Who are Oppressed, and all Beings that Suffer Wrong.

13. You Shall Be Mindful of Your Words as Words Have the Power to Shape Yours and Other Spirit Animal's Lives in a Positive or Negative Way.

14. You Shall Live Your Bliss and Do What Your Heart Enjoys.

15. You Shall Live as an Example of the Great Spirit and Light the Way, with Love, Truth, and Patience.

As Zoey read, thousands of images raced through her mind. Images of spirit animals, events, dialogues, hills, trees, lakes, oceans, and tunnels appeared. She knew very well that she was seeing the history of Ohm Totem's epic past. She didn't know why she knew this. It was more of an enormous feeling of truth overwhelming her. The more she read, the harder it was to tear her gaze from the scroll. She even felt herself somehow merging with it.

Then the sounds started. They were the sounds of spirit animals playing, laughing, communing and singing as if she was outside on a bright and sunny day, picnicking with her family and friends. Then the sounds changed, slipping into the noise of chaos, distress, death, mayhem, burning, screaming, slaughter, and hate filled anger.

She gasped, grabbing the feathers covering her heart. Then the positive images reappeared and abruptly stopped a moment later. She looked down, taking her eyes away from the scroll. Instantly, a wave of dizziness swept through her, toppling her over. After a moment, she gathered herself together and stood up, though her legs were very weak and dizziness overtook her again. She managed to lean forward, placing a wing on a rock just below the PureLight Order's list, and made herself stand up straight. That just made her dizzier as her mind started to fade, and then she collapsed.

# Chapter 9

Coda had a feeling that whispering Meli's name would change the jaguar into a PureLight again, but that's not what was happening. Chev was staring, wide-eyed, and his mouth was hanging open as he watched Meli. He was also still holding Shikoba, as Numee held her paws on the writhing jaguar.

Coda's heart beat faster and faster. He hadn't intended to hurt Meli by sending her into these fits. Her body was arching and contracting in spasms and it all looked very painful. It was agonizing to watch.

Numee's shoulder's drooped. "I wish Nova was here." She peered into the sky as if it held the correct answer for her. "Great Spirit, I'd like some help!"

Chev looked up, hoping The Great Spirit would descend to take away the pain from Meli. Coda hoped for the same.

But nothing changed and Meli tossed back and forth, knocking her feet into Numee.

Then it stopped, leaving only silence.

*Is Meli breathing?* thought Coda.

As if in answer, Meli took a deep breath and moved her head, blinking wildly until that stopped, too. After a moment, she spoke, "Thank you, Coda. I owe you my life."

Coda gave an audible "whoa" as he watched Meli's crystals fade from gray, turn clear, then light up with red, which was the same color as his own crystals.

*Wait! Mine are blue now?* he remembered.

Numee stroked Meli's head. "Are you okay?"

Meli's beautiful hazel eyes looked into Numee's. "Thank you for your help. I felt your presence during my transformation. It would have been deathly and horrible had you not been here."

103

"Uh," chimed Chev. "That right there—that thing that just happened to you—wasn't deathly and horrible?"

Meli stood, shaking snow off of her pelt. She leaned into Numee, giving her a silent gesture of love. Then she rubbed against Chev's leg and walked over to Coda and rubbed his side with her sleek body. She gestured with her head. "Follow me." She took off in a semi-fast trot.

Coda smiled, facing Chev and Numee. "Well, it looks like she's doing just fine." He dashed after her, followed by his friends, snow crunching loudly under their feet in the large, wide forest.

∞

"I think we need to stop," said Chev. "Shikoba is beginning to stir."

Shikoba was moving and pushing her wings out as if in a big yawn. Her legs straightened as she stretched her long talons, though her eyes remained shut.

They'd been traveling for half a day. The sun was fading fast, and all the jaguar had told them was that she was leading them to someplace safe, a place that Coda hoped was warm and sheltered.

"It's just around the bent tree up ahead," replied Meli, pointing with her tail.

Indeed, directly in front of them was a tree growing straight toward the sky and then bent to the right at a ninety degree angle about mid-trunk. *That's not something you see every day.* Coda wondered how he'd thought of that phrase, but remembered that it was something his dad always said on long road trips while pointing out elk or bears grazing on the side of hill, or one time when he saw a cat chasing a dog instead of the other way around.

Passing the tree, they headed toward a large thicket of brambles. At first glance, the thorny bushes seemed like something normally growing in the forest with nothing secret or mysterious about them.

Chev's voice boomed, startling Coda. "If we're going in there, then please tell me there's an elephant door somewhere?" Chev's normal happiness was quickly fading and it was apparent in his voice.

Meli turned, nodding. "Elephant's come here often, and some live here, although it's not a door of any kind that you're familiar with. It's a door for spirit animals of any sort."

Stopping at the foot of the brambles, Numee padded up to Meli. "Are there spirit animals in there?"

"Yes, there is a remnant group from the old Shan Tribe that once lived here peacefully in Changyin Forest." She pointed to the thorny brambles with her tail. "Even though these spirit animals have turned Dim, they don't support Crepus. They've remembered some of the ancient ways," explained Meli. "However, they won't know who you are, so be alert and be prepared to defend yourself."

*Ugh!* Thought Coda. *We're going to have to be on guard? I'm getting tired of this. Its exhausting being ready for an attack all of the time.*

The jaguar sniffed and smiled. She pounded her foot several times in a quick rhythm on the ground. Instead of a door opening, a portion of the ground soundlessly moved downward, creating a declining ramp going under the brambles. This opening was definitely fit for an elephant.

Meli slowly backed up, positioning herself behind Coda, Numee, and Chev. They looked back at her, wondering why she did that, but when she put her paw out, gesturing for them to move forward, they obeyed.

Entering into this unknown area under a gigantic thicket of brambles, Coda peered around. There were spirit animals everywhere, speaking in quiet, but happy, tones. They walked around as if they were in a market place or something.

Coda noticed that the landscape was full of hard soil and patches of green grass. The entire area was shaped like a bowl—shallow around the edges that sloped deeper in the middle. Looking up, Coda saw that the brambles were thick, keeping out the snow. The ceiling was high above them, giving enough space for a tall giraffe. Standing here was easy for Chev who didn't have to bend over, crawl, or worse yet, stay outside.

Coda observed that this was quite the clever little hide out. The woody, thorn filled bush went on for what looked to be hundreds of yards that acted like a ceiling. It was perfect. No one would be dumb enough to try to jump or fly through the overhead barrier of thorns, invading this remnant of Shan Tribe—unless they wanted to maim or kill themselves. The brambles hid and protected this group, who, by the way, weren't very observant, since Coda and the rest had entered the area without a challenge or even a look.

That thought must have penetrated the minds of this remnant cast. Bringing his eyes back down from the ceiling to the spirit animals, he saw that all of them, maybe a hundred or so, were very still, staring deeply with ill intent at the new spirit animals who had just arrived.

A very large, aggressive-looking bull walked forward. "Who are you?!" He had gray crystals, much like the Dims.

Numee stepped forward. "We're PureLights from Sihu Tribe. We just want some rest from our long journey."

Coming forward, the bull lowered his gaze, exhaling loudly. "How did you get in here?"

Coda turned, about to say *Meli,* but saw no jaguar sitting behind him. *Where'd she go?* He turned, facing the bull. "We were led here by Meli."

"Who is Meli?" The bull looked over his shoulder and then twitched his ears, telling his friends to come forward and surround this group, which they gladly did.

"She's a jaguar. You don't know her?" asked Chev, still holding Shikoba.

The bull widened his eyes. "The loner? You were led here by the loner? She doesn't know how to get in here!"

A large stag standing to the right of the bull slammed its foot to the ground, then kicked dirt behind him. He lowered his gaze, ready to charge these intruders. Gray filled all of the spirit animals crystals, making them feel even less welcoming than they already were, especially the stag.

The bull turned to the stag. "Stand down." The stag instantly relaxed, though his eyes remained fixed on the group of unknowns standing before him.

Numee took a step forward, placing her front paws out for all to see. "We mean you no harm."

The stag lowered his head even more. "Well, we mean you a lot of harm if you do anything out of the ordinary."

"I said, stand down, Hao!"

Obeying his leader, Hao lightened up. His body looked more relaxed, but his eyes didn't. Whoever these spirit animals under the brambles were, Coda could tell they were living in fear and constantly stressed. The Dims must be doing a lot of damage to the minds of these spirit animals.

Numee bowed her head. "I'm sorry we disturbed you, but we only need a night's rest. We'll be gone in the morning."

The bull's eyelids suddenly narrowed. He moved at a slow pace, coming closer and closer to Numee. Coda couldn't help it. He took soft steps toward Numee, placing himself between her and the bull. The bull stopped and sniffed the ground, then chuckled for a moment as if to say, *you dare face me?*

The bull spoke again, but his tone was that of curiosity. "How did you get the colors in your crystals?" His eyes became suspicious, as if this was a trick from Crepus.

Just then, Shikoba flew from Chev's trunk and in between Coda and the bull. "I'd suggest you back up if you want to stay upright." Shikoba's voice was stern.

The bull exhaled again and did as she said, more out of respect for such a confident creature than from fear. He knew that Crepus's spies didn't act this way. The spies were less deliberate, and held suspicion in their eyes, none of which these four spirit animals did. Shikoba flew lower, hovering eye to eye with the bull. "We're PureLights. That's why we have colored crystals. We come from beyond the

Fog."

The crowd stirred when she said 'beyond the fog', as if that was a mysterious, dangerous place, a place where people go and never return. This remnant tribe of Shan was convinced that certain death awaits anyone beyond the Fog.

A young looking panda padded through the crowd, past the bewildered bull, and stood in front of the four newly arrived spirit animals. She sniffed each of them, and then a large smile enveloped her small, cuddly face. "You wanna play?"

The silence then broke into laughter, none of which came from Coda's crew. The panda dropped her smile and peered behind her, obviously wondering what all the ruckus was about. The bull gently nudged the panda. "I'm proud of you." He pressed his cheek against her body. "They can't play right now."

"But why?" asked the panda, inching backward, her big innocent eyes staring at the bull.

Coda liked this little panda, and couldn't stop himself from replying to her. "We can play, but just not right now, okay?"

Then the bull lifted his head high and put his chest out. "Come with me."

∞

The light of the fading sun poked through small holes in the thick bramble above, hitting diagonally across the ground where Coda stood. He was at the bottom of the bowl-shaped underground hideout, standing with Chev, Shikoba, and Numee. They were watching the bull and stag speaking quietly between themselves—too quiet for Coda to understand.

Chev's eyebrows rose in dismay. "This is a dramatic group. Are we sure we want to stay here? I'm happy to tell them some jokes and leave."

"Should we just go where the wind takes us?" replied

Numee. She seemed to like the thought.

"I like that idea," responded Shikoba.

Coda didn't. He just wanted to rest one night, then head to Crepus's Castle, get Zoey, and get back to the nice comforts of the Sihu Tribe. Then, when the next full moon came, Zoey and he could go home and sleep in their own comfortable beds. He shook his head with that thought, seeing and feeling how far he'd come in just a week away from home. This place, Ohm Totem, had changed him. He raised his brow, knowing that if he ever told the true tale of what happened to him—coming to Ohm Totem, becoming an Art of Defense specialist, being in a couple of battles and watching Nova lift things with her heart and mind—then no one would take him seriously. Could he take people to the talking Snow Tree and prove it all? Would she talk to anyone else in the Cornell Forest besides him and Zoey? Would that even be a good idea? And his parents? What would they think of his new, different personality? He knew so much now, but so much of what he knows is so different from Gladstone.

Coda was jostled out of his thoughts when the bull came forward, saying, "We've come up with a decision. You can stay if you help."

Coda, not liking the idea, growled. "Help with what? We just need to sleep one night and be on our way."

The bull shook his head. "We need help with the resistance. Since no spirit animal that dwells under these brambles has ever seen another spirit animal alive after going through the Fog must mean that you are all very powerful and would be an asset to our cause."

"What's your cause?" asked Numee.

The bull rolled his eyes as if it wasn't already apparent. "To defeat the dragon." He looked up, booming his next words. "To defeat Crepus!"

Shikoba flew up in a hover, again at eye level with the bull. "If you let us stay one night so we can leave in the morning, then we'll defeat Crepus for you. If you keep us

109

here to fight with you, then you'll only be in our way."

The bull looked over his shoulder, eyeing the stag. They both gave out a sharp laugh, jiggling their shoulders as they shook their heads. "You four puny spirit animals think you can take on an entire army?" The bull gestured around with his head. "We have almost a hundred of us here, and all we can do is put a splinter in their foot, yet you can defeat them?"

Chev's trunk swished back and forth in irritation. "I say we just leave now."

Hao the stag leaped from his position, landing in front of Chev. He leaned close, peering up into Chev's eyes. His brows were lowered. "You aren't leaving so easily, my fat faced friend. You either stay, do your duty and help, or we'll feed you to the army ourselves."

"Get back, Hao!" yelled the bull. "That's not true. They can go now, unharmed, or stay and help."

*Why did Meli lead us here?* thought Coda. This was a mistake on the jaguar's part. There was no community here. No help for a stranger.

Chev lowered his forehead and placed it onto Hao's. "I don't think you can make us do anything against our will, stag!"

"That's quite enough," said the bull. The stag moved back to his original position, staring at Chev, who Coda could feel was petrified, but putting on a good show.

Numee padded up to the bull. "What's your name?"

"Kiwu," responded the bull.

"Well, Kiwu..." Numee smiled. "May my friends and I talk about this for a moment and then get back to you?"

Kiwu's eyes suddenly became soft. He dipped his head, bowing his eyes to her, like a giant before a queen. "You may, but for a moment. We have things to do and ambushes to plan."

"Thank you." With that, Numee gestured for her friends to follow her. They walked about ten panther lengths away and huddled.

110

Numee's green eyes shined as she gazed into the eyes of her befuddled friends. "I say we stay for a night and help them. We can escape in the morning and do what we need to do—get Zoey and somehow find Nova."

Coda didn't know what to say. He just wanted to rest his paws and sleep, or maybe play with that panda who was eagerly watching them.

Chev nodded. "I'm going to sing for him."

Shikoba hit her wing across his foot. "You'll do no such thing." She turned to Coda. "You're now a blue crystal. The memories of Orion are coming back, is that correct?"

Coda nodded. "I think so, but I haven't remembered much since I was in the cave behind the waterfall."

"Is there anything you can help this remnant tribe with? Maybe tactics?"

Coda's bottom lip protruded out as he looked off to his upper left, as if trying to bring in a memory of something. When nothing came, he simply shrugged his shoulders.

"Well, that'll convince the bull that we mean business," replied a sarcastic Numee. "Do you remember ever ambushing Crepus? If so, were you successful?"

Coda looked off to his upper left again, and then nodded as a memory filtered through. It was hazy, but he remembered a time when he was crouched behind some bushes. He was with a group of PureLights, waiting and preparing to take Crepus's army by surprise. He remembered that these PureLights were some of the last survivors of a tribe whose name he couldn't quite remember, but when they sprang the attack it took the army off guard, spreading them thin and making it easy for the PureLights to run them back into the Dim Lands. He saw how there was little bloodshed, because this group of PureLights had mastered the Art of Defense, throwing Dims left and right, until the Dims could do nothing more but run away.

He knew that the spirit animals here under the brambles weren't that talented. He could feel it. They were novices

111

trapped in the world of ego, thinking they were better than they actually were. A voice crept into his mind, something he had once said when he was Orion: *The VioletLight Master is precise with her movements. She is always ready, like a VioletLight in the Dim Lands, being prepared for any possibility. She has fluidity, like a stream in the Sango Mountain Range. She has patience and the presence of mind and love of heart to remain still. When she does this, the answer—the way—manifests on its own. She is in the now, neither searching nor expecting the best or worst, but accepting everything that comes to her.*

Like a blow horn in the silence of the night, Coda came out of his thoughts knowing exactly what to do. It had nothing do with strategy, ambushes, or finding Zoey and Nova. It was about the Art of Defense.

He stood tall, flexing his muscles with confidence. "I know what to do."

They looked at him, eager to hear.

He closed his eyes and opened them a couple seconds later. "We stay until a plan presents itself. We don't go in blind. We scope out the area until we understand with all of our senses, how to retrieve Zoey and Nova. In the meantime, I teach them the Art of Defense. I show this remnant tribe how to allow the Art of Defense to come to them without effort and stress."

Numee looked skeptical. "I don't know, Coda."

Shikoba and Chev nodded agreement with Numee's words.

Again, Coda was confident with his next answer. "We stay and help, just as they've asked. It may lead us to what we're looking for. We go with the flow, as Nova once told me."

"And where would it lead us?" replied Chev, still not convinced.

Coda looked down, shaking his head and wishing he had the answer, but also understanding that it would eventually come to them when they were ready. "I don't know."

Numee made a screwed up face. "I don't know, Coda. I think—"

"I do know," interrupted Shikoba. "What Coda says is correct. The plan of action may not present itself right away and may take us farther away from the castle, but if we go with the flow we will surely be led, one way or another, to Zoey and Nova."

Surprised that Shikoba agreed, he now looked less confident, not because of her, but because Shikoba hoped that what he said was true. She was depending upon him. *What if this doesn't work?*

Shikoba spread her wings, stretching them out wide. "Are we in agreement?"

They all nodded, and then Shikoba took it upon herself to deliver the news to Kiwu, who seemed surprised but smiled in return. He walked off with Hao, saying that he would return with their orders.

∞

It was getting darker. The gray day was turning into night as Coda sat, staring up at the brambles and wondering what he had just gotten them into. He took a short, unhappy breath and glimpsed around the hideout for the hundredth time. Chev was conversing with new friends, making them laugh and dance. Shikoba stood in a corner, watching as if she was an assassin looking for a victim or something. She was weird, but a powerful ally, thought Coda. Numee played with the kids, jumping back and forth with them and playing games like tag.

Kiwu, however, was pacing back and forth in front of Coda, his brow furrowed, anger rising in his chest. Coda had just told Kiwu about the Art of Defense, and then about the plan to teach it to Kiwu's tribe.

Kiwu took a deep breath, contemplating as he paced. He stopped, stared at Coda and took a deep breath, paced again and contemplated some more. Finally, he halted. "We don't need any Art of Defense, whatever that is!"

Coda sighed. "I'm pretty good at it and I think it's the best way you can defend yourselves against Crepus."

"What you speak of is nonsense. What you claim you can do is impossible. I've seen Crepus do those things, but it's dark magic." He gasped. "You want to teach us the Dark Arts?"

Coda put out his paws in frustration. "No, I want to teach you the defense *against* the Dark Arts. I want to show you how to maximize your opponent's energy against themselves, throwing them across the forest with very little effort and watching them run for their lives."

The bull sat. "So you say, but can you prove what you speak of?"

Stunned, Coda wasn't expecting such a question. He was put on the spot. He never had to 'prove' how good he was, he just did it when the moment came. In fact, he wasn't very good when he practiced. This idea of his was backfiring.

Shikoba, overhearing the conversation, flew over and landed beside Coda. "Coda can prove it."

*I can what?*

Shikoba turned to Coda. "You can."

Coda closed his eyes, hiding the fact that he was rolling them under his eyelids. He opened his eyes and tilted his head. "How would you like me to prove it, Kiwu?"

"By facing my best fighter." The bull looked over his shoulder. "Hao!"

*That mean stag? Not him...anyone but him!* A blast of nervous energy engulfed Coda. He stared at his paws, not wanting to see the stag walk toward him.

Shikoba, like a trainer in a boxing match, whispered in Coda's ear. "Empty your mind, proceed from your heart. Watch the stag's fighting style. Be patient, but don't become it."

"Okay." Coda nodded, remembering how going into the heart made things much easier.

The stag trotted over to Kiwu. "Yes?"

114

"Do me a favor. Show this panther what a true fighter does to its enemy, will you?"

The stag smiled. "My pleasure."

Without thought, the stag lowered his head, exposing his large, pointed antlers, and rushed toward Coda at a very fast speed. Coda, without hesitation and acting through instinct, jumped into the air and landed his back paws just below the base of the stag's head, and pushed down. The stag went face first into the dirt, making a loud grunt as he did so.

Coda's heart beat faster, bringing his adrenaline up, which made him more alert. From all around him, he sensed eyes shifting his way. He heard the laughter in Chev's direction stop and the playing in Numee's direction ceased.

The stag got up slowly, shaking his head and flinging pieces of dirt everywhere. He turned, enraged and glaring at Coda, making him cringe. Coda did not want to 'prove' himself. Not here, not anywhere.

Learning from his mistake, Hao didn't run at Coda a second time. He slowly stepped forward, making sharp clopping sounds as he approached.

Coda, trained to wait for an opponent's attack, remained still, all senses alert for any quick movement from the Stag.

There it was.

Hao turned on his front legs, twisting his body and flinging his hind legs around, almost like a roundhouse kick. Coda simply stepped backward and watched the kick take place, completely missing him. But, on the way around, the stag was fast, kicking his hind legs toward Coda, which would have easily hit an untrained, unobservant warrior, which Coda was not.

Coda saw his opponent's lightning reflexes, so he followed the momentum of the kick, seeing that it was going clockwise and would hit Coda sharply against the right side of his body if he didn't move quickly.

Coda spun, knocking his back legs against Hao's hind legs, spinning the stag at twice his original speed. This sent

115

Hao twirling wildly through the air to land on his side. He continued to spin on the ground, making a large circular impression in the dirt.

If Coda wasn't so good at this Art, the stag could have easily overtaken him. The stag *was* a supreme fighter, and had probably done a lot of damage to a lot of Dims.

Hao stood and the crowd seemed to stiffen, as if they knew what was going to happen next. But Hao had a different emotion in his eyes this time. Instead of rage, there was a numbness in his eyes, as if a switch had just flipped in the stag's mind, but the switch turned on Hao's kill reflex. This, Coda thought, was turning into something really negative, really fast.

Kiwu, sensing the stag's shift in energy, ran toward Hao, blocking him from getting any closer to Coda. "Stay put, Hao!"

Hao's mind was no longer functioning correctly. He didn't hear, or even recognize, his leader. He seamlessly pushed Kiwu away with his antlers and rushed at Coda.

Coda had to end this, and end it now.

Running at full speed, Hao lowered his head. He was going to spike the black panther, ending his life once and for all. Coda reared back on his hind legs and jumped high into the air. This made Hao miss him, but barely. Coda then landed a paw on the stag's gray crystal, quickly twisting it and the stag was stunned.

Hao dropped to the ground, skidding several feet, pushing dirt against his chin and face. He was unconscious, looking as if he was sleeping peacefully under the light of the moon.

Coda, not turning to look at his opponent, walked casually toward the bull. He stopped at the bull's feet and sat on his hind legs, curled his tail around his front paws and dipped his head. "I can teach you and your friends the Art of Defense and more."

Kiwu looked at Hao, then at Coda. He looked surprised. "Why did you kill him? This was just a friendly

116

competition."

Coda shook his head. "He's stunned, not dead. He'll be up and at 'em soon enough. I..." Coda was about to tell him that he didn't think this competition was friendly at all, but caught himself. He was talking to this bull more confidently than he'd ever talked to anyone before in his entire life. Coda again noticed that he was changing, which slightly frightened him. He lowered his eyes. "I'm sorry, Kiwu. If Hao is hurt, then know that I didn't mean it." *I wish Nova was here! She'd know what to say.*

Kiwu saw Coda's shift, which took the bull off guard. However, it gave him the upper hand, the right to still be leader, which Coda never thought of taking away from him in the first place. "Tonight, you go on patrol with my night crew. In the meantime, I'll think of a training schedule."

Coda nodded and Kiwu walked off. Then Coda noticed that all eyes were still upon him, so he kept his eyes low and walked up the bowl shaped landscape toward Numee, who looked proud of her friend. Before she could say anything, a voice caught his attention. It was the small, cute panda bear. Her eyes were wide. "Well, will you?"

Coda cocked his head to the side. "Will I what?"

"You said you'd play with me." She smiled as she spoke.

"Oh yeah," replied Coda. "Let's play."

# Chapter 10

"Zoey?"

Zoey jerked back, waking from whatever dream she thought she was having, and gave a barely audible, "Yeah?"

She felt her body being slowly jostled back and forth, and then a voice that seemed distant echoed in her ears. "Wake up."

Pushing her head up to see, she found herself lying on fresh, green grass. She was in a meadow, and in the distance she could hear the pounding of ocean waves. It was very peaceful, wherever she was.

White, yellowish sunlight caused her to blink several times.

"I have something to show you."

It was Lao the Wolf, her friend. But, to make sure, she spoke his name, "Lao?"

"It's Lao. I'm here by your side." His soft cheek grazed across her body, warming her while making her feel loved and comfortable. She sniffed the air. It was alive, as usual, and filling her body full of energy.

She stood up and glanced at Lao. He dipped his head with a smile. "Welcome, Zoey."

"What happened?" she asked. But before he could answer she gazed around, asking another question, "Where are we?" She noticed some familiar areas, such as the rock wall in the distance. It had descending stairs built into the side of it and there was a line of trees to the west. The sounds of the ocean were everywhere around her. She was in the heart of Ohm Totem, the place where the 'Opus' books were located.

Lao nodded. "As you suspect. You're in the heart of Ohm Totem, your home."

Zoey shook her head. "I live in Gladstone, next to the Cornell Forest. This isn't where I live." She smiled, wondering why Lao had said such a silly thing. Then she frowned, because the feeling had come over her again...that empty feeling. She missed home, her family, Coda.

"Come sit next to me." Lao tapped his paw on the grass for Zoey to accompany him.

She walked over and plopped down on her rump. "Why do I miss them so much?" Her eyes welled up. "When can I see my mom and dad again? And Coda?"

"You miss them because you love them. You are attached to them in a way only a parent and child, or a loving brother and sister, are attached. You miss that connection."

"But, when can I go back?"

Lao slowly shook his head, his eyes lowering to the ground. Zoey's shoulders lowered in a feeling of despair. "It may be longer than we thought, Zoey."

Guilt instantly riddled Zoey's body. She had kept Coda here in Ohm Totem, demanding to stay and help and not thinking they'd be here for more than another full moon. How much longer was Lao talking about? Her parent's would be sick if they knew they were here, fighting for their lives. They are probably sick to their stomach looking for them right now with the police, detectives, and with helicopters flying over Cornell Forest and throughout the skies of Gladstone. Pictures were probably plastered on the back of milk cartons and her parents were probably crying all the time, thinking the worst.

Lao gave a little laugh. "Your imagination is vast."

"Vast?"

"Yes, vast—gigantic and far-reaching," responded Lao. "When you worry, you make things worse than what they really are. Remember," Lao looked deeply into Zoey's eyes, "Many, many moons, here in Ohm Totem, are only moments where you're from."

Zoey frowned. "But, what does that really mean?"

"Just know that when you return to Cornell Forest, it will

119

seem like ages since you've been gone, but in reality, it would be less than a day, a lot less than a day. Your parent's will think you've been playing in the forest—nothing more."

This took some of the pressure off Zoey for a moment, but before she could question Lao anymore he flicked his head to the left, indicating for her to follow him.

They walked toward a throng of bushes and long grasses, which looked to be in a circle, as if growing around something. The light from the sky was shining brightly on the wolf's gray coat, showing red and tan highlights slightly intermixed in his fur—something Zoey hadn't noticed before.

Lao stopped in front of the circular bushes and gestured with a paw for her to enter. She looked up at Lao, wondering why he wanted her to go through the tangle of plants in front of her.

"It's for you to see," said Lao.

"See what?"

He simply nodded with a smile.

She stepped into the bushes and thick grasses, weaving her way around sharp, pointy blades of green and tan shoots growing out of the soil. The grasses were hard, and she pushed them away as she ventured forward, but every so often a piece of grass would dig into her wing like a spike, causing her to cringe. As she continued to walk, she found herself under an old-looking fallen branch that was covered with dead moss. Not paying attention, she bumped her head on it. "Ouch!"

She sighed and shook her head. Wading through grasses, bushes, and dead branches wasn't easy as a small bird. *What does he want me to see, anyway?* She bumped into another sharp grass stalk. *I don't know about this. I bet there's another book here somewhere. Why do I have to walk in here for a silly book?*

Lao's voice boomed over the bushes. "If you want the answer, then you must follow the path of truth—the path of not-knowing. Presuming to know is a sickness of the mind.

Once you recognize you're ill, you can move toward perfect health and wellness. The VioletLight Masters are their own natural healers, curing themselves of all-knowing, bringing themselves to a place of extraordinary wisdom. We're here to help you as long as you allow it—without any assumptions."

*What's that supposed to mean? Ugh! Another confusing riddle that makes no sense!*

Continuing to push forward while rolling her eyes at what Lao had said, she felt the ground becoming damper. Water was either seeping up from the ground somewhere, or water had recently been here. She hopped over a damp clump of grass, then stopped and gazed into—water. Rolling her eyes yet again, she eyed a small pond shaded by a large Weeping Willow tree weeping branches over the surface of the water.

Zoey called over her shoulder. "I can't go on any further. There's a pond here!"

For several seconds, there was no reply. For several more seconds, silence still filled the air.

"Lao?"

"Yes?"

Zoey looked into the pond. It was clear, but shaded in some spots and lit by the sun in other spots. "What do you want me to see in here?"

Just then she saw it. As she stood over the pond, she noticed something peculiar on her forehead. Her crystal was different. In fact, it was a completely different color than before.

"Why is my crystal this color?" asked Zoey.

"Because you read the PureLight Order."

Zoey scrunched up her brow. "I did?" Thinking hard, she shook her head. "No I didn't."

"Where were you before you came here?"

Zoey looked around, seeing that the circle of plants and trees lining the edge of the pond thinned out the closer they grew to the water. Then she remembered the large, dark cavern she was in before she had arrived in this beautiful place. But how did she get here? She must be dreaming again, but didn't remember lying in her nice, comfortable nest to take a nap.

"Oh, yeah, I read it. Why did that change my crystal?"

"The PureLight Order is the most important item in all of Ohm Totem. It was created to give truth to those who read it. It was created to allow you to remember The Great Spirit's suggestions for a successful life—a life you can be happy with."

Peering into the water one more time, she gave a whisper, "Ahhh...it's beautiful". Then she bellowed, "I've never seen a spirit animal with crystals this color before. Am I the only one who has read it?"

"All VioletLights have. A lot of of PureLights have, as well."

Zoey was confused. "But, why aren't your crystals this color?"

"There is only one in Ohm Totem who carries the gold crystals. There are never two. Zoey, you are the 'Golden Keeper'. There hasn't been a Golden Keeper since Aria the VioletLight disappeared. She was the Golden Keeper eons ago."

A tingling sensation crawled through Zoey the moment Lao said, *Aria*. Why she tingled she did not know. Then a memory approached her from the back recesses of her mind, struggling to come out in the open, but her mind kept it in the dark.

"You are the song of the sacred heart, Zoey, and now the Golden Keeper. It's a lot to have in one life. You're now marked for all to see, which used to be a blessing in moons past, but now it's a curse in the moons of the Shiver—the period of the Dims."

Baffled, Zoey scrunched up her face and asked, "What's the Golden Keeper supposed to do?"

"The Golden Keeper is the keeper of the PureLight Order. You are charged with keeping it safe. The PureLight

Order will give you more instructions when necessary. All I know is that the keeper is chosen not by you, but by the PureLight Order itself."

Zoey about fell over. "What? How?" *How can a scroll talk to me, let alone talk to anyone? And it can choose certain spirit animals over others?* "Am I supposed to carry it around?" she asked, half joking.

Zoey's eyes widened when Lao responded with a "yes".

Zoey put her wings up, as if measuring the length of the scroll. She put her wings down and walked through the grasses, pushing the sharp shoots to the side with her wings, saying, "But, the scroll is ten times my size!"

Pushing away the last bush and peeking her head out of the grasses, Zoey noticed that Lao had a large smile on his face as he stood above her. He dipped his head. "You'll find a way. Your ingenuity will—your divergent thinking."

"Huh? I don't even know what you're talking about."

"You will, Zoey. You'll remember."

Zoey rolled her eyes, but felt the warmth coming from Lao like a warm summer breeze. "I don't know what you all want me to remember. Just tell me, like you tell Coda." With the thought of Coda, she looked into Lao's eyes with sadness.

"Coda was Orion. He left clues for himself all over Ohm Totem to help reawaken himself when he returned. Orion knew what he was going to do before he left Ohm Totem, and had prepared for it many moons before he left. That's why Coda is remembering so quickly and easily. You don't have that luxury." Lowering his eyes, he frowned. "I'm sorry, Zoey. I really am."

There was nothing Zoey could do, but just listen. She felt that in the days ahead she might remember more of her true self, if there really was a 'true self'.

"And, Zoey." Lao appeared sad. "I won't be coming to your dreams anymore."

"What?" Zoey was stunned, suddenly feeling alone and heart broken. "Why not?"

"Aderyn is your appropriate teacher. She is a Wing, such as you. There are many things she can teach and help you to remember that I cannot."

Zoey stared at Lao and then looked down. "But," she mumbled. "I like having you in my dreams."

"That's why this makes it so much harder for me, Zoey."

∞

Zoey suddenly awoke. She opened and closed her eyes several times, blinking the sleepy fog out of them. Standing over her was Aderyn, perched on a landing that held Zoey's resting nest.

"You fainted. The information that the PureLight Order holds was too much for you to bear. Most children see the PureLight Order and nothing happens, simply because they don't fully understand it yet, and move on. But you, of course, are different. Somehow your aura was able to download it. The PureLight Order, once read, will find any emotional pain you hold and bring it to the surface. Since you're young, the emotional pain brought to the surface was very little, if any. Although, the massive download it gave you made you pass out, which is actually one of the best ways to fully recover from such a strong download."

Zoey strained her neck, looking around. She was inside of the massive redwood tree. The zytes were on, meaning the window was closed. Was it dark outside?

"How long have I been sleeping?"

"I don't know how long you've been out, but when I came back to the Redwood I was surprised that you weren't where I left you. I had a suspicious feeling that you had found the underground tunnels and caverns." Aderyn blinked and nodded. "Before I reached the bottom of the redwood, I saw Gart pleading for my help. He led me to you, thinking you were about to die. I brought you back here and gave you some healing energy. He thought you'd just read a couple of lines of the PureLight Order, then move on and explore the rest of the cavern. He apologizes profusely for his mistake, though I told him it *was* no mistake. The Golden Keeper never reads a couple of lines. They merge with the PureLight Order."

Zoey's mind was rocking back and forth, either from Aderyn's explanation or from reading the PureLight Order. She then yawned. "I'm tired."

"I can see," replied Aderyn.

Closing her eyes, Zoey heard Aderyn's last fleeting words of the night. "Dream softly, child. You'll be training in the morning."

# Chapter 11

Night was even colder than the day, something Coda wasn't expecting. Thick flakes of snow fell heavily onto his pelt, making him wish he was cozy and inside the bramble hideout. In Gladstone, back at home, he was usually inside of his house during snowy nights. He'd either be sitting next to a burning fire, sipping something hot, or laying snugly in his bed, covered with thick, comfortable blankets. He'd never think about going out at night to patrol a forest compacted with snow and searching for ways to ambush opponents—such as he was doing now. For the first time in his life, he realized how plush his life really was in Gladstone. It's something he wouldn't take for granted when he got back, "if" he got back. He stared up at a pale moon through falling snow, doing his best to peer at it for just a second. In Ohm Totem, the moon was one of the few similarities to home. It didn't change. It was always there at night, just as the sun was in the day.

*Home. I wish I was there now.*

As he followed the group sent to scout the night, he sniffed a frozen shrub as he walked past it. He lurched back and stopped. He peered at the group, wondering if they smelled the same scent, only to see them walking onward. He shook his head. It couldn't be. He smelled it again.

*He's here?*

He took a big sniff, hoping the scent wasn't as fresh as he thought it was, but it was fresh—very fresh. He let out a silent gasp. *Sigun!* There was no way he could ever forget that tiger's smell!

Coda leaped forward, dashing as fast as he could to the patrol leader who wasn't too far ahead, which allowed him to catch up to her rather quickly.

"Psst," he whispered. The patrol leader, a small female cougar with a plain, tawny colored coat, turned to him. She was annoyed.

"Yes?"

"A Dim is nearby. I smelled him."

The cougar became interested. "Where was the scent?"

Coda gestured with his tail for her to follow him. She put up her tail, motioning to the rest of the group to stop and wait. They all turned and watched as Coda led the cougar back to the shrub.

The cougar leaned down and sniffed around, then nodded. "Duck down and be as quiet as possible. The Dims are in the area. There are about six of them." She patted her tail softly against the snow and the troop of large cats—cougars, lions, tigers, and cheetahs—moved silently across the snow and huddled around her. Their hearing must have been been incredible, because although Coda was only mere inches from the cougar, he had barely heard the taps on the snow she'd just made. *Perhaps they felt the vibration?*

"You seven go around the trees fifty steps to the east. Keep an eye on us as we head into the group of Dims ahead. Cover our backs. I don't want to run into an ambush. If you see anything coming at us from behind, then attack. If not, stay back until I give the order."

The seven nodded and softly loped off to the east, leaving a total of eleven patrol cats remaining, including Coda and the cougar, who gestured for them to follow.

The muffled silence only heard when snowflakes landing on snow filled Coda's ears as they trekked ahead. Many of the trees looked frozen and almost ready to break. He half expected to hear the sounds of a frozen tree splitting and crashing to the ground. Though, at the moment, everything was quiet and eerie, making him even more cautious as he traveled along.

He eyed the patrolling pack in front of him, assessing them the best he could. They walked quickly, making muffled crunching sounds with each step. They didn't seem

127

to care much about hiding from the Dims by moving from bush to bush, or being cautious and invisible. This was strange to Coda. *Wouldn't it be best to sneak up on them? Listen to what they have to say?* He didn't want to intrude on the cougar's plans, whatever they were, so he kept his mouth shut just in case the cougar knew what she was doing.

Snow was falling faster and Coda saw that it covered their tracks within minutes after a paw left a print in the snow. This was good if they were the ones in danger, the ones being tracked, but they weren't. They were the trackers. They'd have to rely upon smell through the snow.

Sigun drifted into Coda's thoughts. When Coda first met him, he really liked the giant tiger. He felt he was a friend, even though the introduction was short and sweet. Coda shook his head, frowning and remembering how quickly that had changed when Sigun tried to stop him from leaving the Marble Burrow several days ago. Sigun had no right or business in doing so, but Coda knew why the attempt was made. Sigun was working for the other team—the Dims. Perhaps, when Coda was Orion, he may have done something so bad to Sigun that it made him want to play on the other team? He didn't know. It probably didn't matter anyway.

The cougar put her tail up and everyone stopped. She perked up her ears, prompting Coda to do the same. He heard movement and slight whispers up ahead. The cougar gestured with her tail for all to follow her. Coda ran, catching up to her, and just as he was about to tell them to be quiet and to sneak up on Sigun, six Dims appeared—two coyotes, two weasels, a bear, and Sigun the tiger. They were in a small clearing surrounded by a semi-circle of bushes and large trees. They were sitting and talking amongst themselves, as if taking a rest from a long night's journey.

The Dims instantly stopped their discussions and took defensive positions. Sigun, in the lead, bared his fangs and gave a low growl as he started walking slowly toward the cougar's group. But suddenly, Sigun abruptly stopped and tilted his head. His eyes widened in surprise. "Coda?" A small grin appeared across his face. "You're a sight for sore eyes. What are you doing in this neck of the woods?" Sigun straightened up and moved his head left and right a couple of times. "You owe me a fight, young man!" He said this nicely, gently, as if they were definitely old friends.

Coda didn't know what to say. He didn't want to fight if he didn't have to. He was getting rather tired of it so he inched backwards, allowing the cougar to do her thing.

The cougar screwed up her face and spoke up. "You know this panther?"

"I know Coda, or should I say I know Orion very well." Sigun walked forward, creeping in a slow, steady pace. He tilted his head and narrowed his eyes at Coda. "Hi, Orion." His eyes shifted to Coda's forehead. There was a new color sparkling in Coda's crystal. Sigun gave a wry smile. "Congratulations, kid. You're getting your old color back."

It took a moment for the cougar to fully understand why Sigun kept saying Orion. Who in her group was named Orion? "Wait," she said. She took a quick breath and her head darted from Sigun to Coda, then back to Sigun. "Orion? Orion deserted us thousands of moons ago." She looked back at Coda. "What? Is he saying you're Orion?"

"He came back, missy," replied Sigun, who'd now crept only steps away from the baffled cougar.

The cougar turned to Sigun, her mouth gaping open. She didn't understand. This couldn't be true. Orion had run away, hid someplace far away, or was perhaps even dead. He hadn't been heard from or seen in ages. How could this young, black panther be Orion? She turned toward Coda again. "Is this true?"

Before Coda answered, he let out a low growl, then crouched on his hind legs and jumped toward the cougar. The cougar's startled eyes opened wide and she ducked, not anticipating the sudden attack. A moment later, she felt a breeze sail over her head and hissing and growling erupted just behind her, prompting her to turn and look. It was Coda and Sigun. Coda had him on the ground, pinned. Coda's strong paws were pressed against Sigun's thick chest. The Dim's went to attack.

"Stop!" came Sigun's voice, making them halt.

Coda, sensing a shift, moved off of Sigun's chest, allowing the tiger to get up and sit on his rump. Sigun laughed. "So, the deserter comes back, near his old homelands." He stared into Coda's eyes. "What do you have to say to those you turned your back on?"

Coda eyed his paws. He had no idea why he, or Orion, had left. Was it because Orion was scared, or because he had found a way to make things better in Ohm Totem? He gazed at his patrol. They all eyed him suspiciously, as if they were remembering what Orion had done to them in the past, and thinking that he'd most likely do it again. He didn't know he had deserted them, or if it was just rumors or a story Sigun or Crepus had concocted, or perhaps Skint. He didn't know anything, really. He was speechless. He gazed at the moon, seeing how lonely it was.

The cougar looked at her group, and then eyed Coda. "We have some things we need to discuss." There was a cool ire in her voice, sending a chill down Coda's back. He didn't know what he had done to create such emotion in the cougar.

Sigun gave a little chuckle.

The cougar stepped forward. "Sigun, I suggest you take your ragtag crew and leave our territory. I don't want to have to fight you."

Sigun sniffed the air. "*Your* territory?" He shook his head. "No, no, Crepus's territory and *my* territory. You and your bunch of misfits are trespassing."

"We've lived here longer than you have, Sigun!" replied the cougar.

"And, where is it you live, exactly?" asked Sigun, eyeing her suspiciously, knowing she wouldn't fess up no matter how much he asked.

The cougar narrowed her eyes. "You'll never know." She went into a defensive crouch. "You'd better leave, tiger!"

Coda inched quietly backwards. This was getting out of hand and he didn't want to be in the middle of it. Both of these groups were going to tear each other apart without any strategy to it. There would be no Art of Defense at all, just a plain and simple death match. If he were to participate in such a conflict, he'd rather be on the outskirts where he'd be able to see the entire skirmish, assessing the strengths and weakness of both sides. He wondered if this was why Orion had left, because of these pointless fights. There was no sense in fighting to the last spirit animal standing. It was insane. These types of things went on and on, around in circles, always repeating until complete annihilation occurred. He then knew, without a doubt, one of the reasons why Orion had left Ohm Totem. It was to step outside of the box to see through different eyes, to be born a human, and to one day re-enter his old world, allowing him to see Ohm Totem from a different perspective. "Whoa," he said out loud. Everyone turned and stared, as if he was in class interrupting his teacher's lesson of the day. Sigun's eyes were at full attention, darting around the snowy landscape, searching for hidden attackers, and thinking Coda had just given the sound for attack.

The cougar pursed her lips, obviously wondering why he'd make such a noise, especially now. She tilted her head, saying, "Yes, Coda? Do you have something to say?" When Coda simply shook his head, she looked back at Sigun.

The cougar twitched her tail, and for a moment Coda thought that meant to attack. Perhaps he *did* accidentally give the sign to start a brawl, but when seven large cats came out of hiding he knew she was signaling for the others to help. It was smart of the cougar to have the seven other cats stay out of view and scent range. This took Sigun off guard and he clearly made some quick calculations. Coda then wondered if the Dims were hiding any of their own, as well. He surveyed the surrounding area.

131

Sigun's demeanor lightened up. "You win, cougar."

"I didn't plan on losing."

Sigun took a deep breath and gestured for the rest of his group to follow. "I'll see you later, Orion."

Coda caught a glimpse of a movement near a tree, ten panther lengths away, right behind Sigun.

*What was that?*

Sigun grunted, pointing his nose toward Coda. "You have a lot of explaining to do with your new friends tonight. They'll want to know why you abandoned them."

Coda ignored Sigun's words, not because he wanted to, but because of the movement he just witnessed. There it was again!

A *tail!*

It was the same looking tail that poked out of the clump of grass just before he almost drowned in The River Ohm. This time, it had poked out from behind a tree, and then went out of view just as quickly.

Coda waited for Sigun and his group to disappear out of sight. Once they did, he looked to the cougar with worry. "They've left a spy."

The cougar slowly shook her head. "If you are who Sigun says you are, we have no reason to trust you. You have no business speaking."

"What? Why?" What could he have done so wrong when he was Orion? Thinking hard, he couldn't bring up any memories from Orion's past. Did he really abandon them, perhaps when they needed him most? "I thought I left with good intentions."

The cougar gave a curt laugh, shaking off his remark as if he hadn't said it. "Good intentions? We're going to have a tight watch on you from now on, Orion the VioletLight. Come with us."

She motioned with her tail and all of the cats surrounded him, prodding him forward. He was being led back to the brambles. Not a smart idea, especially with Skint on their path. He looked behind and saw the bushy tail pop up, only to vanish again under shrubbery.

"I'm telling you, they've left a spy." He gestured with his head toward a shrub in the distance.

The cougar looked, but when she saw nothing she turned with raised eyebrows. "I see nothing. We don't trust your kind, Orion."

"You've got to trust me. You're leading the Dims to your hideout," Coda said through gritted teeth.

The cougar pointed to a lioness with her tail. "Check it out."

The lioness dashed off without question, making loud crunching sounds as she ran.

Coda rolled his eyes at the lack of the lion's stealth. "Why don't you just yell to the spy that you're coming? It's Skint, the squirrel."

She continued to walk as if it didn't matter. "She can handle a pesky little squirrel."

"Not this one."

A moment later, they all heard a grunt and a thud. The surrounding cats stopped, making Coda do the same. When they looked back in the direction of the lion, they saw that she was lying on her side, not breathing and most assuredly dead. Whoever did this to the lioness had used the Dark Arts.

The cougar gazed into Coda's eyes and he could see a flash of fear in hers. "A squirrel couldn't have done that." Without waiting for a reply, she cursed his name. "Orion the VioletLight, you have sent her into a trap! This won't go unpunished."

"What? You sent her. I didn't." Coda defiantly shook his head. His eyes moved from one cat to the next. "Let me go and investigate. The spy has no power over me. I promise you."

"And let you go?" responded the cougar. "To join your friend, Skint? I think not!"

"But you're leading your tribe into danger if you go back to your hideout. We have to continue patrolling to flush out the spy. If not, he'll know where you live and send the rest of the Dim army."

This brought a shudder amongst the cats, but no one responded as they pressed forward. Everything was silent as falling snow coldly stuck to their backs. Coda wondered how he was going to get out of this and how he could save this remnant tribe from having their home being found by the Dims. Everything was suddenly feeling hopeless and his heart was getting tighter the closer they got to the brambles.

"Look," said Coda. "Just leave me right here and I'll make sure Skint doesn't find you. You have my word."

The cougar shook her head and gestured with her tail again, sending two more large cats on their way to look for the spy.

Coda dropped his head. *Did she really just send two more cats to their death? She must not know who Skint is, or at least not know of his knowledge of the Dark Arts.*

The cougar read his expression well. "Those are my two best. They'll come back with your spy." Coda peered over the cougar's head, watching the two cats run in the direction of the dead lion. A hefty wind suddenly blew, bringing with it a new kind of snow, one that pelted down diagonally instead of straight down. That would have been fine, but the snow was dropping ten times as much in a matter of seconds, blinding him from seeing the cats looking for Skint. A storm had come in.

The cougar and the rest of the cats lowered their heads to keep the snow out of their eyes and to make sure they could stare in the direction their two friends were sent. They were waiting for them to return, hoping they'd be carrying a dead spy.

Coda sat in silence. The chill was picking up, making him shiver slightly. He gazed into the thick falling snow, looking up at it, seeing how it fell. He'd never been in a blizzard, if this is what it was. It had to be. He could barely see a panther length in front of him. If they all stood here much longer, they'd be covered in white flakes and have to burrow

134

their way back to the hideout.

The crunch of paws running on snow took his focus away from the sky and into a crouch. Who was it? Sigun and his gang coming back to fight? Coda crawled slowly to the area where he remembered the cougar being. When he was a couple of panther lengths away, he saw the outline of her through the flood of falling snow. He was going to back her up if he needed to. Relief crept through him when he saw that the crunching snow had come from the two cats the cougar had sent to find the spy. They were safe and alive. They had come back with nothing, though. No spy. No sign or evidence that there had been a spy. Not even a paw track. Their eyes, though, were heavy with confusion. After they huddled close to the cougar, Coda saw the cougar abruptly give an ominous look to the sky, as if something terrible had happened. She glanced in the direction of her dead friend, looking for something she couldn't see. She took a gulp of breath, shook off the snow, and padded several steps toward Coda.

"They say the lions tongue was hanging out as if she'd been choked." She paused, frustration coming over her. "It was the Dark Arts, such as you said." She sighed, flicking her ears in frustration. "Let's go."

"No. He's still out there. Let me at him," replied Coda.

The cougar lunged toward Coda, stopping an inch in front of him. They were nose to nose, her brows lowered. She sent a low growl. "Don't speak, Orion. You do as you're told." She stepped back. "We march."

"If we go to your home, then your home will be found." *Why doesn't she understand that?* Coda stepped up to her, his blue crystal glowing. "Do not do this!" He pointed with his tail toward the dead lion. "You are leading the Dims right to us—to the hideout. Don't be stubborn. Please be smart!"

The cougar pushed Coda back with her front paws. "Don't tempt me, panther." She spit on the ground. "Don't you see this snow storm? Whoever is out there can't track us

135

in this, they can't see in this, and they can't hear in this. They can barely smell in this."

Coda, calming his temper, spoke low, "The one who killed your lion knows the Dark Arts. He has the ability to find us, to follow us." He swished his tail back and forth. "You are leading him to your hideout. Do you understand this?"

"I understand that you're a traitor and a coward. Nothing more." She turned on her heels, walking home. The cats surrounded Coda, making him follow the cougar back to the brambles. Coda knew this was it. *How long until the Dims arrive?* How the Dims would get into the brambles, though, was another story. It would be difficult. This gave him a glimmer of hope.

∞

Morning light blasted through small openings in the ceiling, waking Coda. Looking around, he saw that the place was busy again. Spirit animals were walking around and talking with each other, cubs and kits were playing, and Kiwu was pacing back and forth, obviously in deep thought about something.

Chev, who was still fast asleep, grunted every so often as if he was in the midst of battle. Coda got up to find Numee, but as he did he felt a sharp jab in his back.

Turning to see what it was, he saw Hao give a cruel grin. He, again, jabbed Coda with his antlers. "I've been asked to watch over you." He puffed out his lower lip. "Orion, is it?" Rolling his eyes, he gave a little laugh. "Orion's a coward. If you could choose any VioletLight to be, then why choose that cat? He ran away like a little baby, not wanting to get hurt by big old Crepus." He shook his head. "Nice lie you gave the cougar last night, kid."

Coda wanted to say he wasn't lying, but that wouldn't do any good. Instead, he ignored the stag and peered around the landscape looking for Numee. There she was, playing with the young ones, making them laugh. Coda whispered in his mind, *there's Numee.* She stopped what she was doing and looked at him. She then mumbled something to the youngsters, and padded on over. When she noticed what Hao was doing, keeping watch over Coda, she purposely bumped into him, jostling him from his guard. "Keeping us against our own will is one thing, but hovering around us as we're helping you is another. You either leave Coda alone or—"

"Hao!" interrupted Kiwu. "I need your advice."

Hao turned, wiggled his butt at Numee, and walked over to his leader, making clopping sounds with his hooves as he went.

Coda stood, then yawned and stretched. "Thanks Numee." After another stretch, he asked, "Where's Shikoba?"

"She's over there, calling Nova."

For a moment, Coda pictured Shikoba pressing buttons on a telephone and putting it to her ear, making a phone call to her VioletLight friend. When he saw Shikoba near the entrance of the brambles, he knew for sure that that wasn't the case. Plus, they didn't have phones here.

"How is she calling Nova?"

"It's easy. She's simply doing what you just did to me."

"What I did to you?" questioned Coda.

"Yes, silly." Numee scratched her back with a hind paw. "You looked at me and spoke my name in your mind. I picked up your vibe and responded. All Shikoba needs to do is picture Nova in her heart and speak her name with intention."

Coda suddenly felt sick to his stomach. Not from pain, but from sadness. "Do you think Nova is even alive?" He missed her, almost as much as he missed his sister. According to Nova, Zoey was safe in the hands of Crepus, which was a strange thought, *safe with Crepus?* He knew that wouldn't be the case for Nova. She wouldn't be safe anywhere in the Dim Lands.

137

An unexpected commotion was occurring through the tribe as the light from above started to fluctuate. Looking up at the ceiling, Coda could make out several shapes through the little openings of the bramble ceiling.

*What is that?*

Examining closer, Coda saw that the shapes had wings. He gasped when he saw that many more were coming, landing by the dozens. The Dims had arrived.

"You have no place to go," called a voice from above. "We have you surrounded on land and in the air."

The voice had the familiar hiss of Crepus. He was out there. Coda lowered his eyes, imagining the worst of the worst. He'd do anything to get at that dragon and get his sister back.

Coda whispered to Numee with confidence in his voice. "I'm going to step outside and try to speak with Crepus. In the meantime, gather everyone you can. I'll try and start a fight with Crepus. When that happens, most of the Dims will take their eyes off of here to watch the fight. That will give everyone a chance to run toward the fog and into the Sihu Tribe. I think it will give you all a chance."

Numee closed her eyes, slowly shaking her head no. "Coda, they'll rip you apart. You think that if you get the upper hand on Crepus, that the Dims will just sit there and watch? You'd have all them on top of you in an instant."

Coda thought a moment, then said, "I'll run to the north before that happens. I'll draw them away."

A loud bang echoed throughout the hideout, causing an even louder commotion within the remnant tribe. A rock, the size of Coda, fell through the brambles, barely missing several youngsters. Kiwu sprang into action, running in a circle around his tribe, screaming, "To the passage! To the passage!"

They all nodded in understanding, running to a wall opposite the entrance.

A moment later another rock tumbled through the brambles, smashing hard against the ground and again missing several spirit animals.

Chev and Shikoba came to Coda's side. "Why, in all of the Dim Lands, is Kiwu running the opposite way?" asked Chev.

"It's not just him. It's all of them," replied Shikoba.

Chev nodded his head and shrugged. "I'd say we follow."

Coda and Numee looked at each other. Coda nodded to her, hoping she'd do what he'd asked. It was their only chance to survive. He padded off toward the entrance, figuring he'd open it and meet his opponent—Crepus.

Coda heard another bang and jumped just in time to dodge a big boulder barreling through the ceiling, and this one left a large hole above. An instant later, large birds— ravens, eagles, hawks, and vultures—swarmed through the opening, undercutting Coda, causing him to lose his balance and fall on his side. As he went to get up, he saw several spirit animals, mostly young ones, snatched by the birds and pulled up through the hole.

*Oh no!*

Coda swiped at a raven taking another cub, only to see that the bird held the small panda he had befriended yesterday. He remembered she called herself Pangli. Swiping the raven's back with his claws, Coda saw the bird lose its grip and drop a squealing Pangli to the floor.

She looked up at Coda, wide eyed and scared. He grabbed her by the back of the scruff, then noticed a yelling Numee way in front of him. "Come on Coda. Hurry!"

Coda was both astonished and elated. He now knew why Kiwu was running in the opposite direction of the entrance. At the back of the hideout was an escape tunnel. As Coda ran, he realized that a portion of the back wall opened and closed, just like the entrance. Chev stood at the escape tunnel's entrance, gesturing with his trunk for Coda.

Just ahead, Coda saw Kiwu and Hao moving around, busying themselves by aggressively pushing their tribe- mates into the tunnel entrance, escorting them out of their once safe home.

As Coda quickly approached the tunnel, he gulped in fright. The tunnel's door was shutting. Why would they shut the door on him? Unless—*No! It must be on a timer or something.* If so, then the door may not be able to open back up after it's shut—at least for a while. There might be a mechanism in the door that this remnant tribe created, not allowing the Dims—or anyone else, for that matter—to open it back up right after it closed.

"Hurry!" yelled Chev. Coda picked up speed, running as fast as he could while still carrying Pangli. His heart raced faster and faster while his mind leaked doubt. He wasn't going to make it before that heavy door, made of earth and rock, shut, leaving him and Pangli to face the Dims alone. Slowing down, all Coda could do now was to protect the little panda with his life. Then he tripped on something, somersaulted forward, and landed on his back.

Getting up, he saw what had happened. A large crow had rammed his back legs, making him lose his balance. Pangli had slipped from Coda's grip and was violently shaking, waiting to be taken, or worse yet, killed by the Dims. She was much too young for all of this. Coda scrambled to his feet and hovered over her protectively, making sure no more Dims could harm her, not if he could help it. He'd defend her until his last breath; something he figured was coming quickly.

Standing over her, Coda took a grief stricken glance back at the escape tunnel. His mouth gaped open. There, in between the closing doors, was Chev using his elephant body to prevent the door from closing. "Hurry!" Chev screamed, his eyes telling the story of the strain the heavy door was placing upon him.

Another bird, an eagle this time, swooped in, screeching at the top of its lungs, bumping Coda out of the way, and grabbed the panda with its talons.

"No!" yelled Coda. "Let her go!"

Angrily, Coda crouched and leaped at the eagle, biting down hard on the eagle's tail. He expected the eagle to drop his young friend, but the eagle did the opposite. Its strength almost pulled Coda into flight until Coda leaned back, causing the eagle to lurch backwards with him. The eagle was strong, but its strength didn't compare to Coda's and it couldn't carry all of the weight. His blue crystal shone brightly as they dropped to the ground and he shook the eagle back and forth until it finally let go of the helpless little panda. Then he threw the eagle against a side wall and picked up his friend and ran to the tunnel. Peering over his shoulder, he saw several birds in hot pursuit. This was going to be close.

Glancing ahead, Coda nearly stopped dead in his tracks. Antlers were coming at him. It was Hao!

*Hao wants to fight me now?*

Thinking he'd have to maneuver around Hao, he was happily surprised when Hao ran past him, spiking a large bird.

He wanted to help the stag, but he had to save Pangli and a mouth full of Pangli's scruff prevented him from saying thanks. Running toward Chev, Coda saw how close he was to the opening. He leaped through it, entering a bleak tunnel. Turning around, he set Pangli on the ground and saw Chev still holding the door open. Chev was waiting for Hao to return, but Hao had other things in mind.

Hao thrashed his body, kicked outward, and waved his antlers wildly about, hitting several birds. Then it happened. Something Coda had feared the moment the first boulders had crashed through the ceiling.

Near the entrance of the hideout, the larger of the Dims—gorillas, wolves, and lions, were jumping down through a huge hole in the ceiling, landing skillfully inside of the hideout. Seeing that most of the remnant tribe, except for Hao, were in the process of escaping, the Dims moved forward at full speed.

Hao, though, was oblivious, crazy as could be, tossing birds everywhere. Coda knew Hao would be taken down the moment the large Dims got to him.

141

Leaping forward, Coda landed next to Chev. Glancing at the elephant, he saw a face full of terror and pain. It was obvious that the weight was becoming too much for him. He was struggling and shaking. His legs wobbled back and forth, his eyes scrunched as he used all of his might to keep the door open.

"Chev, I need you to use that inner power of yours and hold this door just a little bit longer," said Coda.

Chev nodded as tears of pain started running down his cheeks.

Coda sprinted toward Hao, but saw he wasn't going to be able to reach him before the lions and wolves did. Coda then did something he had never done before—magic. A feeling took over, opening a channel inside of him, pulsing energy. Everything slowed down, giving him an even bigger advantage.

Coda felt life expand around him as his heart became certain; certain that these Dims were about to feel a force more powerful than fear—the power of love for another Being. Halting, Coda felt a wave of energy rush through him. Taking a deep breath, he lifted on his hind legs and drove his front legs down, slamming his paws onto the ground. Exhaling, he felt the flow of energy draining through his paws, blasting the ground, expanding outward through the earth. A roar came from his mouth, sending the energy even faster.

Looking up, Coda watched as Hao and the rest of the Dims fell backwards, toppling head over heels and sliding across the ground. Coda's eyes beamed with astonishment. *How did I do that?* Right now, it didn't matter. He had to save Hao. He shook himself and leaped in Hao's direction, landing by his side. Glancing around, Coda noticed the Dims were having a hard time regaining their bearings. Many simply fell back over when they got up and others, including Hao, managed to lift themselves off the ground, only to walk in circles, confused about what had just happened.

142

Coda couldn't wait for Hao to compose himself. He grabbed one of the stag's antlers with his teeth and back peddled to the escape tunnel, dragging Hao along with him. Numee, Kiwu, and Shikoba joined him, each pulling the stag with all of their might.

"I can't hold it any longer!" cried Chev.

Coda peered over his shoulder, seeing Chev's struggles. Coda pulled harder.

"I'm losing it, Coda!" Chev shouted.

*Just a little bit farther. Come on Chev, just hold on!*

# Chapter 12

"Magic has a purpose and *we* use it purposefully. When used for menial tasks or, for example, to show off in front of another...that abuses it. And when abusing something, you run the risk of losing that something. Magic shall only be used when absolutely necessary. Does that make sense, Zoey?"

Aderyn had her wings folded in front of her. They were perched on a cliff that stood just behind the redwood, easily hiding them from view, just in case the Dims decided to show themselves in the canyon this morning.

Zoey nodded her head, knowing that yesterday she had abused her power by conjuring the key into reality, then making it disappear over and over again. Anxiety swept through her. What if she had abused her power yesterday so she can't use it ever again? For a moment, she wanted to manifest the key right there, right now, just to see if she had truly lost her privilege to use magic. She wanted to make an excuse, to ask for a bathroom break or something, so she could hide and speak the secret words to manifest the key into physicality to see if it still worked. But then she rolled her eyes. Aderyn would see right through that.

As she continued to fill her mind full of thoughts, a small flake of snow fell on her beak, and then more and more started to fall. Her body shivered and she imagined herself suddenly turning into ice, and then shattering into tiny pieces if she tried to move.

Aderyn observed Zoey, tilted her head, and smiled. "Sit down."

Zoey, looking behind her to make sure there weren't any sharp rocks on the spot where she wanted to sit, smiled back at Aderyn and sat on her rump. She peered into the owl's eyes. Aderyn, from what Zoey could see, wasn't cold at all.

Aderyn blinked. "Close your eyes and inhale deep, slow breaths. Do this for twenty breaths."

Zoey complied, taking in a deep breath and exhaling. She did this over and over again, until her body started to tingle. Opening her eyes, everything seemed sharper and she could see more clearly. Her body was even warm and comfortable. Her mind, usually full of chatter, was calm and ready for anything.

*Maybe this training isn't going to be so bad after all?*

"You must master the elements if you want to use magic effectively, and with any sort of accuracy. Right now the elements of nature overwhelm you, causing your body to react in an unsuitable way. You don't have control over yourself. The first aspect of magic, when used appropriately, delves into continual mastery of Self."

Zoey nodded, thinking she understood. "So, when you say master myself, do you mean to do everything right?" Zoey was shocked at how powerfully she spoke. There was something to this breathing trick and she liked it.

Aderyn placed her feather tips together. "I mean to identify the mistakes you've made and for you to learn from them, keeping them always in your memory and doing your best never to repeat them. To learn compassion for yourself and others, to remain centered when you're in the most difficult of circumstances, and discovering ways to accept the elements of nature by not allowing them to affect your mind and body. These are but a few examples of mastering yourself. I'm working on it every day, as does every VioletLight. We are Beings that have worked hard and progressed in order to be who and what we are—and it's not easy. Not until you've been on the path of Self Mastery for many, many moons does it start taking affect. It then becomes a habit, as effortless as a thought." Aderyn paused, then continued, "I can tell you haven't mastered the chill of the Shiver yet. Let's start there." She put her wing on Zoey's shoulder. "Close your eyes."

Zoey did so and Aderyn walked around her as she talked. "Most spirit animals feel the essence of nature throughout the day, allowing it to bring them energy and abundance. But, when nature is at its harshest, these days spirit animals run from it, fearing that Nature will harm them in some way. When they feel there is no escape, their mind flips a switch, activating the fight or flight mechanism in their brain. This causes their body to react to the elements, such as shivering in the cold. Yes, this momentarily keeps them warm by getting the blood flowing, causing heat to enter their body. However, this is only a temporary solution to a challenge that is easily overcome through Self Mastery."

"Element?" questioned Zoey.

"An element is an individual activity of Nature. When the sun shines, the warmth that it sheds is an element of the sun. Does that make sense?"

Zoey nodded. It made a lot of sense.

Aderyn continued, "In a moment, I'll take you through a process of warming your body in the coldest of temperatures. Are you ready?"

Zoey shrugged, but then realized that shrugging was really not a good answer. She puffed out her chest, confidently nodding a yes to Aderyn's question.

"Wonderful," replied the owl. "With your eyes closed, take a long, deep breath, imagining a beam of warm light coming from the sky and surrounding your body." Aderyn paused and asked, "Do you have that image in your mind?"

Zoey gave a nod.

"Excellent. Now remember a moment in your life when you were really warm, then bring that into the forefront of your mind. Once there, exhale deeply and drop that memory and feeling down into your heart, and imagine it spreading throughout your body." She paused again. "Continue for thirty breaths. When you're done, feel your body. If you're still cold, then continue breathing."

Zoey did so, and as Aderyn took her through the steps

146

again she followed along easily. But, it didn't take any more than ten deep breaths for her body to start warming up. As Zoey concentrated, she became warmer and warmer. Finally, she opened her eyes and felt like a furnace generating heat.

"Very good," said Aderyn. "That was your first training."

*What? That's it?* "Well, how long will it last? I mean, will I get cold again right after I finish doing the deep breaths?"

"The moment you think of getting cold, your body will respond in kind and you'll become cold. Trusting your body to regulate itself at the correct temperature at each given moment takes a lot of practice. Soon, though, the practice will become a habit and you won't need to go through these steps anymore. Your body will automatically breathe deeply throughout the day, helping it to adjust to the temperatures around you, no matter how hot or cold the weather."

Then Aderyn bowed to Zoey. "You are magnificent, child. I'm doing my best to keep my excitement inside, but for you to warm your body to the degree you did in just one practice session is amazing."

Zoey didn't know how to respond to that. It wasn't difficult. She thought anybody could do it. Smiling at Aderyn's adoration, she went to get up, but Aderyn interrupted her. "Continue practicing. I feel Gart needs me in the Hall of Scrolls. I'll be back in a while."

With that, Aderyn spread her wings and lifted off the ground and flew upwards, spiraling around the redwood.

Zoey sighed. *This is why I don't like to train. It gets to be so boring.*

Shaking her head and doing what Aderyn asked, she closed her eyes and started breathing deeply, imagining herself becoming warm. She kept still, sitting on her rump for hours, taking the rich air into her lungs, then exhaling.

After a while, she noticed Aderyn was right. When Zoey would think of being cold her body temperature would instantly plummet. When she refocused and imagined warmth, doing the steps that Aderyn had taught her, she'd

147

become warm—toasty, in fact. For a while she played with that; warm, cold, freezing, warm, and hot. Back and forth she went, until she felt an incredible urge to sing.

She opened her mouth, and instead of a beautiful, soulful voice coming out, she heard herself chirping skillfully. It was enchanting.

The wind picked up for a moment. *You're finding your voice, Zoey.*

Snow Tree?

*Yes, it is I. You're doing well.*

*I miss you,* replied Zoey.

*I'm always with you, Zoey. Remember, you are here for a purpose. Everything you do in Ohm Totem, everything taught to you here, carries a reason with it. Please accept all that comes to you. It's all a lesson and when learned well, it's the way to mastery, the way to magic, the way of love.*

*But,* responded Zoey. *I'm so confused. What am I to do here? How can I know what to do when no one will tell me who I am or why I'm here? Why does everyone practically bow to me when they meet me? Why do they do that?*

*You are greater than you imagine, Zoey. Trust me when I say you'll start to discover who you truly are in moons to come. When your memories surface they will have the answers you seek. You just have to find the physical place where your fondest memories are.*

*The answers? The place where my fondest memories are? Is that somewhere in Ohm Totem?* asked Zoey. When there wasn't a response, she asked again. After a long pause, she realized that the Snow Tree had left. But, if the Snow Tree is always with her, then she must be around here somewhere, thought Zoey.

*Snow Tree?* she asked one more time.

When she didn't hear a response, she opened her eyes. Standing there was Aderyn.

"You look sad, child."

Zoey looked away. She didn't want to go through the

148

explanation of why she was sad. She didn't want to tell Aderyn that she felt confused and alone all the time here in Carwyn Canyon. She didn't want to tell her that she wanted nothing more than to find Coda and go through the portal to see her mom and dad. In fact, it was easier to speak with the Snow Tree back in the Cornell Forest and she felt she was losing the connection to the tree while stuck in Ohm Totem. If she could talk with the Snow Tree like she did before she arrived on this island, then perhaps she could convince the Snow Tree to tell her everything. She took a deep breath. *Who am I? Snow Tree, please tell me!*

"Zoey?" came Aderyn's voice.

Realizing that she hadn't replied to Aderyn, she gazed into the owl's eyes. "I'm sorry. I miss home."

Aderyn nodded with understanding. She felt Zoey's pain. She sat down next to Zoey and put her wing around her. Zoey instantly felt warmth and love from the snow owl. It felt similar to her mom's energy, but not quite the same. Nonetheless, she felt a little better and started to sit up a little straighter. She leaned her head against Aderyn's chest and her eyes began to well up with tears. For a while they sat there in the quiet, accepting each other's company and feeling at peace with it. This warmed Zoey's heart even more, making Zoey stand up.

"I feel better." She lowered her eyes. "Thank you."

"You're a strong child. You came here to Ohm Totem to help us even though you didn't remember us, nor fully understand what you were getting into. There aren't too many souls brave enough to do such a thing. For that, thank you."

Zoey saw Aderyn's violet crystals glow, then felt Aderyn's comforting energy beam to her. A second later, Zoey saw Aderyn shuffle her feet, much like a child would do when feeling a little unsure about something. "Can I teach you what you once taught me? It was something you discovered on your own."

Zoey wondered how she could have taught the owl

149

anything, but refrained from asking. It didn't matter. Aderyn would just tell her that the answer would come soon. For a moment, however, a memory surfaced. She saw a large tuft of green grass moving in a gentle breeze. In that grass, she noticed a portion of it that didn't move at all. It shimmered and looked like rippling green water, but without movement. An instant later, she was shown a snow owl, with violet crystals, emerge from that shimmer, as if appearing out of thin air.

Zoey, coming back from the memory, sat down. "I just saw you in my mind. You were the grass, but weren't the grass." She shook her head, trying to figure out how to explain what she'd seen. "You looked like the grass, but I noticed you because when the grass moved—you didn't."

Aderyn's beak formed a wide grin. "Yes, that was the first time you taught me how to shape-shift. You taught me, from that moment forward, to move with the breeze, instead of being a hard rock, unless of course I'm shape-shifting into a rock. You explained that we're not only to blend into our surroundings, but to become our surroundings. What I found, and what you knew, was that the more I practiced this sacred magic, the easier it was to follow the movement of what I was blending into."

Again, Zoey didn't know how to reply to something she didn't understand. She really wanted to know how she had taught Aderyn anything. She'd never met her before she came to Ohm Totem. But, where did that memory come from? Did she just imagine that? Did Aderyn or the Snow Tree send it to her? Zoey glanced at her feet, frowning. The memory felt just as real as the dreams she had with Lao.

"I think you're ready for our second training."

Zoey's mouth formed an 'oh' as she lifted her head and eyed Aderyn. "I have another training today?" Zoey was a little discouraged. She eyed the redwood tree, searching the bark for some way out of this, as if it would actually tell her.

"You'll learn the Art of shape-shifting," responded Aderyn. Zoey's eyes moved from the tree to Aderyn. Zoey didn't want another training, especially one about shape-shifting. It didn't sound as easy as the first training had been. Her shoulders drooped and she nodded her head in resignation. "When?"

"Now."

∞

Aderyn and Zoey flew side-by-side, gliding silently toward Gwenfree Forest, heading in the direction of Crepus Castle. Looking down, Zoey noticed two large apes and a small pack of white wolves running toward Carwyn Canyon, as if in chase. Some of the pack stopped, sensing something, and gazed up into the sky, seeing Aderyn and Zoey fly by. Luckily for Zoey, she was much too high for them to do anything about it. They yelled things that Zoey couldn't quite hear and the apes pointed, jumping up and down in a chaotic frenzy. A sudden fright engulfed Zoey. *Are they going to report us to Crepus?*

"They are harmless, Zoey."

"What about flying Dims?"

"What about them?"

"What if they spot us, too?"

Aderyn flapped her wings a couple of time, then held them out in another glide. She turned her head to Zoey and winked. "Then we show them a thing or two."

Before they had gone on this flight, Aderyn had explained to Zoey about their second training. Zoey was a little shocked. Not at the aspect of shape-shifting, but at the idea of actually flying into Gwenfree Forest on purpose, knowing that Dims may be in there, not in the dozens, but in the hundreds or thousands. They would practice there, making sure not to be seen. "It's a perfect place to train," said Aderyn.

Coming closer to the forest's canopy, they swooped lower, dodging and swerving around branches as they entered the forest. Zoey saw patches of snow here and there, reminding her of how cold it was. Her body shook from the chill as she maneuvered around a thick tree. Then she remembered to think of warmth, bring it to her heart, and spread it to the rest of her body. Within minutes, she was warm and feeling good again. Her senses were sharper, her reflexes were fluid, and her wings were stronger.

Aderyn suddenly went into a hover and landed on a thick branch. Zoey did the same, landing next to the owl, and almost slipping off of it because of a sheath of frost on the bark.

Glancing around, they seemed to be in the middle of the Gwenfree Forest. It was quiet, and beautiful icicles hung from branches all around them. The cold mist coming from their breath dissipated only inches from their beaks and Zoey realized she was breathing a lot faster than Aderyn. Below them, the forest floor was covered with frost covered dead fall, sticks and branches. The sudden freeze was taking its toll on the old, but strong, forest.

A bird, far off in the east, screeched as it flew away. For a moment, Zoey wondered if they had been noticed, thinking they were definitely going to be reported now.

"It didn't see us." Aderyn stood tall, showing Zoey that she would deal with any Dims if they came close enough. The owl had confidence, just like all of the VioletLights she'd met, but what was amazing about Aderyn was the motherly quality that she held. It was a nice addition to Aderyn's energy and made everything feel nice and calm. Zoey knew she was safe in her presence.

"VioletLights are not here to keep you safe," informed Aderyn. "We will, however, do everything in our power to protect you—or any other being, for that matter. We are here to show you how to be safe on your own, sharing wisdom from our own experiences. If you want safety and security, then dig a hole in the middle of nowhere and hide. Perhaps then, and only then, will you be safe and secure. Otherwise, you're in a world where your senses must always be aware, even when you are asleep. This is what we're

152

teaching you and it's up to you to listen and master. The Dims learn in the same way, but there's a huge difference in our philosophy. They teach stress—to be on alert with fear in their heart, thinking that at any moment death may come, trapping them in its terrible, unforgiving grip. We teach peace—to be on the alert, but to take your breath into consideration while doing so. When you consciously breathe deeply, your senses open up and you feel danger approach long before it is upon you, thus keeping you more safe and secure. Does that make sense?"

Zoey nodded, then winced. Another bird swooped by far off in the distance. *Another Dim.* Her heart pounded a little faster. She didn't want to be seen.

Aderyn pointed at the bird with her wing. "That one's looking for us. Those apes and wolves must have ratted us out."

*Uh oh!* thought Zoey. "Should we go back to the redwood?"

Zoey hoped the answer would be a resounding yes, but when Aderyn shook her head, Zoey about fell out of the tree. Shocked, Zoey responded. "If they are looking for us, then aren't we in danger?"

"What do you feel, Zoey?"

Zoey thought for a moment, and when it was fear that she felt she told the owl.

"I understand, since we are close to Crepus Castle, but we need to know more than that. Close your eyes and breathe. Then see and feel."

As Zoey closed her eyes, she inhaled. She didn't know what it was she was supposed to feel, but within minutes her body started to find its calm again. Then, out of the blue, she felt and saw several Dims, as if they were right in front of her. A band of rushing, flying birds—eagles, hawks, and osprey—the worst winged predators that the Dims had, were heading their way. They had flown out of the large entrance of Crepus Castle and they had determination in their eyes. Zoey could tell they wanted to get Aderyn once

153

and for all.

Opening her eyes, Zoey looked at Aderyn with horror.

"You see them too?" asked the owl.

"They're coming," replied Zoey.

"Now comes our second training of the day." Aderyn spoke as if there was no hurry, and as if it hadn't crossed her mind that she might get caught, or worse, be killed by these menacing birds.

"Shape-shifting is magic that can be used during these types of situations." Aderyn walked to where the branch grew out of the tree and leaned her back up against the bark. In a flash, Aderyn disappeared. Gone.

*What the heck?*

Zoey closed her eyes and saw the flying Dims approaching much faster, twirling with the anticipation of finding Zoey and Aderyn. She gasped. "They're getting closer!"

Aderyn suddenly reappeared out of thin air and was leaning against the tree. "Then it's best you learn the Art of shape-shifting, and quickly." There was a hint of a smile on Aderyn's face, as if she knew Zoey could do this with no problem.

Zoey turned her head, gazing in the direction she knew the flying Dims were approaching. Small snowflakes fell between the branches in front of her and her body shivered. Taking a deep breath, bringing warm images to her heart, she brought her body to the temperature it needed in a matter of seconds. She liked this new technique. It worked well.

The sounds of enraged birds filled the forest canopy, but Zoey couldn't see them yet.

"They're just about on us," said Aderyn, jolting Zoey out of her little daze. "Let's begin." Aderyn extended her wings toward the gray sky, as if pointing toward The Great Spirit. "Come stand next to me."

Zoey walked over, listening to the coming ruckus and feeling that the Dim's were gaining speed, getting closer which made Zoey flinch. "Don't let them bother you." Still holding her wings high, Aderyn smiled. "Magic originates from The Great Spirit, who purifies it, then washes it through you." Dropping her wings, she stared into Zoey's eyes and leaned back against the bark of the tree. She whispered something and then vanished.

Zoey sighed, leaning her head back against the bark. *Great! Just teach me already, so we can—*

The crack of small branches breaking caused Zoey to do a quarter twirl. She peered out into the branches, searching the forest for the squawking birds. After a time, she didn't see anything—but heard them coming closer. She scrunched her face in confusion. The cracking sound had come from somewhere in their own vicinity.

"It's Skint."

Twirling around again, Zoey saw Aderyn standing next to her. Her eyes looked worry. She put a wing feather to her lips, blowing a soft "shhh" sound. She whispered. "He's here, so keep quiet."

Skint had been a thorn in Zoey's side from the moment she had met the little squirrel. And to think, she had once felt sorry for the liar. *Skint the Lying Squirrel should be his name*, she thought. He was good at being a spy, although he proved too quick in using his Dark Arts on her and Coda. It had exposed the fact that he was most likely working for the other team, which they soon found out for certain when they were in the tunnels. The last time he tried the Dark Arts on Zoey, he was blasted backwards by some invisible force that Zoey managed to create. Suddenly, a confidence surged through her. She could take these Dims. When she used that same force in the tunnels, she had knocked two large apes on their backs and they were apes that were ten times her size.

Aderyn tugged on her wing, gesturing to Zoey to follow her lead. She put her beak up to Zoey's ear. "Lean back and touch your feathers against the bark."

Zoey did so, feeling the cold, rough surface.

Another crack, but this time even closer. Zoey looked left and right, trying to find Skint, but was interrupted when she saw the first winged Dim coming into view. It was an eagle that clearly hadn't seen them yet, or so it appeared.

"Now, imagine you're the bark," said Aderyn. "Nothing more, nothing less. Once you imagine that, whisper 'Lemla Semta'. Do you understand?"

Zoey nodded.

"Good." Aderyn's eyes grew fierce. "I'll be back."

"Huh? Where are you going?"

"The birds are almost on top of us and Skint is one tree over. He sees me—"

Another crack and Aderyn flew off the branch, gliding to the next tree and doing her best to make as much noise as possible with her wings.

*She's distracting Skint.*

Suddenly, Zoey saw several Dims land and perch on a branch a couple of trees away and they were waving to the rest of the flying crew to land next to them. A crow pointed directly at Zoey and spoke something, although Zoey couldn't hear what it said. She could easily guess, since they all flew off the branch in unison and headed her way.

"Lemla Semta," whispered Zoey.

Nothing happened.

"Lemla Semta." Zoey looked at her wings, noticing that they were exactly the same as before. She was expecting them to change to the color of the bark, which wasn't happening. It wasn't working like Aderyn said it would. She went to fly to Aderyn, but saw the VioletLight going from branch to branch, doing her best to make as much commotion as possible. The problem was that the birds and Skint weren't taking the bait.

"Lemla Semta."

The scratching sound of a squirrel climbing up a tree filled her ears. When she felt the small vibration of Skint's tiny feet moving fast against the bark she was leaning against, she knew he was on her tree, and about to get her.

156

"Lemla Semta, Lemla Semta."

She remained the same.

*Why isn't it working?*

In front of her, she saw that the birds were very close. In fact, too close. The lead eagle had his sights set on Zoey.

She panicked. She needed to get to the other side of the tree to hide from the coming danger. She glanced to her left, noticing another branch that jutted out of the tree. She jumped on that one, then to the next branch and the next, until she was on the other side of the tree, hidden from the hideous eyes of the coming Dims. Placing her back against the bark of the tree, she inhaled a deep, anxious breath, filling herself full of fear. That wasn't good, and almost paralyzed her with concern. She didn't know what to do.

An instant later, she felt something soft against her shoulder. She gasped when she saw that it was a squirrel's bushy tail.

"Welcome to the Dim Lands, Zoey."

The high, but menacing, voice was Skint's. He was above her and she could feel his breath against the top of her head. She was petrified and couldn't move.

He reached down and placed his paw on her wing. "If you come with us, we won't kill your brother."

*What? Coda?* Her eyes darted everywhere. *They have Coda? How?*

"We took him at the Circle of Elders." He let out a soft laugh. "Just after we snagged you. What a nice prize he is, don't you think?"

He could be right about taking Coda. Zoey didn't remember much after she was snatched by the eagle. Maybe the Sihu Tribe lost the battle and the Dims have them all captive? *Oh no!*

A whack of something hit against the tree as an owl screech filled the air. A moment later, she saw Skint fall, hitting branches on his way down and landing clumsily on the cold ground. He stood up immediately, shaking himself off, and then headed back up the tree.

Aderyn was now standing next to her. "Close your eyes. Imagine you're the tree and become the tree. Lemla Semta!" she said, and disappeared the instant she spoke the magic spell.

*That's right,* she remembered. *I have to imagine I'm the tree.*

A large bird landed on a branch on the other side of the tree.

*They're here.*

She closed her eyes, took a very deep breath to calm her nerves, and imagined she was the tree. She let out a slight whisper, soft enough for no one to hear. "Lemla Semta."

The sound of static entered her ears, and when she opened her eyes everything was the same, except for a reddish tint, almost like someone had placed a red filter over her eyes.

Skint appeared on the branch they were on. And even though he sniffed and sniffed, he couldn't find Aderyn or Zoey. He came up to Zoey, smelling wildly, as if confused. Several birds landed next to him.

An osprey spoke, "Where are they?"

Skint stopped looking wildly about and stiffened. There was rage in his eyes. "Do you think I'd be sniffing around if I knew where they were?" He pointed to the next tree over. "Find them!"

All the birds flew off but one, the eagle. He narrowed his eyes at Skint. "I had her in my talons at the Circle of Elders. I could have squashed her in my grip. Why wasn't I allowed to?" There was anger in his voice and Zoey could tell that he was holding something back. No, she felt something else from the eagle. Was he lying to Skint about something? Perhaps, lying to Skint about wanting to squash Zoey? To Zoey, it definitely felt that way.

"Because that wasn't the order, fool! Crepus wanted her alive! What is it that you don't understand about that?" Skint shook his head in scorn.

"I'm growing weary of Crepus. There's something he's

not telling us."

Zoey could see that Skint paused in thought, assessing the situation, and then he calmed down. His entire body relaxed. "What do you think he's hiding?"

The eagle looked around, watching the many winged Dims circling the area over and over, flying in and out of sight. Zoey was scared and didn't want to move, just in case it disrupted the spell. She felt Aderyn by her side and because of that, she felt a little safer—as safe as you can feel with killers in front of you.

"I don't know, but if he's so hell bent on killing the evil ones beyond the Fog, then why save this one?"

Skint raised up on his hind legs and tilted his head. "You're not telling me what you *really* think."

The eagle shrugged and then screeched loudly, almost making Zoey bring her wings to cover her ears from the terrible sound. "Don't think you can intimidate me, Skint. I'm not one of those lackeys scouring the forest for Aderyn and the skylark. Crepus put me in charge of the winged Dims for a reason. I lead well, and do so with honor."

Skint's shoulder's tensed—fury was there. "Then tell me what you think, oh honorable leader of the winged Dims."

"I think Crepus isn't telling us something. I think Crepus wants that skylark for reasons other than what he states. I know this, because I felt her, Skint." The eagle's eyes saddened. "I felt her deeply. She has a power I haven't sensed before, even more so than Crepus'. I think he wants her power for his own and what he'll do with that power frightens me. It frightens some others I've talked to as well."

Skint shifted uncomfortably. "You've talked with others about this? Who?"

The eagle became indignant, looking over Skint's shoulder, eyeing a hawk patrolling the area. "Just a few."

Skint became still, then started breathing deeply, closing his eyes. The eagle, now staring directly at Skint's forehead crystal, started shaking and doing his best to look away, but couldn't.

159

"What are you doing?" asked the eagle. He was clearly uncomfortable, wanting desperately to move.

Skint opened his eyes, a malicious grin forming. "Just let it happen."

"My head...it hurts!"

The eagle went to grasp his neck as his airway swelled, then shut. His wings fell to his side against his will, making him look like a soldier standing in front of a sergeant. Zoey could tell that the eagle was desperately trying to breath, but to no avail. He was dying right in front of her eyes.

Zoey wanted to yell stop, but knew it would give her position away. The eagle's eyes started to fade.

"Die with honor," said Skint. "You don't deserve it, but do it anyway you worthless eagle."

Before Zoey could jump in front of the eagle to stop Skint, Aderyn broke her spell and came into view, startling the squirrel. This took away Skint's focus, releasing the eagle from the energy grip.

Skint lunged for Aderyn, swinging both claws at her. She ducked each claw effortlessly. Just then, the eagle smashed into Skint with his shoulder, pushing him over the branch. Skint fell with his arms flailing about, bouncing off one branch after another, until he landed on the snow covered ground. He stood up, shook off the white flakes, and glared up the tree.

Zoey took her eyes off Skint and looked back at Aderyn. She was standing, gazing at the eagle as if saying, *I dare you to make a move.*

The eagle lowered his eyes and bowed. He stood straight, raising one wing and motioning toward Carwyn Canyon to the west. "You saved my life. Now please, go home safely." He flew off in the opposite direction, screeching and fibbing to the others that he had seen Aderyn and the skylark heading east, away from Carwyn Canyon.

"He has integrity," said Aderyn, taking her eyes off the eagle to scan the ground. She was watching for Skint, who had disappeared from sight shortly after falling to the ground.

"Where is Skint?" asked Zoey.

"I don't know. He could be anywhere. It's time for more practice." She pointed to a nearby tree. "Follow me."

"What? Now? Shouldn't we do what the eagle says and go back to Carwyn Canyon?"

Aderyn shook her head. "We'd be wasting a perfect opportunity to strengthen your skills under pressure."

Zoey frowned, "Okay."

They both spread their wings and glided to a neighboring tree. Aderyn landed softly on a branch, making no sound. Zoey was the opposite. She nearly slipped on the frosty bark as she landed next to the owl, causing sprinkles of snow to spill from the needles of the tree.

"Landing is more important than flying. That will be your next training session, but now we're shape-shifting. Lemla Semta." Aderyn vanished.

Zoey repeated the phrase and blended into the tree as well. Her vision turned reddish again and the sound of static entered her ears. She almost felt as if she was in a different dimension, but didn't know what that really felt like. Her body tingled all over, but the sensation felt right and good. The forest around her was even more vibrant, in a red tint sort of way. She turned her head, expecting to see Aderyn, only to see nothing except the end of the snow covered branch.

A moment later, Aderyn reappeared. She was right where Zoey expected her to be. "Zoey, we'll glide to the next tree."

Zoey broke the shape-shifting spell and flew to the next tree, again landing next to Aderyn. A rustle of leaves from a nearby tree grabbed their attention.

"Skint senses us," said Aderyn. "We'll glide to the third tree over. Upon landing, we'll fly to the tree to the right. There we'll whisper the spell, hiding from view. Do you understand?"

Zoey nodded, spreading her wings. They jumped and

161

flew through the air, dodging around several branches until they reached the third tree. They landed for less than an instant, then sailed to the next tree over. They quickly moved down the broad branch and leaned against the bark of the tree.

Whispering the words out loud, creating the shape-shifting spell, they watched the forest for any sign of Skint. Were they hiding from Skint or trying to draw him in? Zoey was too nervous to ask, just in case she might give away their position. Or, were they just playing cat and mouse with Skint? Was this a game Aderyn played every so often, simply because she was usually alone and maybe bored all of the time?

Again, the sound of rustling leaves engulfed the area, bringing Zoey to the present moment. The sound was just above, loud and too obnoxious for it to be clumsy feet. Skint didn't seem too worried about being quiet, or was he trying to get them to change their focus to end the spell?

Zoey felt the feathers on the back of her neck stand up. Something wasn't right. Something was about to—

"Go!" yelled Aderyn.

In a start, Zoey leaped forward, flapping her wings quickly. Looking over her shoulder, she saw Aderyn in a tussle with Skint. He had been just above, ready to pounce. Zoey wondered if his loud sounds caused her to break the spell, showing herself to him. That's why she had felt the sudden shift of energy. She had been located.

Zoey landed on the next branch, turning to watch the tussle take place. She knew Skint didn't have a chance against a VioletLight and she was correct. In a matter of seconds, Skint was pinned to the branch. Aderyn's talons were planted firmly across his shoulders. He kicked high with his legs, hoping to catch a portion of Aderyn's tail feathers, but missed with each attempt.

Zoey straightened her wings, flapping them. She felt a rush of wind against her feathers and looped around, heading back to the large branch she had just flown off. She landed next to Aderyn and eyed Skint as he squirmed under Aderyn's grip.

"I could end you right now, Skint. Leave us alone!" Aderyn's eyes were full of rage. Zoey hadn't seen this part of Aderyn before.

Skint cruelly grinned. "Really? Then do it, Ghost Shadow!"

Aderyn sighed. "I'm Aderyn, not that Ghost Shadow gibberish you keep spouting." She tilted her head, as if a new thought had just entered her mind. "I'll do something else, besides killing you."

"You VioletLights don't kill. I'm not that naïve," responded Skint.

Aderyn looked over at Zoey. "I'm going to drop Skint off at Crepus's feet. It's about time I had a talk with the dragon."

Skint laughed, thinking he was obviously seeing an untruth in Aderyn's statement. "You're going to do what?" He shook his head. "I knew you were crazy, but this is a new level, Ghost Shadow."

Astonished, Zoey shrunk back. "You're leaving now?"

The breeze picked up, ruffling Aderyn's feathers as she nodded a yes. "Get back to the canyon. I'll be there shortly."

Skint went to speak, but Aderyn stunned him quickly by pressing her talon on his forehead crystal with a twist. "This should shut him up for the ride to the castle."

"What do I do when I get back to the canyon?"

"Continue practicing." With that, Aderyn picked up the squirrel with her beak, dove to the lowest branches, and then flew forward at an incredible rate of speed. Zoey watched until she disappeared into the thick of the branches, leaves, and hanging needles. About to flap her wings, Zoey paused. She heard a bird whistling and singing. She walked backwards, down the wide limb of the tree, until she felt her back touch the bark.

"Lemla Semta," she whispered.

A female bird, a cardinal in fact, landed on the branch

163

she was on. Zoey about fell out of the tree when she noticed exactly who it was.

*San?*

# Chapter 13

The Shiver had most definitely arrived. Crepus felt its chill as he stared into the fireplace, observing how empty it was except for a few dead logs. He looked out the window. The snow was falling even harder now. It was midday, and by midday he was used to the warmth of the sun filling the room. He didn't know if he liked this Shiver, a prophetic era he'd been anticipating a long, long time.

*You're doing well,* said a voice in his mind. *We are putting things into place. It won't be long now.* Crepus shook his head in defiance, but then nodded his head in agreement a moment later. He was under the spell of The Speaker. Its voice held a lot of power, not consisting of just one being, but of hundreds.

Nonetheless, it was cold and he could do something about that, at least in this gray room.

He turned, closed his eyes, and a moment later a fire blazed in the fireplace, creating a nice orange glow. The warmth comforted him against the chill.

He stood on a large rug in the middle of his stone room. Gazing at it, he peered at the embroidered caricature of himself in the middle of the rug. It was beautiful and he liked the idea of holding lightning between his teeth— something the caricature showed him doing. He felt that he had that power. He felt he held the entire world between his teeth. When he felt such things, he knew he could do anything he wanted. He was unstoppable. Impenetrable.

The sound of flapping wings entered the room. As he turned toward the sound, he heard talons clacking against the stone window sill. There, Aderyn stood, holding an unconscious Skint with one talon, and balancing her weight on the large sill with the other. She dropped down to the stone flooring, demonstrating much agility and skill as she landed on one foot.

Crepus's eyes flashed with hatred. "You dare step into my castle without invitation?" He went to yell for his guards when Aderyn's soft voice immediately calmed him.

"I apologize, Crepus. It's not my custom to come to a spirit animal's home unannounced, but I found this matter a little pressing." She pointed at Skint with her beak and then set him down on the floor. "I'm not here to cause a stir, Crepus. I'm here to simply talk, something we haven't done for many moons."

"What is it you're going to try to convince me of? Let me guess." He snorted. "To leave the PureLights alone and return the Dim's to their PureLight nature?"

Aderyn shook her head as she eyed Crepus. "I'm hopeful, but not dumb. I know you won't change your mind, though I wish for it every day." She shook her head, eyeing the ground for a moment, before lifting her chin. "My hope in you has faded." She blinked. "I have a warning for you. That is all."

Crepus's eyebrows rose. "Really?" He gave a dry, false smile. He was nervous, as if he knew the power of a VioletLight and that their words always held truth, no matter how much he despised them. He'd do his best, like he always did, to push his knowledge of the VioletLights aside, rationalizing away their wisdom.

He gave a short laugh. "Warnings are for cowards. I take what comes, warning or not."

"Then take this warning to heart, Crepus." She cautiously walked up to him, watching his movements; prepared for an attack should it come.

Crepus put his front foot up in a gesture indicating for her to stop. "Don't come any closer, Aderyn. I don't want to hurt you."

Aderyn stopped, wondering why Crepus would caution her.

A shadow appeared from behind Crepus, and then

166

skittered back down, hiding from sight, as if it had shown itself by accident. Aderyn tilted her head. The shadow rose up again, then slowly descended, seeming to merge into Crepus. She knew instantly what it was—one of the shadowed creatures that she and Gart, her prairie dog friend, had seen in Gwenfree Forest on several occasions. She had seen these creatures change in peculiar ways, from oval to flat, from wide to thin. They were an anomaly to her.

"Who has taken you over, Crepus?"

"My, my, my," he replied as he walked past Aderyn and peered through the large window. "I haven't been take over, Aderyn. I've just acquired some help."

"Some help with what?"

"With bringing this little island to its knees." He turned, facing Aderyn. The gray light coming through the window covered his back, creating a shadow of himself on the stone floor.

He continued. "I asked for assistance long ago and they came to help me. They haven't taken over my body like you think. If anything, I have taken over them."

"I don't feel any truth in that, Crepus. They have you in their clutches more than you know." She exhaled in distress. "You required assistance? For what? To take over an island full of beautiful Beings who trusted you with all of their heart and minds? You didn't need shadows to help you with that. Your tribe would have willingly followed you wherever you led them. The Crepus I knew would never lie, kill, or control. Your Speaker has filled you full of untruths.

"I'm not blind," Aderyn continued, "I know what I feel and your words are shrouded in darkness. It's not you who is Dim, Crepus. It's the shadows inside of you who are. They are Beings not of this world. They are Beings willing to corrupt an entire population." She paused, doing her best to assess the shadows by peering deeper into Crepus's pupils. "But the reasons they have corrupted this world is not something I understand."

Crepus stood, listening to all of what his old friend was

167

saying, but not because he enjoyed it, or because he thought her words could help him change his ways or enlighten his heart. He did so to hear her warning, so he could figure out a way to counter it. This would give him an upper claw.

She stamped her foot on the stone ground, her talons tapping loudly against the floor. "They must leave you, Crepus. You are a positive force in the universe shrouded in a blanket of evil that is not your doing. It's not your fault. You were tricked, and somehow allowed these shadowed Beings to take over your mind, your heart, your life. I know there is a small portion of you in there, listening to my truth. Only *you* can push them out of your body." She stopped, looked to her upper right as if a new thought had just formed in her mind. "If you refuse, then there is one who has the power to defeat them. I just don't know if you'd survive it, Crepus. And that is my warning. The Shiver is here, but it has a short life. Though it was a life you and the shadow creatures created, it will be taken away just as quickly as it came. And, to your shadows—if you do not leave Crepus and this space now, then we will destroy you with the Light of The Great Spirit. In fact, you'll tear your selves apart when its Light shines upon you."

"You speak in riddles, Aderyn. Leave! Now!"

Aderyn spread her wings, flapped a couple of times, lifting herself off the ground, then flew over and landed on the window sill. She looked over her shoulder. "Riddles you say? Then let me be frank, but not to you Crepus, but to the shadows." She took a deep breath and blew it toward Crepus. He shuddered and backed up, swiping his arms wildly about as if he'd just run into a spider's web. He fell to his side and slid fast and hard against the wall, as if a large force had thrown him.

"Imagine that force, but tenfold." She gave a nod of her head and flew from the castle, leaving an unconscious Skint lying on the floor.

# Chapter 14

It was dark and everything was silent, except for the panting coming from a few out of shape spirit animals, but then came the sobs and feelings of loss. The loss was little, though, considering what had happened. When no one in a tribe perishes from an attack, you count your lucky stars. This wasn't something that occurred all too often.

Coda took a deep breath of relaxation, but then realized that several of the young *had* been taken. His heart suddenly tightened as he agonized with sorrow, then wild frustration. *What will Crepus do to them? Kill them, or change them into Dims?* Anger toward Crepus churned his gut. He had to stop Crepus and he had to get his sister back. He had to somehow stop this war and somehow find his way back home to his mom and dad.

The pounding sounds of Dims trampling around on the ground directly above pulled Coda out of his thoughts. Then the scraping started.

It was mild at first, making Coda think it was no more than an irritating sound coming from somewhere harmless. As it grew in volume it started to sound like shovels hitting and scraping across hard stone and Coda knew something was desperately wrong. Listening intently, he leaned back on the stone wall of their escape tunnel. When the sound reached the middle of the crowded tunnel, the rest of the remnant tribe within the tunnel started to talk with agitation and fear in their voices. They no doubt worried that the Dims were about to somehow obliterate solid rock and reach their claws down into the tunnel, pulling spirit animals out by the fist full.

BANG!

Coda jumped back, his ears ringing from the loud noise.

Something had smashed against the big slab door.

BANG! BANG! BANG!

The sound pounded against everyone's ears, making them wince each and every time.

*They're breaking in at the door!*

The Dims knew the remainder of the tribe was in the tunnel, and were doing everything they could to get at them.

"They won't be able to break it down," whispered Kiwu. "The door to this tunnel is solid rock."

That didn't resonate with Coda. He knew the Dims would keep at it until they were able to break through. Coda felt that he had to get this tribe moving forward to escape from the deathly grip of the Dims. He looked around, knowing he was one of the few in the tunnel that had good eyesight in darkness. He took a deep breath as doubt crawled through his mind. He'd never been in these hidden tunnels before.

*I wish Nova was here.*

"I could have taken them on," said Hao.

Coda rolled his eyes and shook his head. It was Hao, who had saved Coda when he came barreling at the birds, but his crazy antics proved almost too much. Coda and some of the others had to drag the stag into the escape tunnel just before the door closed on them. If Chev hadn't been able to hold the door, who knows what may have happened.

In truth, it was Chev who had saved most of them. Remembering this, Coda thanked The Great Spirit for help and protection, but then paused for a moment. He'd never thanked The Great Spirit for anything before and it was odd. Was he changing? Was he turning into a full blown PureLight? He couldn't deny that he felt completely different.

"Let's move." It was Kiwu who spoke, pulling Coda away from his thoughts.

Kiwu started the tribe moving forward. With only a single zyte to provide lighting in the tunnel, spirit animals were bumping into each other and the walls surrounding them. Kiwu, the bull and leader of the tribe, seemed to know the tunnel well. He moved ahead without fear or hesitation, and must have been through these tunnels many times before. The tribe followed, unavoidably bumping into each other and the walls during the process.

Coda looked behind him and saw Chev. He was much taller than everyone else and had been the last one to enter the tunnel. He was feeling his way along the wall with his trunk, and carried Numee and Shikoba on his back.

"You're doing well, Chev." said Coda.

"Coda?" It was Numee's voice. "Will you tell this big oaf that my eyes are just as good as yours in the dark? He won't let me lead the way. Tell him to put me down on the ground." Her raccoon eyes were shining in the dark, much like Coda's. The shine came from mirror like tissues that formed inside of their eyes, allowing nocturnal creatures, such as a panther and raccoon, to reflect unabsorbed light in the dark, allowing them a greater ability to see at night or in dark places like this.

Coda frowned. "Chev is just keeping you two safe. Perhaps he doesn't want to step on you."

"Nah, buddy," replied Chev. "I just want them near me. I'm scared of the dark."

"You're what?" Shikoba was astonished by his statement. Her stunned look quickly faded and became stern, the way she normally looked. "Darkness is always temporary. Remember that."

Coda looked ahead, seeing the long line of spirit animals moving slowly around a curve in the tunnel. It was cramped and they were moving at a snail's pace. Then a loud bang bounced around in the tunnel and they all stampeded forward.

"Calm down! Slow down!" blasted Kiwu's voice.

"Kiwu! Where are we going?" asked Coda, yelling over the crowd and hoping his words would reach the bull, who had just rounded a corner.

Another bang behind him caused another stir in the

171

crowd. It was the loudest one thus far and it made Coda flinch. He was certain the Dims had broken through. He looked over his shoulder, but was delighted to see that the rock door still held.

"Chev," whispered Coda, "Let Numee be your eyes."

"I might step on her."

"Just keep her on your back and let her tell you where to go. I'm going to move up ahead to find a way out of this place. We're sitting ducks in here."

"Huh?" said Numee, Chev, and Shikoba in unison. They'd never heard that term before.

"Oh, sorry," replied Coda. "We're not safe here, that's all."

With that, Coda wove his way around spirit animals, bumping them here and there and causing a few annoyed grunts, but ended up where he was trying to go—at the front of the line.

Coda eased up next to Kiwu. He could tell that Kiwu knew the way, not by sight, but by memory. In fact, Kiwu wasn't exactly doing such of an impressive job of finding his way around corners like Coda originally thought. He would bump into a wall the moment the tunnel curved this or that way. However, Coda soon noticed that Kiwu was bumping into them, not because of the darkness, nor from a lack of memory of the tunnel system, it was because he was in a hurry. In fact, Coda saw panic in Kiwu's eyes. He cared for his tribe, wanting them to be as safe as possible. Who knows how long he'd kept this tribe alive.

"Kiwu, I can see in the tunnels. Do you need my help?" explained Coda.

Kiwu stopped and looked around, clearly blinded by the darkness. "Who's there?"

"It's Coda."

Kiwu brought his head down toward Coda's voice and took a sniff. "So, it is you." He walked forward, smacking into a wall and creating a cloud of dust poofing in the air. Kiwu continued, shaking his head to get his bearings back.

"What can you tell me, boy?"

"I can see that this part of the tunnel is turning at a slight bend. If you keep going straight like you are now, you'll keep butting into the wall. I can guide you and the rest of the tribe with my words, if you let me."

Kiwu stopped, prompting Coda to do the same. "It'd be too loud."

It was true, it would be and the Dims could simply follow his voice as they went along. He thought for a moment, until another idea came to mind. "What if we get into single file, making sure each animal is touching the animal in front of him. We can go slowly. You can grab my tail and I'll lead you and the rest of us out of here."

"Your tail? Grab it with what?" replied Kiwu.

"With your teeth, but don't bite down too hard," responded Coda.

Kiwu gave a little nod and grunted. Coda guessed that meant the bull wasn't too keen on the idea, but would go ahead with it. Coda nodded back, but realized Kiwu couldn't see him.

The bull sniffed again. "Then let the others know what we'll be doing."

"Great idea." Coda turned and quickly wove back through the crowd, letting everyone know what to do. When they all formed a line and touched the spirit animal in front of them, Coda went to the front and put his tail out for Kiwu to grab.

"Let's move," voiced Coda in a quiet, but determined, manner.

The tunnel traveled left and right and then downhill and uphill every so often. He occasionally looked over his shoulder to make sure everyone was doing alright, which they always were now that he was in the front. Way in the back of the line Chev followed, looking wild eyed in the darkness, and doing his best to stay close to the spirit animal in front of him by touching his trunk to the spirit animal's hips.

The further they traveled, the less and less they heard the Dims above. The pounding even stopped, as if they had given up trying to get in. *Nah,* thought Coda. *They're just regrouping.*

As they continued to walk, a thought occurred to him. The Dims have to be waiting for them. Why else would it be so quiet? Coda suddenly started to panic, taking short, quick breaths. His sight started to falter and his legs started to tingle, but not the good tingling he was used to when he'd be blasted by Nova's loving magic.

He shook his head, hoping to get the negative thoughts out of his mind. It didn't work.

*What if I lead them into a trap?* What was he doing anyway, leading a group this big? He was just a kid. He had no right to lead an entire tribe of spirit animals. He took a breath, drawing his doubts to his heart and then covering them with white light. He breathed out the negativity, and then inhaled positive energy, in and out as he pushed onward, bringing a lightness to his body and taking away his fear. His confidence grew, pushing him forward at a strong pace with his head high and his chest out. Plus, his new energy seemed to vibrate throughout the tribe as each one, even Hao, looked more positive and determined than before.

Suddenly, a light splashed against a wall from around the bend. Coda smiled. There must be an opening just around the corner, perhaps a door to the outside world. What else could it be?

Coming around the bend, he saw just that, light pouring through a large hole in the wall. It looked as if the tunnel had stopped, and if there hadn't been a hole it'd clearly be a dead end. Kiwu saw it as well. But instead of being happy, a grim energy gripped him. In fact, Coda saw a great deal of unhappiness on Kiwu's face.

"There's supposed to be a wall there, not a hole in the wall. The secret knock opens the wall, leading us out of here." He thought for a moment. "Yes, the hole wasn't there

174

last night. It's fresh. Someone's waiting for us. Use caution, Coda."

Coda quickly approached the hole and gazed into it. It did have scratch marks on the inside of it. Was Kiwu correct? Were the marks fresh?

Sniffing intently on the markings, Coda could sense that they were definitely fresh. In fact, they smelled familiar...very familiar, but how? It wasn't something, or someone, dangerous. It was someone he knew very well.

"I think we're safe. But, how do we get through it?" asked Coda. "It's only big enough for the little ones to pass through."

A bump jostled Kiwu. He looked behind him. The rest of the tribe didn't know Coda and Kiwu had stopped, so one by one they bumped into each other, causing a commotion that Kiwu quickly calmed down with a single, "Shhh!" Kiwu then gazed ahead, staring at Coda. "We do the special stomp to open the door." He heaved in a big breath, making his chest wide and large. "Step aside, boy."

Coda moved to his right as Kiwu took a step forward and tapped several times on the ground with his hooves in a strange and rhythmic way. Then the bull stepped back, watching the wall.

A soft click sounded through the tunnel, and then the rocks that made up the door moved down like an elevator into the earth, exposing the outside world. Light, like Coda had never seen before, erupted into the tunnel, almost blinding him. He stiffened, then squinted his eyes to see better. When that didn't work, he turned his head away from the entrance, opening and shutting his eyes in order to get his eyes to adjust. The rest of the tribe seemed to be doing the same. After a minute, Coda looked back at the entrance and his jaw dropped because of who he saw.

With a smile and a feeling of overwhelming relief, all that came out of Coda's mouth was a soft, almost inaudible, "Nova?"

# Chapter 15

San was peacefully perched on the same branch as Zoey, looking over the forest while taking in its beauty, even though it was rather cold and in the middle of a snow flurry.

Zoey didn't know what to do. She was sitting right next to San, still in her shape-shifting spell and invisible. Should she wait for San to leave? Should she get her attention somehow? If she released the shape-shifting spell, would it scare San, causing her to yell or scream?

No. She'd sit and wait it out. Maybe San would just go away. That's the best idea. Wait for her cruel, traitorous friend to just leave. Zoey had never known what the feeling of betrayal was like, until she felt its crushing blow when San entered into her life. *How could she do that to me? Weren't we friends?*

It didn't matter. San did it anyway.

The more Zoey waited, the more she thought about San and the sadder she got. It was as if San was doing this to her on purpose. Did San know she was right beside her? Was she sent here by Crepus?

Looking around, Zoey wondered if other birds were lying in wait, also. If Zoey eventually showed herself, they'd spot her and immediately pounce. They probably hoped, sooner or later, that Zoey would be stupid enough to turn off the spell.

Shaking her head in anger, Zoey focused on San again. *Would she apologize to me if she saw me? Would I even accept her apology?* Thoughts raced through Zoey's mind, feeding an already large grudge. And how could San be on Zoey's branch right now? What kind of a coincidence was that? *This has to be a trick*, thought Zoey.

"I know you're there, Zoey." San turned around, staring

directly at her.

Shocked, Zoey froze. Was this a bluff, or did San really know that Zoey was there?

"I was watching you and the owl. I was sitting on the branch of that tree over there." She pointed with her wing, but Zoey didn't follow where she was pointing. She didn't trust San, and wasn't going to take her eyes off of her no matter what.

"I saw the owl stun Skint. Then I saw you disappear into this tree." San paused and blinked a couple of times. Her eyes were innocent and Zoey saw that San was scared.

*Why is she scared?*

San took a step closer to Zoey. "Can I touch you? Or, are you completely invisible? How do you do that?"

Zoey watched as San raised her wing, then felt the red crested cardinal touch her. San pulled her wing back in surprise. "I touched you! You *are* there!" She held her wings up with joy.

Zoey almost smiled, bringing back the not too distant memories of San's usual over-excitement. But Zoey shook her head no, scolding herself for allowing San to get this close to her.

Not waiting for Zoey to reply, San continued to poke and prod, as if it was a game. "Come out. I want to see my best friend."

Zoey moved to the right just as San went for another touch, making San miss. San's eyes widened in confusion and her beak formed a baffled 'o'. "Where did you go?"

*Just go away, San!*

San moved forward, spreading her wings and doing her best to find Zoey within the shape-shifting spell.

When San touched her again, Zoey appeared. San was delighted, but her happiness quickly faded when she saw the look on Zoey's face.

San looked down. "I know. I didn't want to do what I did, but Crepus made me. I tried to back out of it in the tunnels when we rode the Zolts to deliver you to Crepus and Skint,

177

but it was too late. I'm so sorry." She looked up at Zoey, searching for something in Zoey's energy that said everything was alright. But, she didn't see anything of the sort.

Zoey's eyes were piercing. "You almost killed us, San! In fact, you were leading us to our deaths!"

San jolted back a little, as if stabbed in the heart. Zoey walked past her on the thick, wide branch they were standing on, and then flew to another tree, not caring if the Dims were watching her or not. San followed, landing on the branch next to Zoey. "Crepus said he'd kill my parents if I didn't do what he asked."

*Parents?* For as long as Zoey had been in Ohm Totem, she hadn't really thought much about the spirit animals having parents, or even kids. But, of course they did. How else could these Dims and PureLights be created in the first place? Did they have two different kinds of spirit animal parents, like a bear and a tiger? Could a bear and tiger have a bird somehow? Or, did it only work with a bear and a bear giving birth to yet another bear? How did that work?

Coming out of her thoughts, Zoey shook her head. "You acted like you were dead after Crepus threw you against the tunnel wall—you wanted to fool us! And you did a very good job of it, too. You should be an actress, acting the way you did." Zoey looked away, not wanting San to reply. She spread her wings and flew to another branch.

San again followed, landing next to Zoey. "That wasn't an act. He threw me hard! It knocked me out and I wonder if he meant to kill me!"

"Gee, I hope your parents are fine and dandy...*Saaannn!*"

Then Zoey jumped, flapped her wings and zoomed past several more trees in the forest. Instead of heading toward the redwood, she zigzagged from tree to tree, hoping San wouldn't discover the direction of Aderyn's redwood. She finally perched on top of a large fir tree, watching the trees rock back and forth in the cold wind. The sky was a menacing gray and turning darker by the minute.

Zoey wanted to smack San a good one as she landed and perched next to her a third time. Then San looked at her with sad eyes. "They're dead."

"What? Who's dead?" Zoey was suddenly numb with panic. *Her brother, Nova, and the rest are dead? How could that be?*

"My parents are dead." San looked away as her eyes started to well up with tears. "Crepus killed them anyway." She shuddered and her shoulders moved up and down as she started to cry. Zoey didn't know what to do. She wanted to put her wings around San, to comfort her, but wondered if this was a trick, too. Crepus was very sneaky and he seemed to stop at nothing to get his way.

Regardless, Zoey put a wing around her, leaning her cheek against San's head. "I'm sorry, San. I would be so sad if my parents died."

San nodded. "He killed them, even though he promised that he wouldn't." She gazed into Zoey's eyes, tears streaking down her feathered cheeks. "Don't trust him, Zoey. No matter what. Promise me you won't let him get into your head like he did mine."

Zoey nodded. She wondered why San would even think to trust Crepus.

"I just want to go back to the Sihu Tribe and live my life," announced San. "That's where I was happiest. And then I was even happier when I met you."

Zoey understood. She didn't like the Dim Lands either. She'd much rather be with the Sihu Tribe, amongst her new found friends. The next time around, Zoey could be with the bards instead of the Art of Defense trainings. She could sing like she did on the beach several days ago. *Wow, it's only been a couple of days since then? It feels like weeks ago!* She started thinking about San and how much fun they'd have with the bards—

*Wait! San is a traitor.*

Zoey remained quiet, not responding to San's last

179

comment. San had done something so terrible that it would be hard to ever forgive her, let alone trust her again. She had led them directly to Crepus, who would have killed her brother if Nova hadn't shown up. She wasn't going to let San off that easy—ever.

"Oh," said San, who was even more melancholy than before. "I see. You don't like me." Her voice was low. "I understand. I wouldn't like me, either, if I were you."

Zoey kept quiet, but San suddenly became interested in Zoey's forehead. "What is that?" She put her wing out to touch Zoey's forehead crystal. Zoey pulled away. She didn't want San to touch her, but San continued to inspect it. "How did your crystal turn golden?"

Zoey held her breath. Should she tell San? Shaking her head, she frowned. "It's just golden, that's all."

"Why did—"

A loud crack echoed behind them, as if a branch had just snapped. They both turned around with a start. Zoey then eyed San suspiciously, who simply shrugged her shoulders, indicating that she had no idea who, or what, had created that sound.

Zoey, not taking any chances, walked backwards and leaned against the bark of the tree. She whispered, "Lemla Semta," and vanished, or rather, blended into the tree right before San's very eyes.

San gasped, putting her wings to her beak. "How did you do that?" She lifted her wings in excitement. "I want to know how to do that! Tell me, tell me, tell—"

The excitement was short lived because a crow twice the size of San landed next to her. He flicked his wing in her face, knocking San back a couple of inches. Zoey almost lurched forward to stop the crow, but willed herself to remain still.

"Who are you talking to, San?" asked the crow. He put both of his wings on San's cheeks.

San pushed his wings away. "Leave me alone."

Astonished that San would push him away, the crow

180

poked his beak into San's chest. She hopped backward from the sudden pain. He poked again and again.

"Stop!" yelled San. She crouched, covering her body with a wing and doing her best to hold off the annoying crow.

"Then tell me who you were talking to. Was it that skylark we're scouring the forest for?"

San hesitated, looking over the crow's shoulder and directly at Zoey, who stood camouflaged against the tree. The crow looked over his shoulder, then back at San. A cruel smile developed on his face. "She's somewhere behind me, isn't she?"

San slowly shook her head. "I don't see her there."

"It's because she's hiding, San. You imbecile." He poked at her chest again, and then turned and walked toward Zoey.

*Can he see me?* Zoey wondered, and then slowly moved to her right until she was at the very edge of the large branch she was standing upon. If she took another step to the right, she'd fall, which might be what she needed to do, just in case she needed to escape quickly.

"She's not there," announced San.

"We'll just see about that." The crow waddled forward, coming closer and closer to Zoey and her heart started to beat faster. She decided to crouch, just in case the crow put his wing out to try to touch her.

When he was just a few inches from her, he stopped. "I can sense her, San. She's near us." He spread his wings and flapped them, giving him lift. He twisted in mid-air to face San, and then landed. "Do you feel her? I hope you do and I hope you feel her pain when I find her and rip her open." He flew forward, landing next to San. "Tell me where she is, because I know she's close by."

San looked to her left, pointing to a nearby tree. "She's over there."

The crow slapped San's wing down. "Stop that at once! You know where she is—don't lie to me, San!"

Both San and the crow were silenced as a large eagle

181

landed next to them. The branch bobbed up and down because of the sudden change in weight. Zoey tilted her head, noticing it was the same eagle she'd helped earlier.

"What's going on here?" The eagle gave a serious look at the crow. "Leave San alone."

The crow shook his head, less in defiance and more in disgust with San. "She knows where the skylark is."

The eagle glared at San. "Yes, I know she does."

"Then make her tell us this instant," replied the crow.

The eagle stood tall. "Where is she, San?"

San stared at her feet, speaking softly. "I don't know."

"San, take Punzley away from here and show him where you last saw the skylark." The eagle pointed to a throng of trees to the north. "Earlier, you told me she was over there. Now go!"

San nodded her head, confusing the crow. The crow asked, "The skylark's not in this area?" He was suspicious at what was taking place.

Shaking his head, the eagle continued to point to the north. "Take him, San. I know she was a good friend of yours, but orders are orders. We're to find the skylark and hand her over safely to Crepus. Is that understood?"

San nodded and jumped off the branch and flew north. The crow screwed up his face and glanced at the eagle. "I don't know about this." Regardless, the crow flew north as well, following San.

A large sigh came from the eagle's mouth. He perched on the branch, looking west and staring at the many trees of the forest. After about ten minutes or so had passed, the eagle turned his head and stared at Zoey, making her heart skip a beat.

"My name is Freedom. At least that's what I named myself, here in the Dim Lands. You can just call me Free. I will not tell you my real name, though."

Zoey wanted to ask why he wouldn't tell her his real name, but refrained. She was still in hiding mode, and didn't want to come out of it unless she knew that she was

182

completely safe.

"I saw that you are the Golden Keeper. I once knew the one before you. She was a skylark, as well. She was a light among lights." He paused, as if waiting for a reply. When none came, he nodded in understanding. "You and Aderyn saved my life, and for that I owe you mine. This won't be the last you see of me. I'm part of the prophesy. Look on the hallway walls at the bottom of the redwood tree. There you'll see me." He gave a nod. "Thank you for saving my life." Then he spread his wings and flew off to the north.

*Prophecy? What prophecy? Aderyn and Nova didn't tell me anything about a prophecy with an eagle in it.* Then, as if beamed to her from The Great Spirit itself, a memory entered her mind. It was of the etchings on the wall at the bottom of the redwood tree, in the first hallway that she entered into. *Were those prophecies? Was he the eagle carrying the scroll toward the pyramid?* Some of the etchings seemed like the past, but some could have easily been of the future.

"Zoey?"

Zoey jumped in a start as her name echoed across the tree. The sudden fright instantly removed the shape-shifting spell.

"I'm sorry to scare you, child." Looking up, Zoey saw Aderyn perched on the branch just above her. "Use this as a lesson to stay focused no matter what happens, not giving away your position to anyone or anything, including my voice. We'll have to practice on that when we get back to the redwood."

*How did Aderyn land there without making any noise?*

Aderyn merely lowered her head, smiling at Zoey. She gathered herself, jumped, and flew west. Zoey spread her wings, jumped, and started gliding after her.

# Chapter 16

Nova sat on her haunches as Coda padded on the soft snow leading to her. He sniffed her as if in doubt that she was actually real, instead of a figment of his imagination. He slowly and cautiously touched his cheek against hers and the touching brought wonder to his eyes. *Am I dreaming?*

"It's me, Coda. I'm alive." She smiled. "Though this is not a dream, know that dreams are as real as the very ground that you stand upon. They have lessons just as important as the lessons during your waking day."

Coda nodded, not from understanding her, but from the knowing that this was definitely Nova. Who else spoke like that? A tingling sensation traveled through him, giving him that peaceful energy Nova sends to those around her. This calmed him, along with knowing that Nova was back and unharmed.

Standing a ways behind her, Coda spotted Meli the jaguar. She was sitting on a small clump of snow with her head held high, her red crystals glowing brightly, and her eyes watching a line of spirit animals exiting the tunnel. Coda followed her gaze only to see a worried Kiwu. The bull didn't know what to think of these two new large cats. Coda could tell the bull recognized Meli, but he saw mistrust in Kiwu's eyes. To Kiwu, Meli was a coward who stood for nothing, while living a loner existence and perhaps passing his tribe's secrets over to the Dims. In his mind, there was no pride or warrior spirit in any spirit animal who didn't help Kiwu and his tribe's cause.

Kiwu approached Nova with a blank stare. He hadn't met this cat before, nor had he seen a VioletLight up close. He'd only heard of them. Nova was calm and Kiwu could sense that she possessed something deep within her that other spirit animals didn't have. Was it wisdom? There was also an energy about her that made him think that everything was going to be alright, though nothing had ever been alright, but yet he felt that way right now. There was something wrong with that, so Kiwu lowered his eyes and walked past her.

Coda looked back at Nova and noticed that she was using some of her magic, sprinkling a sparkling aura of tranquility over the bull. His reaction was instantaneous as his body and mind seemed to relax, allowing him to stand up straighter as he strode beyond Nova, heading in Meli's direction.

Coda felt a bump at his back. "Watch it."

Coda didn't need to look to know that it was Hao. Coda moved aside, letting the testosterone filled stag be on his way. Nova dipped her head to him. "Greetings." She blinked softly, sending him a gush of love directly from her heart. "I'm Nova."

Hao staggered for a moment, as if caught off guard by the love sent to him, or was it because of seeing a snow leopard with violet crystals? He shook his head in annoyance and then looked down, taking his eyes off Nova. As he did so, Nova spoke. "Look at me, Hao."

Hao stopped, baffled, as was Coda. *How did she know his name?* As he raised his eyes, she placed her paw on his foreleg. He suddenly stood tall, eyeing something off in the distance, but Coda could see that there was nothing in the distance to look at other than snow on top of some bushes and trees. After a few moments, Hao took a long, deep breath. There was a peace now inside of him.

Hao placed his forehead crystal against Nova's. Coda began to move toward them just in case Nova needed protecting from the unpredictable stag.

Nova held up her paw, indicating for Coda to stay put.

Taking his forehead off Nova's, Hao took a step backward. "Thank you. I remember now." He brushed

185

against her pelt as he stepped forward, following Kiwu.

"What did you do to him?" asked Coda.

"I gave him a different perspective. I showed him what he'd forgotten—the love that he held for his child, who has been with The Great Spirit for many moons now." She tilted her head. "Let's see which path he chooses, the light or the dark. It's up to him, since now he has a conscious choice. He can continue to feel the love, or he can seek revenge against life and the Dims for taking away his only child."

"But," Coda scratched the snow covered earth. "How did you know his name?"

"We used to be friends, long ago. He and his son were two of your greatest students."

"Mine?" Confused and convinced that he'd never met Hao's son, Coda thought for a moment. His tail shot up. "You mean Orion's students?"

"Yes, I mean Orion's students. You *are* Orion. Don't forget that."

"Is that why he didn't like me?"

"He didn't know why he didn't like you. Now he knows."

Coda twitched his tail left and right, trying to figure out why Hao wouldn't like him. "Did I do something to him, or his son? Does he blame me for something? If so, what is it?"

"It's not for us to speak of right now. You and he will figure it out. If you don't, well..." she paused, looking off into the distance, as if seeing a future event of some kind. "Let's just say that you two *must* figure it out if you want to make the transition go smoothly."

*Transition?* Coda wanted to ask more, but knew better. As she had said, it wasn't for them to speak of right now. He'd most likely speak with Hao later on about the subject. Although, how was he going to bring up the subject? He sighed. *More drama.* He was glad that Hao was at least sane at the moment and he hoped it remained that way.

As the tribe continued to exit the tunnel, Coda could hear a commotion far off in the distant forest and the sounds were growing closer with each passing moment.

186

Kiwu heard it as well, and even though he was way beyond Meli by now, his voice was heard loud and clear. He bellowed, "We're not out of this yet! Keep moving! We need to hide deep in the eastern portion of Changyin Forest. Move!"

With that, the crowd of spirit animals moved faster, coming out of the tunnel in a straight line, and fleeing quickly into the thick of the forest. Coda saw that Kiwu was definitely good at organizing, and had what was left of his tribe well trained. They didn't freak out; they just accepted orders and followed their leader. That's a sign of a loved leader, or a feared leader and Coda couldn't decide which of the two it was.

Then Coda heard a gasp. He turned toward the tunnel to observe a shocked raccoon. It was Numee. She had just exited the tunnel, and for the first time in several days she saw her VioletLight. "Nova? Is it really you?"

Then it was Chev saying the same exact words. Then his expression went from excited to teary eyed. He ran over, clomping across the snow and placing kisses all over Nova with the end of his trunk.

The hawk, Shikoba, came next and simply nodded, almost as if she'd known Nova would be waiting for them.

Nova looked behind her, glancing at Meli. "You can thank Meli over there for showing me this place. We saw the Dims break into your hideout, but she knew that if you were to escape, you'd exit here and I had no doubt that you'd be here. I'm very happy to see you all."

Still not fully understanding, Chev's mouth gaped open until he asked, "How did you get away? Well, where did you go?" He furrowed his brow, scratching his head with his trunk. "I mean, how did you escape? Are you okay? We saw you—"

Nova held her paw up and smiled. "I have many answers for your many questions, Chev. But not now. We must get moving."

Numee frowned. "Why is everyone hurrying into the

187

forest? Are the Dims here already?"

Meli stepped forward, closer to the group. "No, but they are on their way. We must go now."

"Where?" asked Chev. He surveyed the area, obviously looking for the coming Dims. When he didn't see anything, he shrugged his shoulders. An instant later they heard voices from the west, heading their way and they knew the Dims were hot on their trail. He shoved Coda ahead. "Let's go, buddy. I'm not sticking around."

Shikoba hovered twenty or so feet up in the air and her eyes narrowed. "They are near, very near. Wings and Paws, we must get going if we're to survive!"

Nova turned and gestured with her tail for the rest to follow her. Meli walked by her side.

"Let's go!" shouted Nova. A moment later, Nova and Meli took off, snow flinging about from their feet as they ran straight into a thick line of trees. Coda went to move, just like the rest of them, but slipped and fell straight on his chest, causing snow to smack into his face. *That wasn't so coordinated.*

He shook his head, then stood up and brushed the snow off his face with his paws. He felt a little nip from Numee, and then a nudge from her. He got the point and ran after the group just ahead of him. The Dims were still hunting them, which quickly dampened the immense joy and relief that Coda felt about Nova still being alive, and best of all, that she was here with him.

∞

This eastern portion of the Changyin Forest was thick with brush and trees, which was always a good thing when it came to hiding. The snow, however, wasn't helping. It was falling faster and thicker, making it difficult for Coda to see. He jogged along with his head down, following the disappearing tracks of his group. He was in the back, not because he was slow, but because he wanted to face any adversary that came close to his group of friends, giving them more time to escape. He knew Nova could defeat any Dim, but he didn't want to chance losing her again, nor did he want the rest of his friends to get hurt. He knew he could take on the entire Dim army long enough for everyone to get away. At least he hoped he could. He had never actually put that thought into practice.

A voice broke his concentration. "If it's hard going for us in the snow, it's hard for the Dims, as well. Snow is our greatest ally right now."

Coda looked up to see that it was Nova. She had slowed down, trotting next to Coda's side, the very place he didn't want her to be. Now she was in the back of the pack.

"I'm fine back here by myself. I can handle it." Coda wanted Nova to do anything but be back here.

"If I can survive a dis-incarnate, I can survive a Dim. Trust me."

Yes, the dis-incarnate, that black, shadowy creature—something Coda would love to know more about.

"How did you get away?" asked Coda, doing his best to stay a little bit behind her. She didn't have a scrape on her, yet when she was taken by the dis-incarnate he saw some of Nova's fur covered in dried blood. Then Coda remembered how quickly Nova could heal herself.

"It wasn't a matter of getting away. It was a matter of retrieving knowledge from the dis-incarnate, whether the dis-incarnate knew it or not. I know who controls Crepus. I know why they are doing what they're doing and it makes me sick to my stomach." She screwed up her face, unhappy with what she had seen. "I will brief you on it when we're out of harm's way."

Coda bit his lip as he looked up at the gray sky. It all looked like one massive cloud, not wispy like a giant cotton ball flying high above, but perfectly flat against the sky and blocking the sun. "Where are we going?" Coda glimpsed ahead, seeing Chev's large feet creating holes in the snow.

"Before I made my way back here to be with you, I was at

189

the front of the pack for a moment. I was able convince Kiwu to go to The Pyramid of Ohm, a place he'd never been before. He was resistant, but finally willing. We'll be safest there."

Coda wanted to ask a million questions about the pyramid, but knew this wasn't the place to do so. It was cold and it was starting to become too much for Coda. He simply gave an "okay", putting his head down to shield his eyes from the fast falling snow. His teeth started to clatter and he was shivering.

Nova padded up and leaned against him. He felt instant warmth, not only from the love that she carried in her aura, but from her thick fur that kept her dry. "We're in the era of the Shiver, but we needn't carry it with us."

Coda, trotting alongside Nova and close enough for her body warmth to comfort him, wondered how she was able to stay warm. Answering his thoughts, Nova responded, "Prana. It's The Great Spirit's gift to us all. It not only helps us breathe infinite energy, it also keeps our body the exact temperature it needs to be in order to be comfortable."

"What?" Coda was amazed, opening his eyes wide, which accidentally allowed a few snowflakes to brush against his retinas. He blinked, causing the flakes to instantly melt away. "You can stay warm in this weather?"

"Yes. We all can." She pointed her tail to Numee and Shikoba. Even though they were ahead of Chev, he could still see them between the falling snowflakes. Those two were warm and dry, just like Nova. However, Chev was another story. The only thing that kept him warm was his continuous long strides. He must have known this, because even though he looked tired he kept going, creating more and more heat within his body. The snow was melting on Chev's back, forming skinny trickles of water that fell to the ground.

Coda was just thinking how now wasn't the greatest time for him to ask Nova to teach him all about prana, when she said, "We need to speed up if we're to make it to The

190

Pyramid of Ohm before the Dims catch us."

Just as Nova spoke, Coda heard loud voices behind them. It was the Dims.

"Yes, they get closer and closer. Let's move faster," said Nova as she rushed forward, dragging her tail over Coda's spine.

With that, Coda felt a sudden burst of energy. Whatever Nova had just done to him gave him more energy than he'd experienced in a very long time. He leaped ahead, quickly gaining on Chev. Then Nova touched Chev's hind leg with her tail, giving Chev a sudden jolt of energy, as well, turning his long strides into a gallop.

They ran hard and fast, passing branches and bushes, sometimes bumping into them and splattering snow all over the ground. It didn't matter, though. Being stealthy and quiet wasn't their goal. They were trying to get to a place that Nova deemed safe. And because Nova had deemed it, Coda knew that it would be safe.

Then came the hills. They were large and daunting. Trekking up them, climbing over and around boulders as they moved wasn't so easy. For Chev, it was very difficult. The snow beaten trail created by the many hooves and paws of fleeing spirit animals made it slick and Chev wasn't used to climbing hills covered in snow drifts. His round feet weren't built for such travel, nor was his bulk. But, going down the hills was another story. In fact, it was fun. They all slid, and not necessarily feet first, and hoping it was leaving a wider gap between them and the pursuing Dims.

Shikoba had it the easiest by flying. Coda bet Shikoba could get to The Pyramind of Ohm right away, but understood that she was staying with the group to help them if the Dims caught up.

After climbing the ninth hill—according to Coda's count—he found himself in the rear again. When he reached the hilltop, he almost ran into the tribe greeting him with their rumps and tails. They had all stopped on the hill top and were gazing ahead like they were seeing something spectacular. They almost looked frozen, but Coda could tell that they weren't. They were breathing with heavy wafts of fog coming out of their mouths with each exhale.

*Why are they all stopped?*

Chev pointed with his trunk. "Look." He peered down at Coda. "Shall I lift you up?"

Coda shook his head, choosing to walk softly around the crowd, weaving his way to the front. When he got there, he noticed something quite different. Just twenty or so feet in front of him was dry, green grass.

*How can that be?*

But, that's not the only reason they were all staring. In the distance, there was a white pyramid with a shiny gold capstone shining like a beacon of light. All around it was clear, beautiful, and free of snow. In fact, the sky above it was blue and sunny, almost as if there was a large, circular force field that didn't allow clouds to move over the pyramid to block the sun shining on it and the land around it. He noticed that the sun was gleaming off the golden capstone, making it look like a second sun. He wondered how he had never noticed the sheen of golden light glaring in this direction before, especially when he was back in the Sihu Tribe standing on top of the Large Boulder. Perhaps the tall hills they had just climbed blocked it from view.

Changing his focus, he surveyed the area around the pyramid, seeing flowers of all colors sprinkled everywhere. Why the Dims didn't attack this place and take it as their own, he did not know. It was perfect, magical, and seemed very important. *Well,* he thought. *Maybe they've tried several times without success.*

"Isn't it gorgeous?" said Numee's voice. She was standing next to Coda, eyeing the view below.

Coda nodded, thinking they should get to the pyramid as fast as possible. The Dims had to be closer now.

And he was right.

The sound of horses galloping at full speed came from behind. He turned, along with the rest of the tribe, to see a

192

couple dozen horses, elk, moose, and other spirit animals of the like, racing over the crest of the hill they'd just climbed.

"We must—owe!" Coda fell back as a large hawk swiped down and dug its talons across Coda's side. The hawk flew off, carrying a tuft of his fur. Wincing from the sting of it, he looked up to see the hawk turning in mid-air and heading down at him for a second pass, not allowing Coda an instant to assess the damage to his side.

Coda crouched and spun out of the way as the hawk swooped and missed him. Coda jumped and grabbed the hawk by its tail feathers with his jaws, catching the bird by surprise. The hawk screeched and flapped its wings, and was quickly pulled to the ground. Coda flopped the hawk onto its back and pinned the bird's flailing wings with his paws, causing reddish brown feathers to fly about, peppering the ground. Coda glared into the hawk's eyes. "Have a good nap."

As Coda went to stun the hawk, its eyes widened, but instead of seeing hatred or rage in its eyes, Coda saw something else. He saw sadness, coupled with a plea for help. Coda, baffled, withdrew his paws from the creature and stood back. He nodded, which surprised his opponent. He was letting the hawk go free, taking the chance that it wouldn't fight again, or worse yet, attack him from behind as he helped the others.

Then Coda twisted around to see an intense fight taking place. Since Kiwu's tribe also had gray crystals, it was hard to tell the Dims apart from the tribe. The worst of it was that they all fought alike, making it even harder to decide who was who. He recognized Hao just fine, who was his usual insane self, pummeling his attackers with ease. Coda went to enter into the fray, but stopped as a voice came from behind.

"Thank you, Orion."

Startled, Coda looked over his shoulder to see the hawk still there, looking hopeless and weak. The hawk was slouching with her shoulders rounded forward in defeat, but she was holding her head up and looking into Coda's eyes.

"Go," said Coda.

The hawk slowly shook her head. "I used to know you."

Coda blinked, not knowing or remembering this spirit animal. He thought for a moment, hoping a memory would surface. If so, maybe he could say the hawk's name, and bring her back to her PureLight state. When no memory or feeling of remembrance came to him, he took a deep breath, bringing calmness to his heart. "Don't let the rest of the Dims see you talking to me. Go!" He flicked his head toward the west—where he thought Crepus Castle might be.

"This is the second time you've saved my life. I will always be in debt to you."

Firstly, Coda didn't care about anyone being in debt to him. Secondly, he just wanted this hawk to fly away to someplace safe, and to not attack the PureLights ever again.

Coda dipped his head. "Thank you. Now, please go."

"I can tell you where your sister is, Orion."

Coda's heart skipped a beat and everything else around Coda fell to the background, dull and noiseless. "Where is she?"

"She's—"

The hawk went flying backwards, almost as if it had been punched by an unseen force. It raised its wings, doing its best to flap, but Coda could tell the hawk was gripped in an energy clasp.

*Crepus?*

Coda ran to help the hawk, but before he could reach her Nova leaped over him, having caught the hawk between her teeth as it traveled through the air. Placing the hawk on the ground, she shook her head as sadness filled her eyes.

Looking at the hawk, Coda frowned. The hawk was dead. "How?"

"Crepus," replied Nova. "He's here somewhere. I feel him. He used the Dark Arts to kill this hawk."

Then a blast of Chev's trumpet sound reverberated across the hill. Coda and Nova immediately ran across the

194

hilltop, seeing Chev slowly backing up, warding off a small group of elk cresting the hill. They thrust their antlers at Chev, stabbing his chest several times. His trunk wasn't fast enough to push away so many attackers.

"Help, anyone?" yelled Chev, scared out of his mind. As Coda and Nova ran to their friend, they watched Shikoba tear across the sky, shrieking. She attacked the eyes of the lead elk with her talons and then grabbed its antlers as she twisted her body, causing the elk to lose its balance and topple over. She stunned it and went to the next elk, who slashed his antlers through the air, barely missing her. This one had been ready, but it didn't see a slightly smaller adversary coming at its back legs—Numee.

Coda and Nova leaped through the air, just as Numee undercut the elk's back legs, making it lurch back to strike at the fearless raccoon, but it was too late. Nova landed on the Elk's back, reached over its forehead and stunned it. The elk slumped to the ground.

Coda had landed next to Chev, ready to fend off the rest of the attackers. As he leaped, something in the battle drastically changed. Instead of continuing to fight, the rest of the elk fled back down the hill. For a second, Coda thought it was because it was him—the great and mighty Orion. Perhaps they thought he was the greatest of all fighters. But, as he glanced around, he saw the rest of the Dims running back down the hill as well, shrinking his ego. It wasn't because of him, it was something else.

"Look," called Kiwu, who was limping toward Coda. The bull flicked his ears toward the pyramid.

Coming from The Pyramid of Ohm were hundreds of spirit animals, racing up the other side of the hill to help them fight on the hilltop. Coda could see their indigo crystals beaming brightly, almost like flashlights strapped to their heads. These were PureLights and they meant business. No wonder the Dims ran.

Nova laughed, twitched her tail, and started to make her way toward the oncoming PureLights. Coda watched her,

195

but noticed that the PureLights rushing up the hill from the pyramid weren't exactly slowing down. In fact, they were speeding up and heading right toward her. A mean looking bear was in the lead and it looked like he wanted blood.

*Are these really PureLights? They can't be!* "Nova, watch out!" screamed Coda. In desperation, he leaped, landing in front of Nova to block the bear's advancement. Before Nova could speak, Coda spread his claws wide and slashed at the oncoming bear. Coda wasn't going to lose Nova a second time.

His swipe, however, went right through the bear as if it was a ghost. All Coda felt was air, nothing more. He reared back and swung a second time. Again, all Coda felt was air where there should have been fur. *What's going on?*

Coda, mystified as to what had just occurred, backed up, pushing Nova behind him during the process.

Nova laughed again. "The bear isn't really there, Coda. It's a trick coming from the pyramid's capstone."

"What?" asked an astonished Coda. The bear vanished in front of him, and like a domino effect the rest of the PureLights charging up the hill, shining their beautiful indigo crystals, disappeared.

Chev raced over with Shikoba on his back. Numee was close behind with a "what the heck" look on her face.

The rest of the tribe started down the hill to the pyramid, following their leader, Kiwu, with Hao, the stag, right behind him. Several of the tribe were limping, taking their time with their first steps down the long hillside, making sure they didn't fall. Some were wincing, clearly in pain, and some were dragging their injured friends who were too damaged to walk. Coda didn't know if some of them were actually dead, which he feared might be the case.

Looking past the tribe, his heart dropped when he saw his small friend, Pangli, being pulled down the hill by Meli. He quickly forgot about the vanishing spirit animals and ran to her.

When he arrived, Meli's red crystals glowed, not of

196

happiness, but of sadness. Coda's heart lurched, fearing the worst.

Meli stopped pulling, letting the panda rest limply. "She won't make it if we don't get her help immediately."

Coda nodded, seeing blood all over the little panda's body. *Who'd attack a child?* There was a slit across her side—the source of the blood. He glanced over his shoulder to see Nova and Numee already on their way.

Standing beside Coda, Numee placed her paws on each side of the slit, and pulling her paws together, closed up the wound. Then she closed her eyes and took a deep breath. Nova placed her paws over Numee's paws, and closed her eyes as well. Just as Coda had seen before, a faint light came from the sky, down to the heads of Numee and Nova as their bodies relaxed. Within moments, the slit started to shrink and heal.

"Thank you, Nova," said Numee, taking her paws off the panda. "But, I don't know if she'll make it. The internal injuries healed some, but not all."

Coda bit his lip. There had to be a way of keeping her alive. "Where can we take her? To the pyramid? To a better healer?"

Numee jolted her head back, feeling the sting of Coda's assertion that Numee might not be a good enough healer.

Nova nodded. "There may be a way if we can get her inside of the pyramid." She flicked her tail toward Chev. "Can you give Pangli a lift?"

Chev was further down the hill, speaking with Shikoba and watching as the tribe cautiously walked toward the pyramid. He turned to Nova and nodded, then ran back up the hill with Shikoba flying slowly behind.

"How can we be of assistance?" asked Shikoba.

"Who needs the lift? Coda?" He flicked Coda's shoulder with his trunk. "You can't make it down the hill?" he asked, clearly teasing him.

"It's for our panda friend," replied Coda.

Chev immediately shifted his eyes to Pangli. He'd just

197

noticed her there and she didn't look good. His happy expression went serious. "She's barely alive."

Nova gave a solemn purr, then walked up to Chev and pressed her fur against his leg. "That's why we need you to lift her onto your back and carry her to the pyramid. Any more pulling across the ground will make her worse."

"I'll keep her stable," Shikoba remarked. "Is it okay if I accompany her on your back, Chev?"

Chev tasseled the feathers on her head with his trunk. "Yes, anything to help."

Meli shifted her weight on her paws. "Go quickly. She doesn't have too many moments left in her."

Shikoba jumped up and flew onto Chev's back. Chev gently lifted the panda over his head, tenderly placing Pangli next to Shikoba. When it was done, they faced the pyramid and proceeded down the long slope of the hillside.

Nova pressed her flank against Numee's. "Numee, will you stay with Chev? Coda and I have some business to attend to."

"We have business?" asked Coda.

"We do." She slapped Coda's backside, then took off in a sprint. "Come!"

Coda followed, wondering what business she could be talking about.

# Chapter 17

The day grew darker and lighter throughout the day, not because of the falling and rising of the sun, but because of the density of whatever clouds would block the sun at any given moment. When Zoey finally thought it was dusk, it suddenly got lighter as a thick, gray cloud layer moved slowly away from the sun, allowing a thinner sheet of clouds to replace it and making it seem like a regular, gloomy afternoon in the Dim Lands. And, Zoey was glad of it because only moments earlier, she had thought it was dusk, making her wonder how the day could have gone by so fast.

Zoey and Aderyn were sitting on the flat cliff behind the redwood tree. They'd been quiet for a while, just listening to the sounds around them—the rushing river, the ocean waves a mile away or so to the west, the wind careening around the redwood tree and the pebbles dancing across the canyon top as they tumbled in the breeze. Life was relaxing at the moment, something Zoey needed.

"Who's San?"Just when Zoey was getting comfortable, Aderyn asked about her terrible friend.

"She's just an old friend."

Aderyn gave a friendly nudge. "How can you have an old friend in Ohm Totem if you've been here only seven moons, at most?"

Zoey sighed. "Well, she was one of my first friends when I arrived here." Zoey paused. "How do you know San?"

"I was sitting on the branch just above you and your friend when we were in Gwenfree Forest, and listening to your conversation. I arrived when San did, and didn't want to cause a stir by revealing myself to her. I followed you from tree to tree. I didn't want anything terrible to happen to you, so I was silent and remained ready to defend you if the need arose. You did a masterful job, flying the way you did. I'm proud of you."

Zoey shrugged, looking up at the gray sky and laughing with embarrassment. "Yeah, but when you spoke my name it kind of scared me. That wasn't so good."

"Good? Bad? Who's to know what good or bad really is? What may be good for one individual is bad for another. It's all relative. I see your startle as something positive, something that can be learned from, and then mastered."

Zoey nodded, getting herself ready for another training lesson. She wanted to rest, but her body and mind were getting used to the fact that she must train in order to survive this place. "Are we going to train now?" She checked her body, feeling that it could sustain another lesson. "I think I'm ready."

Aderyn tilted her head, gazing at Zoey. "Right now? I think not."

Relieved, but confused as well, Zoey furrowed her brow feathers. "I thought you said I should work on *not* getting startled when I'm doing the shape-shifting thing?"

"Yes, but at this very moment? No. I'm in need of some rest and meditation. You are, too. And if I were you, I'd bring your friend San into your heart. We're in a world of unforgiving creatures aptly named the Dims. Don't be one of them. Forgive her, but keep your wits about you when, or if, you're ever around her again."

Zoey held her wings out, almost in disgust. "How do I forgive someone who tried to kill my brother?"

"Good question, child." Aderyn closed her eyes. "Know that we, the PureLights and the Dims, are all teachers in your life, just as you are a teacher in our lives. We, including you, came to Ohm Totem with certain lessons to learn about unconditional Love. These lessons were created before we came here. And, before we were born, some spirit animals volunteered to be the villains in our lives in order for us to learn very important lessons. Others came to be helpers in our lives, also to teach very important lessons."

200

Aderyn smiled, looking at Zoey to see if she comprehended what she was saying. She saw little understanding. Nonetheless, she continued. "Both villain and friend are essential in your life. In many cases, a villain is actually a friend in disguise. They've come to teach you a lesson that a helper cannot. If you continue to blame that villain for the wrongs that you claim they've done to you, then you give them no gratitude for the difficult lesson they provided, thus furthering the villain's attachment to you and your attachment to the villain. Once you feel truly grateful for the lesson, or lessons, you received from the villain, then and only then, will the lessons stop repeating themselves, allowing you a rest before you go onto the next lesson. Just understand that when you don't 'get the lesson', especially from a villain, it keeps repeating until you've learned it. Does that make sense?"

Zoey thought for a moment. "Aren't we supposed to stop the villain from doing bad things?"

"Yes, and that's perhaps one of the major lessons in our lives—the lesson of stopping a villain, without becoming a villain."

Zoey shrugged. "San led Coda and me to Crepus, knowing what he'd do to us. She knew he'd beat us, kill us, enslave us, or whatever bad things he does." She stared at her toes, shaking her head. "I should forgive that?"

"You can do what you want. Just know that holding on to this grudge of yours isn't doing any good for your heart, mind, or body. You're creating unneeded stress, making it affect every cell inside of you. And it has an effect on those around you. If you hold on to this grudge long enough, you'll create dis-ease in your body, perhaps killing yourself sooner than Crepus could. Once you forgive San, she'll either go away and never come back, or she'll return with another lesson, or perhaps you'll simply enjoy the friendship. Perhaps she's not so *bad* after all? And maybe the lesson she'll learn from you is forgiveness, truth, and loyalty. Did you ever think of that?"

201

Zoey shook her head. She'd never thought of any of those things. She put her wings out in front of her, observing her feather tips, and wondering how she could ever forgive San.

"Freedom is found in forgiving all, Zoey. Prison is the lack of forgiving. You can be trapped in that prison your entire life if you don't let go of your anger toward another Being. Your grudge only hurts you, not anyone else. It burns in your heart, slowly consuming your soul."

The conversation shot tingles down Zoey's body, vibrating truth throughout her, because a burning in her heart was exactly what Zoey was feeling whenever she thought of San. Zoey sighed. "I feel so much..." Zoey paused, bringing her wings by her side and staring off into the distance. Then she scrunched up her wing tip feathers as if she was clinching her fists, "...so much anger for San. I don't know if it will ever go away."

"Close your eyes and bring her to your heart. Find a way to understand why she did what she did and forgive her. Forgive yourself."

Zoey did just that. She closed her eyes and brought San to her heart, swallowing her up in pink light, doing her best to forgive San. Zoey felt Aderyn close her eyes as well, perhaps to do the same thing. Maybe Aderyn had to forgive another spirit animal, and if that was true it was probably Crepus.

Zoey took a deep breath, feeling her rhythmic breathing matching Aderyn's. They were in perfect sequence with each other. They did this for hours.

∞

Flapping her wings and reaching the top of the redwood tree, Zoey looped in the air and then fell into a fast nose dive toward Aderyn, who was about fifty bird lengths below. Zoey thought she was going to catch Aderyn by surprise.

They had been training in The Art of Air Defense, a modified style of the Art of Defense created for the

PureLight Wings, for quite some time now. Before they started, Aderyn had explained that The Art of Air Defense was a defensive technique that Orion had taught to Aria. Then Aria taught Aderyn. Apparently, both techniques were the same, except that the air version had obviously been designed for air combat.

Zoey zoomed downward, closing in on Aderyn, but just as Zoey was about to catch her by surprise, the snow owl rolled out of the way, letting Zoey pass on by. Zoey extended her wings to slow down so she wouldn't smack into a cliff top, but, as she was doing so she felt sharp talons gouge into her back.

"Owe!" Flipping backward, more in fright than anything else, Zoey maneuvered out of the way, successfully breaking Aderyn's grip. "Hey, I thought we were just practicing!" Zoey hadn't expected to be clawed in these training sessions.

Landing on the cliff top and rubbing her back with a wing, Zoey reared around to see Aderyn standing next to her.

"Zoey, right now, if I had been a Dim, you'd be their meal for the night."

Aghast, Zoey stepped back. "They'd eat me?!"

Aderyn's eyes fell to the rocky ground. She didn't necessarily mean that the Dims would automatically eat her, only that it was possible to be killed if Aderyn had been a true Dim, but sometimes words came out of a VioletLight's mouth in an unintended way for a reason.

"Yes, there have been times when they have feasted on their enemies. It's a warrior's ritual that Crepus created to lower the Dims' vibration level in their bodies and crystals. He did this in order to keep their crystals gray, maintaining their Dim-like denseness."

Zoey defiantly placed her wings on her hips, shaking her head. "Nova would have told us that! San would have said something! I've not seen them do anything like that...to actually eat someone?"

"I know, child, and you have not been here as long as I have been, observing the things that Crepus has done. It's not something that they do often, but it's a way for Crepus to maintain fear within the hearts and minds of the Dims, making Crepus' minions more susceptible to control. It lowers their will power, their intelligence, their thoughts and feelings. It dulls and dumbs them down."

"Is that how he turned all of their crystals gray? Why would spirit animals agree to eat another spirit animal in the first place?"

Aderyn folded her wings across her chest and then walked over to Zoey to place a wing around her shoulder. "That's not how they went gray. No PureLight would have voluntarily consumed another PureLight. We still haven't figured out how he managed to turn so many PureLights into Dims. We've been baffled about that for moons upon moons. That's another subject I have Gart researching in the Hall of Scrolls."

"It's not so baffling," said a voice behind them.

Startled, Zoey spun around, nearly carrying a stumbling Aderyn with her.

Aderyn's beak turned into a smile. "Maldwyn?"

She flew over to him and Maldwyn grabbed her into a soft bear hug. "It's nice to see you too, Aderyn."

Aderyn pointed to Zoey. "This is Zoey."

Maldwyn, setting Aderyn on the ground, dipped his head. "We've met." Zoey remembered him from the tunnels, the time they'd almost been caught by Crepus. Maldwyn was the one who had mouthed the words, "Empty your mind and proceed from the heart." They were words that had kept her alive, giving her the idea and the power to use that strange magic that had come out of her, blasting energy at her opponents and making them tumble backwards.

The ape bowed to her. "It's nice to see you again, Zoey."

Zoey bowed back, hoping it was the correct gesture of response. "Nice to see you again, too."

Maldwyn then turned to Aderyn who was standing near

his feet, beaming with happiness.

"Are you ready?" she asked.

*Ready for what?* thought Zoey, but saw what she meant only seconds later as the ape bent down on one knee, kneeling in front of the owl. Aderyn flew into a hover at Maldwyn's forehead and whispered, "Lemla Sanctum." Then she blew on his gray crystal.

The gray in the crystal started to peel off, falling away as Aderyn blew on it, revealing a beautiful, shining indigo crystal. She did the same for his chest crystal, as well.

Zoey gave an audible, "Wow." Then scratching her head, she asked, "How did you do that?"

Aderyn faced Zoey. "It's another spell we cast into the ethers, making it manifest through our words. Words have power. It's a way to get Maldwyn inside of Crepus Castle to spy on Crepus."

Maldwyn grunted. "That's how Crepus creates his spies. He uses the same spell."

Aderyn gasped. "They know the spell?"

Maldwyn nodded. "I don't know how he got it." He brought his eyes to Aderyn's. "And, he's in pursuit of all of the VioletLight spells. That's why you've become target number two, just after target number one—Zoey."

Aderyn's mouth gaped open, still shocked that Crepus had one of their spells. "Who did they get the spell from?"

"I don't know. I suspect there's a traitor somewhere. Perhaps at the Pyramid of Ohm?"

Aderyn stared at her feet. "That's probably why Luli gave us the key."

Zoey frowned, trying to take it all in. "Can the spell also turn a gray crystal to a colored crystal?"

Aderyn stared off into the distance, as if in deep thought, not because of Zoey's question, but from the news of another traitor. It was a traitor that might be living in the pyramid with Lao's tribe. She sniffed, perturbed and crinkling her beak. "Yes, Zoey. With the spell, you can change your crystal's color to any color you'd like. All you

205

have to do is imagine the color as you speak the words."

"But, how did all of the Dim crystals turn gray? Did he do it with that spell?"

"No, child." Aderyn stared at Maldwyn. "They had gray crystals before we created the spells. That's a great question, though. Do you know the answer to that question, Maldwyn?" There was a lot of interest on the snow owl's face, looking like a child wanting to know everything about the world, which was something Zoey hadn't yet seen on Aderyn before. The teacher was wanting to be taught and informed.

Maldwyn puffed out his lower lip, as if in thought. Then he sighed. "What I've been able to gather is that Crepus was able to convince a PureLight, or even a PureLight tribe through mass suggestion, to change their thoughts from a positive to a negative outlook on life. If their thoughts remained negative for a certain period of moons, then their crystals may have gradually faded to gray. It's brainwashing on a massive scale."

Aderyn tilted her head as her eyes narrowed. "Did he ever try that on you—brainwashing?"

Maldwyn's face went glum as if every nerve feeding his mouth, cheeks, and forehead had instantaneously died. He had just realized the worst. If he had been brainwashed by Crepus, even a little, then the dragon would have access through his eyes and worse, his memories. He nodded his head. "He walked in my mind, doing his best to find your home and The PureLight Order. He even tried to find Zoey."

Aderyn lowered her head, but kept her gaze upon Maldwyn. Zoey could tell that Aderyn had just realized that something terrible had occurred. "How much did you show him?"

Maldwyn lowered his eyes, feeling ashamed. "I fought him the best I could. I maintained control. He got as far as the redwood tree, but I eventually led him down the Mosazi River toward the Zulu Tribe, where I knew he wouldn't attempt to go."

206

"It might not be too late, then. Lay down." Aderyn patted the ground next to her. Maldwyn complied and lay on his back, closing his eyes as if he knew what Aderyn was going to do. She placed both of her wings on his forehead. Zoey expected Aderyn to bring in Prana, like she had when Zoey first met her, but she did nothing of the sort. Aderyn closed her eyes, her beak slowly moving as if whispering to herself.

After a few moments, the owl spoke out loud, as if in a trance. "Yes, Crepus is still in your mind and he knows that you're here. Even though you defeated his guards to get out of the castle, he was happy that you did so. It was a set up. There was a reason why only your arms were chained. He wanted you to break out. He knew you'd come to me, and that you'd feel safe enough to drop your guard so he could search your thoughts, unnoticed. He would easily access your memories of The PureLight Order's location. Your entire life you've known the special knock to open the door to the cavern where The PureLight Order is stored, and the way to get down to it. Crepus has retrieved that information from your memories, and has sent his minions. They're coming, and they're close...very close."

Aderyn opened her eyes looking as if the worst had happened. She pressed her forehead against Maldwyns, crystal against crystal. "Release him, Crepus. Release Maldwyn! Now!"

Maldwyn shuddered as his eyes opened wide and his mouth let out a large exhale. His chest convulsed and then he screamed, making Zoey cover her ears. A moment later, everything went silent and Zoey brought her wings down to her sides.

Aderyn stroked Maldwyn's head. "It's done. Crepus has left you."

Maldwyn could only muster a nod. He was breathing heavy, as if he had just been running.

Zoey didn't know what to do, or what just happened. She cautiously walked over to them, touching Adery's back with her wing. "Is he okay?"

"He'll live, but I must stay with him all night, bringing as much Prana to him as I can. If I don't, then he won't be with us by morning. Crepus has drained almost all of his energy."

Suddenly, Aderyn looked deep into Zoey's eyes. She whispered, "They're here."

Zoey looked around, seeing no one. "Who?"

"The Dims. Skint's with them. I can feel him."

"Where?"

"There." She gestured toward the top of the redwood tree. "Crepus most likely gave Skint the secret knock. He must not be allowed to take the scroll. We must stop him."

Zoey glanced up, but again saw nothing. All was calm, even the breeze. The clouds even looked a little better than usual.

Maldwyn coughed, bringing his eyes to Aderyn. "Go. Save The PureLight Order. Leave me."

"If I leave, you'll die."

"There is no death," he whispered.

There was sadness in Aderyn's eyes. She knew, just as Maldwyn, that to keep the Dims paws off The PureLight Order, she needed to go to the redwood—now.

A tear fell from Aderyn's eyes and then anger. She closed her eyes, determined to heal her friend. She took in a deep breath.

Zoey, suddenly feeling compelled to do something she'd never done before, placed her wings on Maldwyn, closed her eyes just like Aderyn and took a deep breath, as well. She had never brought in Prana before, but that wasn't her intent at the moment. She had a feeling that her voice could help Maldwyn in some way.

She opened her beak, letting out a chirp, then another and another, until she was singing the most beautiful song she'd ever sung. Her body swayed, flowing with the rhythms of her music. Even though her eyes were closed, her vision filled with swirling indigo colors, then violet, then pink, then indigo again. A moment later, she stopped, as if by some unknown command telling her to do so. She gasped

208

by what she had done, and then looked at Aderyn, who simply nodded back.

"You may have just saved his life," said Aderyn. "You're truly remarkable."

Zoey glanced at Maldwyn, seeing him turn over. He placed his hands on the rocky ground and pushed himself up into a standing position. He still appeared weary, but still alive and moving, nonetheless. Aderyn pointed to several large boulders. "Hide between those until you get better. We'll be back. Do you understand?"

Maldwyn turned and walked like a drunken man. He reached the rocks, sitting down between them and hiding from view. Aderyn lifted up in flight. "We must get to The PureLight Order!"

# Chapter 18

Reaching the top of the stairs and standing on the platform leading to the entrance of the pyramid, Coda, out of breath, looked back down. *How many stairs were there?* It looked as if they had just climbed a mile, and almost straight up. He felt like he was higher than he'd ever been before and gave a breathy, "Wow!" Then he gazed at the sweeping view all around him and he was amazed at how incredibly beautiful everything was from this height.

"It is," responded Nova, following his gaze.

The sky was blue and the sun was big in the sky. And, to make things even better, it was warm here, a complete contrast to the cold, harsh Shiver of the Dim Lands. *Wait; am I still in the Dim Lands?*

Changing his focus, he glimpsed down below again. He saw the remnant tribe standing at the base of the pyramid. Some looked like they were in pain, staring up at Nova and Coda, and others glared at them as if they were aliens from another planet. They seemed frightened of the pyramid, and even more terrified that anyone would have the guts to climb it.

Chev, Numee, Shikoba and the injured panda were at the very bottom of the staircase. Nova gave them a nod, and to Coda's surprise Chev saw her gesture and waved his trunk, though he looked as small as a mouse from Coda's point of view. His friends took their first steps up the stairs, but again the tribe stayed put. *Why aren't they following them?*

"Welcome to the Shan Tribe, Nova—as few as we are. It's nice to see you again."

A little startled, Coda turned his eyes to the entrance, seeing a gray wolf standing there. The wolf's chest was out, his head was held high, and he was smiling. His violet crystals glowed as he bowed his head.

The gray wolf gestured for them to enter the pyramid, and as they did, Coda noticed a flower of life symbol etched in the stone just above the doorway. It was identical to the one he had noticed inside of the Large Boulder just several days ago. He still didn't know what it meant, but according to San it was important. But, San tried to get them killed and was probably lying to them.

Walking past the entrance brought him into a large hall surrounded with gold walls and a gold ceiling. Colorful statues of spirit animals stood against the wall—nine statues, to be exact.

Nova bowed. "Thank you, Lao. It's a pleasure to see you again. It's been many, many moons."

Lao smiled. "It's been far too long, Nova." Shifting his gaze, he looked at Coda. "You must be Zoey's brother, the Night Walker. It's wonderful to see you again."

*Again?* thought Coda. *Oh yeah, he probably used to be friends with Orion, like everyone else in Ohm Totem.*

"I'm sorry to intrude on you Lao, but we need a healing chamber. We have a little one being carried up the stairs that may not make it," said Nova.

Lao's expression turned from happiness to concern. "Yes, I have the perfect place." He turned and walked toward a wall. Coda was about to follow, but suddenly stopped. Tingling sensations were saturating his body. He wiggled his nose and blinked several times, trying to make the sensations stop, much in the same way that he'd end a sneeze before it happened. His forehead crystal began to pulse, as well, making him lower his head and rub his forehead with his fore leg. He was feeling weird, to say the least.

Lao glanced over his shoulder and said, "It's the energy of the room. The entire pyramid is like that. Don't worry, you'll get used to it."

*How did he know what I was feeling?* Coda puffed out his lower lip, realizing that Lao was a VioletLight and a

VioletLight senses those things. Lao continued to walk, heading toward a door that Coda wasn't able to see at first. A large statue, beautifully designed and painted, stood next to the door, concealing it from first glance. Then Coda's eyes widened when he noticed that it was a statue that looked just like Crepus. He wanted to jump back, ready for an attack, but decided that a statue probably wouldn't come to life and try to kill him. And there was another gigantic statue standing on the other side of the door. It was a bear with golden fur—a spirit animal he'd never encountered before in Ohm Totem.

Coda had a burning question, and just before Lao was about to blow on the door to open it, Coda asked, "How did you create all of those PureLights out there? You know—the ones that scared off the Dims?"

Lao gazed into Nova's eyes. Nova nodded and Lao nodded back, as if they both understood each other. "It's very complicated to explain, yet easy to do. I'll show you how, sometime."

"Sure," replied Coda, wondering what the shared look between Nova and Lao was all about. Was it a secret they weren't supposed to tell? Did they have a projection camera of some sort? He knew they didn't, but that was the only explanation that he had for the PureLights that chased off the Dims and disappeared.

Lao blew on the door. It opened slowly, rolling to the side. "Tell your friends to bring the panda in here. This is where it can rest and rejuvenate."

Lao turned, walking away from the door and gesturing for them to follow.

Lao leaned into Nova, whispering, "There's a Dim in our pyramid tribe—the Shan Tribe." He gave a side look to Coda, making sure that he understood. "Whoever it is hides his or her cover very well."

Coda hadn't seen any other spirit animals in the pyramid thus far. All he had seen were the PureLights that had disappeared right in front of his eyes, so he didn't know if

212

this Lao was cuckoo, or if the spirit animals of the Shan Tribe were all somewhere else, perhaps hiding?

Nova simply nodded her head. She eyed the entrance they had come through. Padding over to it, she glanced down the long stairway. "Chev and the rest of our group is nearly half way up."

Lao grazed against Coda, giving him a wonderful, calm feeling. "I must get back to my tribe." He turned his eyes to Nova. "I will see you soon?"

She nodded a yes to Lao. "We will be with your tribe for many moons. I fear the small tribe below won't be here for much longer." She spoke with a melancholy sigh. "We'd be great assets to each other if they stayed."

Lao shook his head. "They won't stay. They fear the energy of this pyramid and our colored crystals. They've forgotten much."

"Hao, the stag, is remembering," replied Nova.

Lao's brows rose. "Really? That's a great turn for the positive. I hope he comes up the steps and joins us." He walked toward another wall, looked over his shoulder, and stared at Coda. "We can change him into what he used to be, if he allows it." He turned and blew into the wall. It opened up and thick golden light, partly from the zytes lining the wall, but mostly from the golden wall itself, greeted them, relaxing Coda for some reason. It made him want to take a big, relaxing breath. Then the gray wolf padded through the opening in the wall and disappeared around a corner. The wall closed an instant later.

Nova nudged Coda, smiling. She twitched her tail, asking Coda to follow him. "Let's get going. Much will be explained to you very soon."

They padded down the hall, toward a long descending ramp also made of gold. *Where'd they get all this gold, anyway?*

She pointed her tail up and forward, indicating for him to stop. "All will be shown, shortly. Your questions about this pyramid, the sensations you're feeling, and even of me, will be answered." She stopped in mid stride. "Well..." she tipped her head to the side as she stared at Coda, "if you ask the right questions."

Coda wondered how, or what, he'd be shown, and how would he know what questions to ask? *What the heck is she even talking about?* He leaned his head to the side. There was one question about Nova he'd like to ask. "Well, I hope I'll be shown how you escaped that weird, black creature."

"The dis-incarnate." She took a big breath, as if there was a lot involved to that question. She pursed her lips and started walking. "It would be a waste to explain. So, I'll give it to you in a dream."

"In a dream?" Coda repeated. "Really? How?"

"It's not a question of how. It's a question of advancement. You are a very advanced soul—an advanced spirit animal. You can do things not many of us can, just like your sister. Your experience, your innocence, and your mastery of past lessons have allowed you to have abilities and senses that even some of us VioletLights haven't yet attained."

"Even you? I mean, I can do things that you can't?" Coda was surprised that he would have an ability more advanced than her.

"Even me. Once you tap fully into your heart, that innocence of yours and your sister's will stop Crepus and his army. I'm confident about this."

Coda frowned. "What's innocence, anyway?"

"Innocence is a place where ego is non-existent. It's a purity of body, spirit, and mind. It's state of Being where choices are made from the heart, not from the ego. The ego requires personal gain."

She stopped, seeing that Coda was looking a little confused. She rephrased her answer. "You see, a lot of our motivations in life are based on how we can individually benefit from a situation. You may have had similar motivations many times in your life, but as young as you are, you didn't know any better, even when you were being selfish with your sister back in Gladstone. We VioletLights are free of ego, but our experiences in life have been tainted by the suffering around us. We've seen a lot of violence, and a lot of shameless killing. We've all been impacted by the events in Ohm Totem in some way or another. You haven't, as of yet. That's why Orion, as best as I can figure, left Ohm Totem and rebirthed as you. He'd have the innocence needed to defeat Crepus, and the downloaded memories of the Art of Defense, among a myriad of other memories. I just don't know how he did it, just as I haven't figured out how your sister did it."

Coda nodded, though much of what Nova had just said went right over his head. He understood bits and pieces, but it was like math class, back at home. When he was first taught how to solve algebra equations, it wasn't until about the tenth time the teacher went through it with him that he finally understood. He figured that's how he'll start to understand these things that Nova spoke about. The more he listened, plus the more she taught, equaled the more he'd start putting the pieces together that would allow him to make sense of it all.

They continued moving forward again, going down a small, golden ramp leading down to a small chamber. "I must stop here," stated Nova.

Coda looked ahead, sitting next to Nova. "What's that room?"

She gestured for him to enter it. "You'll see."

He shrugged and proceeded to the chamber, wishing she'd just explain everything, instead of him trying to figure it out on his own.

He walked into the small room, noticing a small slit in one of the walls. It must have faced outside, because it allowed a ray of sunshine to seep into the room, lighting up the gold floors, walls, and ceiling. He wondered, *why all the gold?*

"This chamber is aligned with a very important star. At a certain point in the night, the star will shimmer through the

215

slit and light up the room for several moments. It will regenerate you, and do many other things as well." She winked at him.

"When do I come out?"

She thought for a moment. "When you feel you must."

"So, I could be in here for a long time?" Coda didn't like the sound of that.

Nova shook her head. "Not a good idea. The chamber would burn you up if you stayed in here longer than a day. You'll just be here through the night, until I come and get you." She licked her forepaw. "Like I said before, you'll know the correct moment to leave and I'll be there at the door for you."

"What door?"

"The door to the chamber. It's like most doors here. It rolls in and out of the wall. It's open right now, as you can see. It will remain that way, unless one of us on the outside shuts it. That won't be necessary, though. So—"

Nova was cut off as a large falcon landed beside her. "Hi, I'm Luli." Her voice was excited, as if she was thrilled to see new visitors. She screwed up her face as she looked at Coda. "Wait, what are you doing inside of the chamber? It's not safe in there if you're not a VioletLight, and by the colors of your crystals I can see that you aren't one. You won't make it past a day."

Coda looked at Nova, hoping she'd explain. Just as she was about to, a large ape, the biggest one Coda had ever seen, came into view. He had indigo crystals, although his head hung low, almost hiding his chest crystal. There was a real sadness about him, which went away the moment he spoke. "Nova, your friends need your assistance. There's an emergency."

Both Nova's and Coda's eyes widened. He went to run out of the room when Nova put up her tail, making Coda halt. "I'll go. You stay. Everything will be fine. I'll make sure of it." She ran up the chamber ramp, through the large room and vanished from Coda's sight.

216

Coda tilted his head, his brows creased and his eyes were on the ape. "What happened?"

Luli frowned, turning her head toward the large Ape. "Yu'an, is everything okay? I've never seen you so panicked, or...is that sadness?"

The ape lowered his eyes. "They're fighting with that tribe at the base of our pyramid."

Luli looked at Coda's startled face. "Don't judge them. This is all that tribe has known for thousands of moons. They were decimated and this is all that's left of them. They've lived a hard and trying life and they're in survival mode, pushing others aside for the betterment of their own tribe."

Coda crouched, readying to jump out of the chamber. "My friends need my help!"

The ape jumped into the middle of the doorway, knocking Luli onto her side and blocking Coda from doing anything. "Nova said stay!"

Luli stood up, shaking her feathers as if shaking off pain. She playfully bit Yu'an's leg. "What's gotten into you?" She shimmied her way in between the doorway and the ape.

Coda padded forward, but Luli put up her wing. "Nova will get everything straight and positive, so please don't worry. She wants you in here for a reason, so I suggest that you stay, but not for too long. If you feel you're about to burn up from too much energy pulsing through your body, then get out of the chamber immediately. If you don't, then you will certainly have a most horrific death. It's not pleasant, I assure you." She then gestured her wing toward the main room where the statues stood. "This chamber's door will be open and you'll be able to see us come and go, meaning that we'll be able to see you. If you can't tell when you've had too much, then know that I can tell."

Coda walked back into the middle of the room where the beam of sun light landed on the gold floor. He sighed, laying down, resting his chin on his paws. "I guess I must stay, then." He was realizing that he didn't have much of a choice. What was so great about this chamber, anyway?

"Thank you," replied the falcon. She careened her head, looking up at the ape and making a funny expression, as if asking him why he was being so weird. "You can move back, you know. Coda's not leaving. Later on, you can tell me why you pushed me down, okay?"

Luli smiled, turning her eyes to Coda. "And, I have a message for you."

"You do?"

"Yes." She nodded her head up and down like a child would emphasize what she was saying to a parent. "Your sister is safe. I saw her a day ago with our dear VioletLight friend, Aderyn the VioletLight."

Coda jerked his head up with his ears perked. "What? How?" A huge weight suddenly lifted from his entire body. *Is she telling me the truth?* He wanted to jump up and down, screaming with joy and excitement. He wanted it to be true, but could it even be possible? With the biggest smile, he listened intently for Luli's answer.

"She was rescued by Aderyn, just after Crepus took her away. So, please don't worry yourself anymore. She's as safe as can be. Be assured that Aderyn is most skilled at hiding from the Dims. She won't let a Dim harm a feather on your sister."

A loud grunt came from the ape, startling Coda and Luli. "I've had enough," he shouted, bringing both fists together just above his head. With one hefty swing, he slammed his fists across the falcon, smashing against her chest and sending her up the ramp and across the room.

"Hey!" Baffled, Coda looked left and right. *What just happened?* He backed up, waiting for the ape to jump into the chamber to try and do the same to him. Coda crouched, ready to use his Art of Defense, even though his mind drifted from fear to anger, and for the first time in a long time, he couldn't focus. Was it the room doing it to him? Yu'an laughed. The ape knew it would be crazy to fight such a skilled panther, so he backed up, mocking Coda with a

218

pouting face. "Like Luli said, if you're in here too long, you'll burn to death. Get ready to burn." The ape whispered something into the wall.

Coda went to leap at Yu'an, but a door rolled out of the entrance wall, shutting in front of him and leaving him in a darkened room. Only that same slit of light came through, the one he saw when he had entered the chamber. He ran to the door, blowing on it, hoping he could open it somehow and stop the crazy ape from killing Luli, or any other unsuspecting spirit animal. Coda waited a moment, remembering that the door would catch his scent, then blew on it again and crouched to leap, readying for it to open.

Nothing happened. He blew again, but the door remained shut. He had hoped it was like the Large Boulder, or the Marble Burrow, and all he'd need to do was to blow. This chamber clearly wasn't like that. The ape had whispered something in order to close the door, making it roll shut, but what was it? He scratched at the wall, doing his best to find a switch to let him out, or make enough noise for someone to hear him. "Nova!" he yelled. It was a yell he repeated over and over again, until giving up and leaning against the door, slid down into a slump.

# Chapter 19

Zoey and Aderyn landed and perched on the lip of the redwood tree's entrance. They both looked down, noticing that the door to the lower portion of the redwood tree was wide open. Somebody had gotten in.

Panic filled Zoey. *They're here!* That's all she knew. *Now what?*

She turned, looking at Aderyn. The owl, however, had something else in her sights as she stared straight ahead with her eyes narrowed. Following Aderyn's gaze, Zoey saw him.

*Skint!*

His claws were clinging to the inner wall of the redwood entrance. He was just across from them, his eyes locked on Aderyn. Neither one of them moved or spoke, locked in some kind of mental or energetic fight that Zoey couldn't see.

Skint's eyes quickly shifted to Zoey's, taking her off guard and making her heart sink into her stomach. Skint energetically grabbed Zoey, using his Dark Arts to squeeze Zoey's throat shut, choking her. Skint smiled a wicked grin, as if telling her that he had her again and that she was an easy target. But his face quickly changed when he saw Aderyn flying at him with sharp talons pointing directly at him. In a stunt as quick as Zoey had ever seen, Aderyn had the squirrel pinned to the wall, instantly releasing his power over Zoey.

Rubbing her throat with her wings, Zoey sucked in a deep breath, bringing in much needed air. Glancing down at the open floor, Zoey wondered, *how long have they been here?*

Zoey knew that the Dims had learned the secret to

opening this floor from Maldwyn's thoughts taken by Crepus, and then sent to his minions. If some Dims had already found their way down to the Hall of Scrolls, that meant that Gart was in serious trouble.

Aderyn interrupted Zoey's thoughts. "I'll hold Skint while you go down and stop them. We must get him as far away from you as possible."

Zoey saw Skint straining to release himself from Aderyn's hold, but to no avail. Aderyn then did something that Zoey wasn't expecting. Aderyn leaned her head toward Skint, almost touching her beak to his nose. "We've given you chance after chance, Skint," spoke Aderyn. "I cannot, in good conscience, allow you to harm any more Beings. I must end this now."

Skint's eyes widened, then fear over took him. He knew what she was going to do, but the sheer surprise of it terrorized him. His body desperately squirmed against the bark of the tree, doing his best to break Aderyn steely grip on him. Aderyn leaned closer, pressing her beak against Skint's throat. Skint started to tremble uncontrollably.

"No, please. I...I won't hurt anyone anymore...ever again." He shook his head back and forth, careening his neck. Then he laid his head sideways against the tree. Holding his breath, he closed his eyes, waiting for the inevitable.

"I'm sorry, Skint. I must do this." Aderyn, feeling Skint's terror, relaxed, easing her grip on him, although he still cringed in expectation. Compassion suddenly filled Aderyn. She felt pity for the squirrel. He still had more lessons to learn, something Aderyn felt she had no right to end. Instead of killing Skint, she pressed on his chest crystal and twisted it by turning her head, stunning Skint for the second time in one day. Then she leaped out of the entrance, carrying his limp body in her talons, while looking back at Zoey during the process. "I'm taking Skint somewhere far from here, to a place beyond our shores, so he can never return. I'll be back soon. Now go and stop them!" Aderyn flew off toward Gwenfree Forest, moving much faster than any normal bird, disappearing from Zoey's view within seconds.

Zoey sighed. *Who am I supposed to stop?* She didn't know what she was about to get herself into. How was she going to stop anyone, especially without Aderyn? Well, she'd been lucky before, perhaps she'd get lucky again.

Zoey spread her wings, ready to fall into a nose dive when a large osprey appeared out of the shadows, making Zoey lose her footing and slip into a free fall toward the bottom of the redwood. Catching herself as quickly as she could, she spun into the nose dive she was hoping to do in the first place. Looking over her shoulder, she saw the osprey coming at her. *Oh no!* Terror filled, she tightened herself up, doing her best to fall at a faster rate. She wasn't fast enough.

A nip on her back feathers caused her to twirl away, slightly grazing the inner bark of the tree. The osprey crashed into her, feathers flying wildly into the air. Zoey could feel the osprey talons starting to grab hold of her. *No! No! No!* Zoey forced herself to twist her body, facing her head up, and then pushed off the osprey with her feet. Zoey hovered, watching the osprey smash against the soft dirt below. Zoey hadn't realized how close she was to the bottom. When she noticed that the osprey wasn't moving, she thanked her lucky stars that she hadn't hit the ground, too.

Zoey was slowly hovering to the ground while keeping her eye on the osprey, just in case it was faking death or being knocked out. As she was about to touch down, Zoey felt another bird from above dig its talons into her, and yank her upwards.

"Let go of her!"

For a second, Zoey thought it was Aderyn who had yelled, but this voice had a higher pitch to it, so she knew it was someone else. Maybe Luli, the falcon she'd recently met? The Dim who had her suddenly lost its grip on Zoey.

Zoey began to fall, but spread her wings, slowing herself to a hover. She then watched two birds fighting each other in the air above her, until they both went down, hitting the soft dirt. Zoey looked around to make sure there were no more Dims coming. When she saw none, she gazed down at the motionless birds in the dirt, until one shook its head. It brushed the dirt off itself with its wings and turned, looking up at Zoey.

"Are you okay, Zoey?"

"San?"

San nodded her head up and down, attempting a jump, but fell back down again in pain. "It's me," she finally said, her voice sounding dazed and weak.

Zoey dropped to the ground, landing next to San. Now there were two downed Dims lying unconscious—at least she hoped they were unconscious.

San put her wings up. "I stunned this one." She pointed to the dirt covered bird lying next to her. She rubbed her neck. "That landing hurt."

"I'll bring you that healing energy stuff," said Zoey with doubt in her voice. All that she knew how to do was sing. She hoped it would help San, like it had done with Maldwyn.

"We don't have a moment to spare," said San. "They're going after The PureLight Order as we speak. They know how to open the wall to get it, so we have to stop them and I mean now!" San lifted her wings, fighting the pain that obviously surged through her, and then flew down the hallway.

Zoey followed, and knowing the way, she took the lead; hoping San wasn't tricking her again by leading her into a trap. Zoey careened around a corner, then flew down a long flight of stairs, down more hallways, and into the root covered Hall of Scrolls. And, to their dismay, they saw three more Dims and they had a scared prairie dog surrounded— Gart!

"G-g-get back!" he yelled. He flung dirt clods at the

223

Dims, only causing laughter, instead of fear.

Just in front of Gart stood that mean crow who had tried to harm San in the Gwenfree Forest. There were two smaller birds with him.

*Wait*, thought Zoey. San had covered for her in front of that crow back in the Gwenfree Forest, saying that she didn't know where Zoey was. She had risked her life for Zoey!

That memory brought a smile to Zoey's face and a wonderful feeling of euphoria welled up inside of her, and her heart started to beat faster. Not because of fear, but because of joy. The joy surrounded her, coursing unconditional love through her veins.

San, thinking on her toes, abruptly pulled Zoey behind a root, hiding them from the Dims.

Zoey screwed her face up in confusion. "What are you doing? We have to stop them!" she whispered.

"It's Gart. He can handle them. He's only putting on a show. We'll sneak up on them and—" San paused. She was staring at Zoey in an odd way. "You're glowing all over. Even your golden crystals—cover them up!"

"I am?" Zoey glanced down at her chest, seeing the crystal glowing brightly. She covered it with a wing, but didn't think to cover her forehead crystal with her other wing.

"Did you see that?" said a voice. It was one of the Dims.

"Yes," replied the crow. They turned, seeing a golden light behind a large, thick root. The light was splattering the ceiling and suddenly Zoey and San knew they'd been found.

"Go see what it is." The crow gave the order, and a grunt was the response.

"I wouldn't do that if I were you." Gart sounded confident. His act was over.

"And why not?" asked the crow. There was a bit of fear in his voice. To the crow, something eerie was transpiring.

Gart's voice blasted throughout the hallway. "What you seek is the PureLight Order, but what you'll find is—"

There was silence. A little too much silence for Zoey, and the Dim looking for them stopped, and even San seemed a bit unnerved.

Emerging from their crouch, Zoey and San peeked over their root. Gart was straining, not of pain, but from concentration. He had the three birds in that strange energy clasp. He had caught the Dims with their guards down. That's how Zoey always got caught in those energy clasps— when she wasn't paying attention.

Zoey and San walked around the root, slowly inching their way to the wall that secretly opened into the cavern housing The PureLight Order. Gart's eyes seemed to strain some more, looking like they were going to pop out of his head. He shifted his gaze to Zoey and San, moving his head in the direction of the wall they were tip toeing toward. His gesture told them to hurry it up.

Just as they moved past Gart, the prairie dog fell backwards, letting out a ghastly blow of breath. The Dims had somehow broken free of the clasp. They shook themselves like wet dogs, doing their best to regain their senses, while Zoey and San were just mere inches away from the wall. If Zoey could manage the secret knock and open the wall before the Dims got to them, then they might have a chance to get away, though the chances were slim.

The crow let out a loud caw, but looked at the wall as he did so. Zoey wondered why, and her question was quickly answered when the wall opened up behind her, making not only San and Zoey gasp in horror, but Gart as well.

"Who opened the wall? No one did the knock!" yelled the Prairie Dog, his eyes darting left and right, trying to find the culprit.

The crow pointed to Zoey. "Get her!"

Zoey felt someone behind her rush through the wall opening and grab her, encircling her body with its large wings. Whoever it was had been hiding on the other side of the wall, waiting to ambush them. An instant later, Zoey felt San bump into her. She'd been caught between the large wings, too. This bird was huge and covered them almost completely with its wings. San and Zoey tried to escape, but at best, their attempts were feeble. They had no room to maneuver, no room to move at all.

Zoey could hear a struggle on the other side of the wings that gripped her. Gart yelled something, but it was muffled so she couldn't tell exactly what he had said. The crows' laughter echoed in the hallway.

Zoey was able to jump up and head bump the chin of her captor. Startled, the bird's feathers opened slightly, letting in light, but then closed them again. The bird started backing up, causing Zoey and San to shuffle backwards with it.

"If we can turn," whispered San. "Then we can stun this bird. I can do that on his chest crystal."

The bird must have heard San, because the wings squeezed even tighter. There was not a chance of turning now. Zoey sighed, wishing she would have thought about that earlier. If she had, she wouldn't have said it out loud. She'd simply turn and try to stun the bird. Zoey rolled her eyes. She had no idea how to stun a spirit animal anyway, so it didn't matter.

As they continued to be shuffled backwards, Zoey knew they were going into the cavern that stored The PureLight Order. But why? Did they need the Golden Keeper in order to take it off the wall? Zoey heard the wall close in front of her, bringing her back to the situation at hand, and when loud pecking noises came from the other side of the wall, piercing the hollow cave, she knew something wasn't right.

The crows' voices muffled through the wall. "What are you doing? You have the girls, now get back here!"

San started laughing, then Zoey felt the strong wings holding her loosen the squeeze, then open up. As the faint light of the cavern surrounded Zoey, she saw a gleeful San giving the large bird a hug. If it wasn't so dimly lit in the cavern, Zoey could swear that the large bird was the eagle named Free. By narrowing her eyes and letting them adjust to the change in light, Zoey saw that it was him.

Free laughed. "Nice trick, San."

"Yes." she put her wings up in excitement. "We tricked them!" She looked at Zoey. "The crow wanted Free to hide in the cavern, and when it was the right moment, Free would open the door and snatch you...or...us." San tilted her head. "No, Free was told to get you, because the crow didn't even know I was coming."

"What?" Zoey's shoulders lifted, not quite comprehending San's words.

His gray crystals glowing, Free stepped forward to Zoey and bowed. "I arrived here earlier, before Gart had arrived to the Hall of Scrolls. I learned the secret knock from Crepus. He'd somehow obtained it." The eagle tapped his head with his large wing. "I don't know how, but he knew it. I was supposed to destroy The PureLight Order when I got here, then capture you and take you back to Crepus. What Crepus didn't know was that I had other plans, including saving you."

Zoey turned to the wall, fear tingling down her feathers. *Did he actually destroy The PureLight Order?* Looking in its direction, The PureLight Order was there. Nice and in one piece. It glowed the moment she laid eyes on it, prompting Free and San to eye it as well.

A pound on the wall jostled Zoey out of her happiness. She twirled around, feeling that at any moment the Dims were going to somehow open the wall. She felt sorry for Gart, hoping he was alright. Perhaps he was an advanced defender and able to handle the Dims with the Art of Defense. Her thoughts then turned to Aderyn. She'd be in the Hall of Records soon and he'd definitely save him. *Hurry Aderyn!*

Free spoke again, "Crepus told only me the secret knock. The crows and the others don't know it. However, they'll find a way in, so we must go now, and do what we need to do." He pointed to the wall, indicating the Dims on the other side of it. "Who knows, they might convince Gart to give them the secret knock." He spread his large his wings, flapping and lifting off, heading toward The PureLight Order. San and Zoey followed him.

"Shall we get it down?" asked Zoey as they dropped down in front of The PureLight Order. San and Free landed next to her, gazing up at the gigantic scroll in utter amazement. To Zoey, it was just another scroll. To them, it was everything. They probably hadn't seen it in eons, or perhaps never.

Free frowned, then gazed over his shoulder, ignoring Zoey's question. "I don't want to risk it, San. Not now. When it's safe, we can read it."

San's shoulder's drooped, her eyes wide, almost pleading for Free to let her read it. "But, that's why we're here, right?"

"We're here to save The PureLight Order first. Our motivation for reading The PureLight Order comes last. Do you understand?" He eyed her like a father disciplining a child.

San nodded, but disappointment was written all over her face. They must have discussed this beforehand, telling each other that they needed to read it, perhaps to change them into PureLights, wondered Zoey.

"Why can't you two read it?" she asked. Maybe because they'd faint just like she had? Would their crystals turn gold, as well? No. She was told she was the only Golden Keeper.

Free looked up and down the entire scroll and said, "We can explain later. Let's get this down."

A loud bang on the wall echoed throughout the cavern, making them turn, half expecting an entire army to barrel through. All they saw was darkness, indicating that the wall was still intact and closed.

San eyed the scroll. "But, how do we get it down without ripping it?"

Free shrugged and doubt spread over him. "I don't know."

Zoey had an idea. It was the idea she had when Aderyn first told her to stop the Dims and save the scroll. "Can I try something?"

"By all means." Free gestured for Zoey to do whatever it was Zoey wanted to do.

"You can't be near me, though," replied Zoey, hoping it wouldn't offend them.

As strange a request as it was, Free nodded.

San's expression was blank. "Why can't we be near you?"

Zoey pondered for a moment, gazing up at the words encompassing the scroll. "I was asked not to let anyone hear what I'm about to say."

San's eyes widened, wanting to be given a better explanation. "Well—"

"San!" Free placed a heavy wing on her shoulder. He gave a sideways glance at Zoey. "Tell us where you need us to be and we'll go." He again looked behind them.

Zoey, feeling a bit relieved, was grateful that the eagle was giving her a free pass. She didn't want to have to tell them that she didn't trust them, that she was told not to say these words in front of any spirit animals unless it felt right.

"Can you go over there?" Zoey pointed to an area she hadn't noticed before. It was a large rock outcropping, high up on a far wall.

Free put his wings together, giving Zoey a slight bow. "I will." He waited for San to do the same, and when nothing came, he slapped her on the back and gave a head nod toward Zoey.

San sighed and shrugged. She rolled her eyes, putting her wings together, and gave a fast and short bow. "Sure."

Free patted Zoey on the back, making her feel that everything was alright, that he didn't have any ill feelings. He spread his wings, then took off, flying in the direction Zoey had pointed to. San jumped and glided after him, flicking Free's tail feathers as they went. San laughed, as if this was all fun and games, making Zoey smile.

A loud bang behind her made her smile disappear. This

wasn't all fun and it definitely wasn't a game. Glancing over her shoulder, she saw a crack of light through the wall. The Dims were breaking in. But how? She had to make this fast!

Zoey took a deep breath and then peered down at her ankle—the one with a golden rope and pouch holding the key. It wasn't visible to her now, but she knew if she concentrated on it and said the words, that it would materialize in front of her and she'd feel its extra weight when it appeared.

Another bang, and this time Zoey could hear parts of the wall crumbling. Her heart started beating faster. Perhaps this idea wouldn't work.

Bang!

Zoey heard more rocks falling to the earth. She wanted to cover her eyes, go to the Snow Tree, or better yet, wake up from this nightmare and run into her parent's room. She was supposed to be enjoying her childhood, not trying to save her life or save a gigantic, silly scroll.

She wanted to cry. Even if she managed to get the scroll down, where would she take it? Where could she hide?

She gave an abrupt, "Oh," and froze. She remembered something. Didn't Gart say there was another secret passageway to the Hall of Records? Maybe it's in this cavern?

A bigger thud behind her was the last one the Dims needed. Light and dust poured through a large, gaping hole. Commotion ensued and several Dim voices, perhaps a dozen or more, filled the cavern. They were here, inside the cavern and there were more of them than she'd expected. She could hear the flapping of their wings coming her way. They could pounce on her at any moment.

Zoey peered over her shoulder, seeing Free attacking the Dims to hold them off until Zoey could get the scroll down. Zoey wondered how long Free could last. Twelve against one, or maybe even twenty against one? The odds weren't in his favor.

Zoey closed her eyes, praying that her plan would work.

Opening them back up, she stared intently at the scroll, whispering, "Lemla Surita."

She blinked. Not because the scroll had vanished or anything, but because the knot in the back of her throat had suddenly gotten tighter. The PureLight Order hadn't moved or disappeared. It was still there. Nothing changed and she swallowed. "Lemla Surita."

Nothing.

She wanted to scream, cry, or whatever else she could do. She felt helpless staring up at the scroll, seeing that it didn't budge at all. She stared at her wings, not knowing why she did that, but figuring that's what you do when nothing works.

"Say your name, child." Zoey turned, seeing Aderyn hovering just above her.

"How did you get in here?"

She gestured toward an area next to the outcropping where San was nervously standing. "Through the secret passageway. I'm sorry I'm late. I couldn't get down the main entrance." She shook her head. "It's swarming with Dims. Regardless, say your name—your *real* name. It knows you by that, not by Zoey."

Zoey put her wings up, then to the top of her head. *What's my real name? What does Aderyn mean?* She could hear the Dims coming closer, fighting their way through Free's defense.

"Your real name is Aria!" Aderyn spoke loudly, making sure Zoey could hear. "Speak it!" Aderyn took off, heading toward the oncoming Dims, joining the conflict. With Aderyn there, Zoey knew it would buy her more precious moments.

She peered at the scroll once more. "Aria."

A big golden flash enveloped The PureLight Order, taking Zoey's breath away.

Zoey turned her eyes toward San. Then she glared into the scroll, letting out an exhale, and whispered, "Lemla Surita."

231

The PureLight Order rolled up, dropped, and just before it hit the ground, disappeared in front of Zoey.

"Go!"

Without looking, Zoey took off toward the outcropping. She felt Aderyn's presence right behind her, and heard the mass swooshing sounds of wings flapping hard. The Dims were right on her tail.

"Fly under the outcropping!" yelled Aderyn. "I'll command it to open—then close it once you get through! It will lead you to a safety!"

Several questions raced through Zoey's mind. *Will San, Free, and Aderyn make it, too? Or, are they staying behind? Will they live?* She ducked below the outcropping and saw a portion of the rock wall open, letting in the daylight. She flew hard and fast through the opening and heard the door shut behind her. She went to look over her shoulder, but flew into branches and leaves. She put her wings in front of her, protecting her eyes and she heard the swooshing of leaves and the cracking of branches. She slammed into a large branch, making her spin in the air and ricochet off another thick branch. She tumbled straight down, crashing into a large bush.

She breathed heavily, eyes open, listening to the sounds of a rushing river that she must have crossed during her flight. A stabbing feeling in her back, most likely from a branch from the bush she was currently laying on, prompted her to roll off to the side. Freed from her weight, the bush shook heavily, making her hold her breath. She didn't want to make a sound.

For a while she lay there on the ground, under a bush and taking slow, shallow breaths, expecting a patrol of Dims to come by any minute. After several moments of listening without hearing the sounds of any flying Dims, she climbed out from under the bush.

There were trees everywhere and she could tell she was in a large forest. Was she in Gwenfree Forest? She hoped not. Gwenfree was always filled with Dims patrolling every which way. The trees all around her were thick with foliage, but no ice like the Gwenfree Forest had. She was in a different forest, one without any snow. She drew in a deep breath and was happy to be alive.

*Alive?* She suddenly felt a heavy weight descend upon her, the usual fear once you realize that something bad has happened. Were Aderyn, San, and Free alive? Did they make it through the secret passageway? Glancing around, she knew they hadn't. They were so worried about The PureLight Order getting through that they had closed the secret passageway on themselves.

She took a few steps forward, but then stopped. She had heard a crack behind her. Turning, she saw a fox standing still. An instant later, a puma came out of a tree next to the fox. Looking around, she saw spirit animal after spirit animal emerge out of thin air and encircling her. She tilted her head in curiosity, though her heart pumped with fear. When she stared at their crystals, she figured something strange was afoot.

*Who are these spirit animals?*

# The Adventure Lives On...

## Book III:

## The PureLights

## &

## the Pyramid of Ohm

www.brandon-ellis.com

50146175R10133

Made in the USA
San Bernardino, CA
14 June 2017